Bad Wing Crow

By Jim Powell

ElderBerry Publishing
CMP Publishing Group, LLC

This novel is a work of fiction. Any similarity to events, places, or people is purely coincidental and beyond the intent of either the author or the publisher.

Copyright 2018©Jim Powell All rights reserved.

No part of this book may be reproduced in any form, by photostat, microfilm, xerography, or any other means, or incorporated into any information retrieval system, electronic or mechanical, without the written permission of the author.

Cover Art by Edie Abnet, artist/illustrator: Edie Abnet is a well known Minnesota artist. She is an Impressionist who works primarily in mixed media watercolor.

Author Photo by Michelle King.
All rights reserved.

All inquiries, including distributor information,
should be addressed to:
Jim Powell: email: yllwdawg@aol.com

Bad Wing Crow may be ordered through any Book Seller.

ISBN13: 978-1-937162-15-3

Library of Congress Control Number: 2018943572

If we blended all together
Countries gods and races
One language on our tongues
One color on our faces

We'd be back to where we started
On the first days of man
To the way we were created
To the way it all began

If again we were one people
If indeed that was our fate
Who would we look down upon
How would we know who to hate

Jim Powell

This story is about hanging on to one's humanity, civility and decency in circumstances that are inhuman, uncivil and indecent without sacrificing one's pride and self respect.

Prologue

Pine Bluff, Arkansas, 1869

Too much for one so young
Would have killed or broken some
Will it scar this gentle boy
And the man he will become

He was a man reaching deep within to find the strength and the control…mostly the control…to deal with the circumstances life had handed him. His gut told him to strike back, but in his mind he knew that wouldn't be the right choice for him or for the boy. The boy was the only thing he had left, and he was all the boy had. Control was the key.

With shoulders slumped and head hung low, his posture reflected his struggle and his grief as he made his way through the darkened room to the boy's bedside. When he lit the kerosene lamp, it flickered, sputtered, and smoked a bit before the flame grew bright and steady.

When the yellow light was strong enough to fill the room, the dark red stains on the strips of rag wrapped tightly around his grandson's left wrist became visible. The sight made him shudder and gasp for breath.

He took some time to compose himself, and then spoke in a whisper. "How you doin', Samuel? Ya feelin' any better?" The boy turned his head toward the wall and didn't answer. "I'm sorry they done ya this way, son. I'm real sorry. It ain't right, an' you bein' only ten years old. It ain't right at all."

The man was nearing sixty. His close cropped, mostly white, hair and beard stood in stark contrast to the dark and weathered skin of his face. Reflected in his soft, brown eyes was the pain and sorrow that had too frequently been his companions over the years. He wore bib overalls and no shirt. Fit and lean as most men twenty years his junior, the muscles of his arms and shoulders testified to the decades of physical labor he'd endured as a slave and a share cropper.

He looked down upon his injured grandson with sadness and frustration. His cheeks were wet with tears. At the same time anger burned deep within him. More anger, perhaps, than he'd ever known before, but he kept it inside. He fought to keep it inside. Keeping anger hidden was one of the keys to survival for men like him. It was something he would teach his grandson, and the lesson would begin now.

Gently placing his hand on the boy's shoulder, he held the lamp over the bed. He felt his little body shaking and saw there were tears in his eyes as well.

"All's I did was pick up that girl's purse an' try to give it back it to her, Grandpa, an' she screamed like I was tryin' to hurt her. She dropped her purse an' I was tryin' to give it to her…that's all I was doin'."

"I know it was, Sammy, I know it was."

"How come you didn't stop 'em Grandpa? My daddy wouldn't a let 'em do me this way. He would'a stopped 'em for sure."

The man's chin sank all the way to his chest. He was quiet, and, for just a moment, he was ashamed. Gently he rubbed the boy's shoulder, took a couple of deep breaths, and spoke.

"Your daddy was a fine man, Samuel. He was my only boy, and I will always be proud of him. He was brave, and you're right, he would'a stood up to those white men for sure."

He wiped his eyes and paused for several seconds while he weighed his words. Words his grandson needed to hear. "Cept they already hung him for standin' up to white men. An if he'da been here yesterday, an if he'da stood up to 'em, they'da hung him again, an 'they'da still cut off your hand."

"It ain't fair, Grandpa. They hung my daddy for tryin' to keep 'em away from Momma, and they did this to me for touchin' that girl, and there ain't nobody can do nothin' about it. Us niggers jes have to let 'em do what they want to us."

The man nodded. "Most of the time that's what we have to do, Sammy. If I'da tried to stop those Coolidge boys, they'da killed me an' I wouldn't be here no more. I wouldn't be here to help with this." He touched the boy's left arm. "Cause they still would'a cut off your hand. An' I wouldn't be here to help you grow up like I promised your daddy I would. Us colored folks needs to know when to fight an' when not to fight. If we got no chance a winnin, if all's that can happen is we get killed or hung, then there's no sense to fightin'."

He paused for a full minute this time, and then reached out and gently turned the boy's face toward his own. "Someday it ain't gonna' be that way, Sammy. No sir, it ain't. Someday you an' me gonna' have a chance, and then we gonna' make this right. An' you know, waitin' for that time don't make us afraid an' it shouldn't make us ashamed. It makes us smart and it makes us alive when the time comes."

"Don't never forget that Sammy. An' don't never call yourself a nigger. There's gonna' be plenty of folks doin' that for ya. We don't gotta' do it to ourselves. When the chance comes along…maybe it comes to me…maybe it comes to you, but when it does, we gonna' stand up, an' we ain't gonna' be nobody's nigger."

The boy's eyes opened wide and he looked to his grandfather as though begging for the truth... for hope... for something to hold on to. "We really gonna' do that, Grandpa?"

"Yes we are, Samuel, but only when the time comes. That's when we gonna' do it."

He pulled a folded piece of paper from the pocket of his overalls and stuffed it under the boy's pillow. "There's three names on this here paper... Robert Coolidge, Buster Coolidge, an' James Howard. Howard an' the Coolidges are cousins. Robert an' Buster... they the ones that done this to you, an' James was with 'em. They was drunk and feelin' mean an' they had guns. An' they was that way five years ago when all three of 'em ganged up on your daddy an' hung him. Keep these names with you... for when the time comes."

Chapter One

Kansas, 1885

Blew in from the prairie
Foul and rank as could be
Never planned on hangin'
From the cottonwood tree

For more than half an hour I'd known I was about to have visitors. The dust they kicked up was visible when they were still three miles out on the dry Kansas prairie. Hardly more than a dot at first, the cloud of yellow dust grew in size as they drew closer.

When they were a half mile or so out, I could make out the black silhouettes of the riders and their mounts. Even at that distance I was pretty sure they weren't Indians. I can't say what it was, but there was just something about them that looked more like white men than Indians. It didn't make me real happy.

"Damn," I swore, "the last thing I need is three white cowboys joinin' me for lunch."

I looked up from time to time to mark their progress. The stiff south wind made the dust drift almost horizontally to the right of the horses' feet. The whole picture was blurred and distorted by the heat waves. It struck me as an erie, surreal sight… like a mirage or apparition of some kind, but I knew I wasn't going to be that lucky.

The first thing to catch my eye as they finally rode into

camp was their hats. Broad brimmed, tattered, and stained from sweat, trail dust, grease and smoke, I would have bet they even smelled bad, although I sure had no inclination to get close enough to find out. I supposed they might have been different colors at one time… maybe white, grey or silver belly, but the trail had turned them all the same dirty, yellow-brown color. Shabby as they were, the hats may have been the best part of this rough looking trio.

Covered with dust, their horses were tired and lean from too many miles and too little feed. One was a seal brown, one a bay, and the third a liver chestnut. The saddle pad and girth of each mount was fringed with the salty white stains of dried sweat.

A big sorrel mule was tied to a string attached to the saddle of the chestnut. Wearing neither saddle nor harness, there was no residue of sweat on the sleek, copper-colored coat of the mule. Showing no sign of the long trail, he was in good flesh and he seemed uneasy.

Without speaking, the men rode until they were within twenty feet of where I sat, leaning over my small fire, stirring some beans and salt pork in a cast iron frying pan. I used my right hand. As was my habit, my left arm was stuffed into the pocket of my gray canvas duster.

The three horses stood quietly with their heads held low. They were happy to rest after the long miles of the trail. The chestnut mare was the only one that moved, and all she did was lay her ears back in a threatening gesture whenever the fidgety mule moved too close. It was clear to me the mule hadn't been in the company of the horses for long, wasn't accepted by them, and felt bad about it. It reminded me of something my grandfather used to say about a mule's affinity for horses: "A mule knows he ain't a horse, Sammy, he knows he ain't, but he wishes he was."

The man in the middle nudged his mount a few steps

forward, removed his hat and wiped his brow with a grimy bandana. No longer shaded by the brim of the hat, the midday Kansas sun revealed a broad face covered with tanned, pock marked skin and what looked to be about three weeks growth of dark scraggly beard. The upper part of his forehead, usually protected from the sun by the hat, was so white it appeared to glow. The look of it made me smile, and I made no attempt to hide it.

For a few seconds he sat slouched in the saddle without speaking. Then the stub of the wet and well-chewed cigar he held in his teeth began to bob up and down in time with the movement of his fat, cracked lips. "Somethin' ticklin' you boy? You findin' somethin' amusin' here, nigger?" The word made my jaw tighten, but I continued stirring my lunch and didn't look up.

A medium sized man, with broad shoulders and a muscular build, I was lean and hard from life on the trail. Like my visitors, I'd gone a long time between shaves and several weeks growth of dense, tightly curled whiskers covered the lower half of my face. My dark, mahogany skin was weathered from long days in the sun and stretched tightly over high cheekbones and a prominent jaw.

Weighing around one hundred and sixty-five pounds, I figured I was at least twenty or thirty pounds lighter than any of the three white men who looked down at me from their mounts. That concerned me no more than did the fact there were three of them.

Not being real worried about angering him, I answered the man, but I did it in my own time. "Yes suh, I did think of somethin' kinda funny. Now what can I do for you gentlemen?" I still didn't raise my head to look directly at my visitors and the smile on my face didn't change. I gave no indication that the racial slur had angered me.

"Well, you can look at me when I'm talkin' to you nigger.

That's one thing you can do."

I pushed my black, flat-brimmed hat a couple of inches further back on my head and lifted my eyes until they made contact with those of the man who had spoken. He seemed to be the leader of the bunch. "This good enough? Is this here good enough for you, boss?"

The cigar bobbed again as the man laughed and spoke to his two companions. "I think we're gonna kill us a darky today, boys."

The man on his left smiled and nodded in agreement. He was short and stocky with reddish hair and a full beard that was long and thick. Even in this group he looked particularly unclean… so much so that I wondered what kind of critters might be making their homes in that nasty looking hair and beard. The thought made my smile grow a little wider.

The rider on the right was blonde and fairly tall with little visible facial hair. He was much younger than the others… perhaps no more than sixteen or seventeen years old. The left side of his face was red and swollen. Obviously ill at ease, he looked down at his saddle horn and made no eye contact with me or his companions.

I take some pride in my ability to quickly size up an adversary, and I had no illusions about these guys wanting to be my friends. Sizing up an adversary is something I've given a lot of thought to and I've worked at it. I consider it one of the keys to survival, and survival isn't an easy job for a man traveling alone in this country… especially a man like me.

These men weren't trying to hide their intentions, so I had a pretty good idea of what they were all about, and I figured there was no need to study them much longer before I acted on my judgment.

Setting the frying pan on a rock next to the fire, I stood up and took a step backward. With my right hand I pushed my coat back exposing the pistol encased in the worn leather holster that rode high up on my hip. "You say you're thinkin' 'bout doin' some killin' today?"

The red head spit some tobacco juice that failed to clear his beard and hung from it like a dirty brown icicle. The spittle fit right in. He was so filthy it didn't really detract from his appearance. The sight made my smile grow wider still.

"Yeah, that's what he said." He smiled now as well; a smile that revealed a mouthful of stained and half rotted teeth. "An' we're fixin' to git on with it real soon."

It was plain that the two who had spoken were feeling brave and in control at the moment. They were well armed, horseback, and looking down at a single man with a revolver. Although there were three of them, the kid was not really a factor and we all knew it. Still, I'm sure it looked to them like the odds were stacked heavily on their side. For the moment, they were brave and more than capable of being cold and ruthless.

Many times I'd encountered men like these. They were bullies; tough, but in a very limited way. Tough only when they could create fear in the man they were facing.

I reckoned they could shoot some, but they weren't gun hands. I was sure of that. There's something in the eyes of a true gun hand that I can't describe; something that reflects his willingness to face his own death. These three were killers, I supposed, but that's not the same as being a gun hand. When I made them think they were at a disadvantage... when I made them face their own death... they'd crumble along with all of the tough talk. I looked forward to watching it happen...to hearing the word "nigger" suddenly drop from their vocabulary.

I continued to smile, and I nodded at the red haired one who had last spoken. Next I turned to the dark haired one. Once we were eye to eye, I held it. I made sure I didn't blink or look away.

"You come from the east I see. That farm back there by the creek, maybe six, eight miles, I seen that mule there. That where you got him? I see he ain't packin' nothin' and he ain't all sweated up from the trail like the rest of you is."

This time the leader answered. "That's right. We got him back at that farm." Pulling the cigar out of his mouth, he laughed. "Bought him."

"So, you gonna kill me then, an'…uh… buy my horse?"

Again the dark haired man chuckled as he answered. "Yeah, nigger, that's what we was thinkin'. Unless you're so fast with that big old Colt you got hangin' on your hip that you can get all three of us first. You reckon you're that fast?"

"No suh… no suh… I ain't fast at all." I shook my head, and looked toward the ground but still kept him in sight. Several seconds went by as I pushed some dirt around with the toe of my boot before I looked up and finished making my point.

"Ain't fast at all… jes accurate. Jes real accurate, that's all. Let me show you. See them rocks over there?" Without taking my eyes off the black bearded one, I slowly drew the six shooter from its holster and fired two shots in rapid succession. Though I made no apparent effort to aim, a small rock, about the size of a hen's egg, jumped into the air each time the pistol barked.

The dark haired man's expression grew more serious for a few seconds and then he laughed and spoke again. "That was pretty good shootin', boy. You have the hammer sittin' on a empty chamber, did ya?"

"Yes suh, I believe I did have it sittin' on a empty one."

"Then you've got just three rounds left, don't ya? With three of us, you can't really afford to miss with any of those rounds, can you? I don't think that was real smart even for a darky."

"Never claimed to be smart…no suh… jes accurate." I then shot two more times and two more rocks flew into the air. Again, I did it without lining up the sights. The eyes of all three opened wide and they looked at one another in confusion.

"I don't never miss. The bullets jes go where I'm lookin', that's all. They jes go where I'm lookin'. Always been that way long as I can remember."

With my gaze locked on the face of the leader, the smile disappeared from my lips. "Can ya see where I'm lookin' right now, suh? Right now I'm lookin' between your eyes."

I pulled my left arm from my coat pocket revealing a leather-wrapped steel stump where my hand should have been. The metal on the end was exposed. It was a piece that resembled a three inch pipe that had been capped off.

The color drained from the face of the leader like somebody'd pulled a cork out of his ass. "You… you… you're Crow! You're Crow ain't you?"

"That's what they call me. Ain't my name, but that's what they call me. Tell your boys to drop their pistols to the ground."

A few seconds passed without a response from any of the three. I spoke again, but more slowly this time. "I'm lookin' right between your eyes, fat boy, an' I ain't gonna ask again."

"Uh…throw 'em in the dirt." He looked from one of his cohorts to the other, and back into my dark, burning eyes. "Do it now! Right now!" With a dull sound the two pistols fell on the hard, dry ground of the Kansas prairie. Turning my attention back toward the leader, I nodded, and his pistol fell as well. "Rifles too."

When all of the firearms were on the ground, I motioned for the three to move back a few feet while I gathered them up.

My manner of speaking changed as I further addressed my charges. I was starting to enjoy the show. "Gentlemen, I'd like you to slip the loops of your lariats around your chests and under your arms. Please remain mounted as you do so."

At this point, I pulled back the left side of my canvas duster to reveal another Colt revolver strapped inside in a cross draw position. Smiling, I shook my head, and spit some tobacco juice into the dust at my feet.

"You never really know what to believe in this uncivilized country… do you? It's so difficult to know when a man is lying, when he's bluffing, and when he's just messing with your mind… your slow, simple mind."

When the three were situated to my satisfaction, I took a few minutes to study their horses and the tracks they made. I committed the tracks to memory.

In my estimation, the liver chestnut mare was the best of the three horses. She was well made and in pretty good flesh… not worn down as much as the others. I decided to take her with me. I pulled the saddles and bridles from the bay and the brown and turned them loose. Saddling my own grey gelding, I mounted and turned to the east with the chestnut mare and the mule in tow.

I turned back to take a last look at my handiwork. Each of the three men was hanging from a different branch of a big cottonwood tree, with his feet about a foot and a half off the ground and his own lariat around his chest. At my urging, their horses had walked out from under them and left them swinging.

"Crow! You ain't gonna just leave us here… are ya?" The leader of the bunch had panic in his voice as he struggled to shout the question. When you're hanging from a tree, with a rope around your chest, evidently it gets a little hard to breathe and harder still to talk. Amusing to me but not so much to them.

"I'll be back." I answered. "I'm just goin' to see how that family you got this mule from is doin'. Maybe give 'em this nice mare for their trouble."

"Crow! Listen… we… uh… we didn't hurt those folks." There was a long pause while he fought for air. "All we done was take that mule… that's all we done. That place was already hit. Looked like injuns done it."

I felt a churning in my belly as I spun the big grey around, rode up close, and faced the three as they hung there like Christmas tree ornaments. "I should gut shoot all three of you assholes right now and let you hang here until you die. If those folks are hurt or dead, I know pretty well what happened to them, but I'll go back to that farm and see for myself."

The red headed one spoke now in a pleading voice. His phrases were short with big gaps between them as he, too, fought for his breath. "How you gonna' know… what happened… Crow? Ain't nobody left… nobody alive there… to tell you nothin'. You gotta' believe us… we took the mule… that's all we done. I swear… that's all we done. We got nothin' against you, Crow… we was just foolin' with you. We wasn't gonna' take yer horse."

Releasing the mule and the chestnut mare, I shook my head and sighed. "Really? I'm glad we're friends now. I'll go to the farm and read the sign anyway. I want to know exactly what you did… each one of you." Turning back toward the east, I nudged the grey gelding into a smooth, easy lope.

That these three characters thought they could steal my horse caused me to smile and wonder at the depth of their ignorance. To accomplish that, they would have had to kill me before I killed them. I don't mean to brag, but the chances of that happening were mighty slim.

The whole idea made me think back nine years to the day this magnificent animal came into my life…back to when I was a scrawny kid and Boone was little more than a colt.

Chapter Two

West Texas, 1876

A skinny black cowboy
With only one hand
Now a horse and a chance
To grow into a man

Wood was scarce on the west Texas plain, and the round corral at the Busted A Ranch was clear evidence of that. The rails and posts were dry and twisted, and few of them were even close to being straight. Scavenged from the river bottoms, most of the pieces had drifted downstream during times of high water and had been deposited on shore over the course of many decades. On this hot August afternoon the rickety but serviceable enclosure was a center of activity.

A thick cloud of dust arose from the center of the corral, and a dry, gusty wind blew it toward the east. Four men stood, side by side, leaning against the top rail on the upwind side. Twenty feet to their left, two others did the same. All six hollered a mixture of encouragement and smart-ass remarks to the cowboy who was trying to stick with the grey colt that was kicking up all the dust.

The man stayed with the big colt for six or seven good hard bucks, but he bailed out when the horse reared and launched himself into space with his body almost vertical and his hind feet three or four feet off the ground.

The young man swore as he picked himself up out of

the dirt. "Sumbitchin' horse is crazy. He like to come over back'ards. He like to come over back'ards right on top of me. Sumbitchin' horse is crazy."

Picking up his hat and wiping the dust from his eyes, the cowboy made a pushing gesture toward the horse with the palms of both hands and turned toward the four men at the rail. "You want that sumbitch rode, boss, you gonna' have to find somebody better and crazier'n me."

The one on the left end of the group of four nodded. He was a tall, raw boned man with a square jaw and thick grey hair. "You ain't tellin' me nothin' I don't already know, Billy. If somebody's gonna ride that bronc it ain't gonna be you."

The face of the cowboy puckered up a little. "Well that suits me fine, boss, but you're gonna' have a hell of a time findin' a man that'll stay with that grey bastard any longer'n I did."

Turning to his left, the big man spoke again. "Henry, how 'bout puttin' the colored kid on him?"

Henry was the only man at the corral who was as big as the boss. He was a colored man, over six feet tall, and powerfully built with close cropped grey hair and beard. Both he and the man he worked for, Luke Hopkins, were on the long side of fifty.

"The kid, boss, is called Samuel. So why don't we just call him by his name instead of his color? Although I suppose it's easier for you to go by color so's you don't have to tax that razor sharp mind of yours by memorizin' a bunch of names."

Luke made a strange noise that was sort of a snort and a laugh mixed together. "I didn't mean no harm, Henry… the two of you are the only colored folks we got here, and you sure as hell ain't no kid… so I figured you'd know who I was talkin' about."

Henry smiled. "Well sometimes, boss, I need to remind you of some things. You see, when they fought the war, some years back, and they freed us folks, they made us into people at the same time. At least accordin' to the law, they made us into people with names and everything."

Luke shook his head. "I ain't your damned boss, Henry, and does makin' me out to be some kind of a slave trader or somethin' make you feel better? Who got you out of Mississippi both free and alive, Henry?"

"It was you, boss. It was you, and I'd probably forget that if you didn't keep remindin' me about it every damned day." Henry turned away and pretended to be angry while Luke laughed.

The discussion between the two men had the cowboy in the corral somewhat confused as he walked up to the rail and spoke to Luke. "The kid can ride some, boss, I got to admit that… he can ride some, but he ain't hardly full growed yet, and he ain't got but one hand."

Luke laughed. "You worried about him gettin' hurt, or are you afraid a skinny, one handed black kid is gonna' show you up, Billy?"

The cowboy frowned. "No…no it ain't that at all, boss. I'm just thinkin' it's too much horse for him… that's the onliest thing I'm thinkin' right now."

Before Billy and Luke had finished their short conversation, Samuel Tucker was inside the corral making his way toward the nervous colt. Not quite seventeen years old, he was about average height with wide shoulders and very little meat on his bones. His blue cotton shirt and canvas pants hung on him like there was no one inside. The big, flat brimmed black hat he wore looked like it belonged on the head of a much bigger man. Strips of rag were wrapped tightly around the stump at the end of his left arm and secured with a couple of leather straps. The coils of his lariat were hung over that arm and he held the loop with his right hand.

He didn't look at the colt as he approached…kept his eyes on the ground. When he was within a dozen feet, he threw his loop with one swift movement and caught the horse by the neck. The big grey scrambled back and to the side and the boy worked the rope up to a point just below the horse's jowls and snugged it up, but not so tight as to shut off his wind.

Positioning himself in the middle of the sixty-odd foot round corral, he stayed even with the horse's shoulder and pushed him toward the rail. The lad went with him when he moved. Trying to overpower the big animal would have been foolish and would serve no good purpose. At just over two years old, the big, muscular colt already weighed more than a thousand pounds. Samuel kept just enough pressure on the line to keep it taut, and he continued to move when the horse moved. When he stopped, the boy released the pressure and walked toward him. Each time he moved in his direction the horse shied away, and each time the boy snugged the lariat and moved with him. This routine repeated itself maybe twenty times.

Billy, the cowboy who'd just been thrown, hollered from the rail. "Samuel, it's gonna' be dark in another six or seven hours. You gonna' ride that colt or dance with him all day?"

Samuel smiled and looked toward the men on the rail. "This here colt's gonna' get rode today, and I'll bet any or all of you a week's pay I won't be needin' to dust myself off when it's over."

None of the men took the bet or said anything at all. Big Henry looked in their direction with a smile on his face. Luke looked back at him with a grin of his own.

Samuel was able to get a little closer to the colt each time he stopped, and before long he was standing next to him rubbing his neck and face. Again Billy shouted. "Watch out fer that mean bastard, boy. He'd as soon bite yer other hand off as look at ya."

Samuel stepped back a bit from the horse and turned toward Billy. "He ain't all that mean, Billy. He's just a might scared."

Moving slowly, he began rubbing the horse with the coils of his lariat. He rubbed him on the shoulders, the neck, the flanks and the hind quarters. Then he moved his hand up and down all four legs. Whenever the horse moved away from the contact and attention, he applied light pressure to the rope and moved with him.

Next, the boy put a twist in the rope and slipped it over the colt's muzzle, making it into a device called a war bridle that enabled him to control his head. Now he urged the colt to move along the rail with no pressure on the rope. With the command whoa, he tightened the rope until he stopped and looked in his direction. If the colt turned his head away, Samuel gave a tug and made him look at him again. Soon, the word whoa, with no pressure on the rope, caused the horse to stop and look the boy's way.

After applying downward pressure on both stirrups a few times and rubbing the colt's neck, he swung into the saddle in one easy motion. At first he just sat there and continued to rub his neck without asking him to do anything. After he felt the horse relax, he urged him to move along the rail at a walk and then a trot.

Now it was Henry who offered his advice. "I believe he'll buck if you put him into a lope."

Samuel smiled at his mentor. "That's what I'm fixin' to do in a bit. We all know he can buck, and he knows it too. An'

Billy taught him he can throw a man off. If he didn't know that I'd work him a lot slower and maybe he'd never know it. What he needs to find out now is that he can't get me off no matter what he does."

Luke Hopkins spoke up. "Looks to me like you got it figured out pretty good, son. Let's have the show."

The young man got the horse moving around the rail at a trot in a counter clockwise direction and then hooked him gently with his right spur. The startled colt hunched a bit and moved forward. The boy touched him again with the same spur.

With his head down between his knees, he began bucking for all he was worth. Samuel took a deep seat, leaned back and went with it. He made no effort to pull his head up to stop the bucking. Instead he applied pressure to his flanks with his heels and spurs. The idea was to keep him moving forward.

With his left arm high in the air, he timed each jump perfectly, and stayed tight in the saddle. After a dozen bone jarring jumps straight up in the air, the colt began to move forward more, and the bucks were less vertical and not so severe. All the while the boy kept urging him onward; applying pressure when he didn't move forward and releasing it when he did.

It wasn't long and he was loping smoothly around the corral. Maybe eighteen or twenty times they circled the enclosure at a lope before Samuel reined the horse in right in front of Luke and the other cowboys.

"This here grey's gonna' be a fine horse, boss. You mind if I add him to my string?"

Luke responded. "I think that's a good idea, Samuel. You done a mighty good job of gentlin' him. It'd make sense for you to use him on the ranch. By the way, how long are you figurin' on bein' here?"

Caught a little off guard by the question, Samuel fidgeted a little before answering. "Oh, I suppose another few months…til winter maybe."

Luke nodded. "I'll tell you what, young fella. You stay on here 'til calvin' is over next spring, and you can leave with that grey horse yer sittin' on and an extra month's pay to boot."

The boy thought for a minute and then smiled. "That sounds pretty good. I reckon I'll do that. Thanks boss."

*****

Henry and Samuel sat on the steps of the bunkhouse under a night sky crowded with bright stars. They could hear the laughter and shouts from inside where the rest of the ranch hands were playing cards. Henry reached over and squeezed the boy's upper right arm. The muscles weren't bulky, but they felt like steel cables. "Mighty stout for a fella your size, Samuel. Mighty stout."

Then he reached out to test the left. The boy tried to pull away, but he wasn't quite quick enough to avoid the older man's grasp. "Ain't much to this one."

Samuel had a hurt look on his face as he turned toward Henry. "Well I can't do nothin' with it without a hand on it. I can't help it if it got shriveled up some."

Henry nodded and his eyes softened. "Let me tell you somethin', son. Me and Luke would like you to stay here on the ranch and maybe even take it over some day, but there's somethin' inside of you that ain't gonna let that happen. You're gonna move on. I can see it."

"Now, anybody who travels this country is gonna' run into a fair bit of trouble. A colored man is gonna' run into a whole lot more than that. He needs to try to duck it when he can, but he needs to be ready for it when it comes. You understand me?"

"Yes sir."

"Well, if you'd build up the strength in that left arm, you'd be a sight more ready to handle what's comin'."

The lad had tears in his eyes as he turned and looked squarely into the older man's face. "They done cut off my hand, Henry. I can't fix it and I don't know how to do anything different with it."

"Well, I got me an idea about that." Reaching into his coat pocket, Henry pulled out a handful of leather thongs that were woven into a sort of sling. "I want you to wrap this around your wrist and put a rock in this here pocket. Work that arm both ways… bend it and straighten it out over your head. Do it fifty or a hundred times… two or three times a day if you can… every day. Don't miss any days. After a while use a bigger rock. Will you do that?"

"Yes sir, I will."

Henry smiled. "Good, and maybe we'll figure out somethin' to put on the end of that thing. Luke was sayin' he had an idea about that. Maybe he can make somethin' that might help you out a time or two. Ain't gonna' be a new hand, but it'll be somethin' that might help you out. Luke was a blacksmith before the war. We'll get him to make somethin' for you."

The boy's face took on a curious look and he turned to the older man. "Luke ain't really your boss, is he?"

"No, Sammy, not really. He's my friend."

"You got to be friends in the war?"

"Yeah, we did, son."

"But you were a slave and he fought for the South, didn't he?"

The big man smiled. "How about if I just tell you about it? You ain't gonna' stop askin' questions until I do anyhow, are ya?."

The boy shook his head and flashed a shy grin. "No sir, I reckon I ain't."

"It was gettin' near the end of the war when Luke and I met. My wife, Essie, had been sold away from the plantation and I'd run off to find her. I found out she'd been killed when the Yanks shelled the place where she was livin'. They'd chased a small bunch of Rebs to the farm and leveled the house with cannon fire. Luke was one of only three Rebs that survived, and he managed to sneak away. We ran into each other a few days later at a nearby farm. We were both tryin' to steal the same horse.

I stood my ground as he approached me with his rifle pointed at the ground. He asked me if I was a runaway and I said I was. He told me he didn't really hold with slavery and that he'd fought for the South because he lived in Georgia and that was what was expected. As far as he was concerned the war was lost and he'd had his fill of it anyway… said his wife and son had both been killed… same kind of situation my wife had been caught in. He told me I could travel west with him if I had a mind to.

I was grievin' for Essie, and I told him I figured on travelin' alone, and we went our separate ways. Two days later I was captured by a rebel outfit and chained up in a chicken coop they'd turned into a brig. They had four other runaways in there with me. There was a granary on the same place where they had several rebel deserters locked up.

These Rebs were just hangin' around waitin' for the war to be over. They'd had all of the fightin' they wanted and they weren't lookin' for any more action. Sometimes, when the Rebs got liquored up, they'd take a couple of the runaways out and make 'em fight. They'd bet on the outcome. The winner was given some extra food.

I was by far the biggest man among the slaves. To find a match for me they pulled a deserter out of the granary. The man they brought out was Luke.

We didn't speak to each other… just started fightin' inside this ring they'd made out of logs. At first we hit each other as hard and as often as we could, but neither of us went down. The Reb soldiers sat on the logs, shouted encouragement to Luke, and drank corn liquor.

After we'd been at it for a while, Luke grabbed me around the shoulders and got me in a bear hug. He whispered in my ear that we should ease up and give these boys more time to get drunk. I told him that was fine with me. I was tired of hittin' the big son of a bitch an' havin' him hit me anyway. We danced around for a good long while just makin' it look good.

We'd been goin' at for the better part of a half hour when I threw a punch with my right hand. It just grazed the top of Luke's head, but he fell back like he'd been pole axed and landed on some of the soldiers who were sittin' on the logs.

For a while he floundered around among them like he was really hurt and couldn't get to his feet. When he got up he had a pistol in each hand. He made the drunken Rebs strip down to their skivvies while I broke open the two brigs and released the prisoners. The slaves were still shackled, but they ran off as best as they could.

One of the Rebs was big enough that I could fit into his uniform. I put it on and Luke and me rode off on the two best horses the outfit had. We kept heading west until we got to this country. I never figured on us stayin' together this long, but that's what happened.

We own this place fifty-fifty. Thinkin' Luke owns it by himself is just easier for folks around here to understand."

The boy turned toward the older man. He had a thoughtful look on his face, like what he'd just heard meant something to him. "That's good, Henry. I'm glad to hear you an' Luke are partners. An' thanks for tellin' me about the war. I can't hardly remember nothin' about it 'cept seein' some Yankee soldiers ride through one time. I was no more than five or six when it ended."

Henry put his hand on Sammy's shoulder. His lips pursed up and his eyes narrowed… like he figured the words he had to say were real important. "There's somethin' more you got to know about the war, son. It ain't over yet. An' it won't be over in your lifetime. You're gonna be fightin' that war as long as you live… not because you want to, but because there won't be any way of escapin' it. An' you ain't gonna win it. No sir… you ain't gonna win it. The best you can do is survive it, and bein' smart is the key to survivin' it. Don't ever forget that… not ever."

Chapter Three

How could they have done it
To this sweet little girl
They left with a mule
And took her whole world

The little farmstead sat in the bottomland next to the creek. None of the buildings was painted, but all were in good repair and probably only a few years old. The forty or so acres that were planted were green with crops. It was apparent the family had put their heart and soul into building and caring for the place. I'd noticed that the day before when I'd passed through.

Mostly, though, I'd taken note of how welcoming the Willis family had been toward me. That doesn't often happen to a colored man in this part of the country. Hell, I doubt if it happens often in any part of the country.

Today, as I neared the farm, I caught a glimpse of movement on the knoll behind the little wood frame house. Whatever it was, it quickly disappeared behind the hill.

Stopping the grey, I took a minute to scan the terrain with my glass. I knew better than to rush head first into trouble. Not seeing anything out of the ordinary, I circled to the left of the farmstead and approached the crest in the cover of some cottonwoods. Some two hundred yards out, in the grassland to the east, I saw a woman running. The wind blew from her to me and carried the sound of her crying.

I hesitated for a moment, to make sure no one else was around, and set after her. The grey ate up the gap between us quickly. "Hold up Ma'am. Hold up! I ain't gonna' hurt you. I'm the fella who rode through here yesterday and visited with you folks. Samuel Tucker…I'm Samuel Tucker."

She stopped running and turned toward me. Now that I could see her face clearly, I remembered her from the day before. Blonde and pretty, she was the oldest of the Willis children and the only girl. She wore a blue cotton dress that reached to her ankles. The wind blew it tight against her in a way that outlined her woman's shape, and it held my gaze for a few seconds. I caught myself and looked away.

I guessed her to be somewhere around eighteen years old. She looked up at me with eyes wide with fear. Her deeply tanned face was stained with the muddy streaks from her tears.

"They killed everyone. Mom and Dad and the boys… they killed them all. They sat there and shot them down. They shot them down for a mule… they could have just taken it… they didn't have to kill them to get the mule." Her voice trailed off and her body shook while she hung her head and sobbed.

I swung out of the saddle, dropped the reins, and walked toward her. The grey stood ground tied and began to graze. "I'm sorry, ma'am. Like I said, I'm Samuel. Your name's… uh… Katherine… isn't it?"

Still sobbing, she nodded and rushed toward me. She buried her head in my chest and wrapped her arms around me. I tensed up and tried to pull back, but she held on.

Nervously, I looked around. Bad things could happen to a colored man who touched a white woman in Kansas as well as Arkansas. Nobody had to tell me that. I'd learned it the hard way.

"I was gatherin' eggs when they rode up. I hid in the barn 'til they were gone, and I saw what they did. They… they just sat on their horses and shot them down," she repeated, "and they laughed."

Gently, I removed her arms from around my body and stepped back. I picked up the reins and handed them to her. "You stay here. Old Boone will look after you. I'll go back to the house and look around. I won't be long."

She was still sobbing as I started to walk away, so I turned back toward her. "Would you feel better in the saddle? He's plumb gentle." The girl nodded and I gave her a leg up. She began to rub Boone's neck and it seemed to comfort her some. He lowered his head to the ground and resumed grazing.

As I walked toward the farmstead I thought about how small and fragile she looked astride the big gelding… and so alone. I glanced back again, and it struck me hard. How terribly alone she was.

She was alone as the result of the three men snuffing out her family. Snuffing out their lives and their dreams and their hard work, and I supposed they'd done it with no more concern than if they'd stepped on as many ants.

I had seen this type of cruelty before. I had lived through this type of cruelty, but I still couldn't understand it.

As I approached the Willis' farmyard, I knew what I'd see would not be pretty. I wasn't wrong at all. The bodies of Mr. Willis and the two boys were lying between the house and barn. There was a hayfork next to one of the boys and their father's right hand was still gripping an axe. He was lying face up with his mouth open and his eyes glazed over. All three bodies were riddled with bullet holes and covered with blood and flies.

Mrs. Willis was lying face down just off the front porch with her feet still on the steps. A rusty, double barreled shotgun was in the dirt next to her. There was an exit wound in her lower back and the top of her head was mostly blown off. I remembered her from the previous day as a pretty woman in her late thirties. Had she not had the scatter gun, I knew her fate would have been much worse. Because she was armed, they'd been forced to shoot her. That was merciful, I reckoned, compared to what they would have done to her otherwise.

Walking back and forth between the barn and the house, I took a good long while to study the sign. When I was satisfied that I knew how it had happened, I dragged the bodies into the barn and covered them with a tarp. Then I walked back over the hill and found the girl, still mounted, still stroking the grey's neck, and still crying.

"I moved the… all of them… out of sight. Why don't I take you to the house where you can lie down?" She nodded and I began leading Boone back toward the house.

"It looks to me like two of them did all of the shooting. The kid stayed back fifty yards or so and there were no shell casings next to where his horse stood. The older of the two boys was leading the mule. They shot your father and brothers and the one with the red beard rode after the spooked mule.

Your mother came out onto the steps with the shotgun. The red bearded one shot her from close range, and the mule broke loose and ran toward the corral. One of 'em, most likely the one with the black beard, caught the mule and held on to him while the other one went through the house. It looks like the kid just sat on his horse and stayed out of it. Is that about right?"

The girl nodded and began speaking in a shaky voice. "Yes, that's how it was. When they first rode up they stopped at the edge of the farm yard and talked. The big one hit the blonde kid with the back of his hand and nearly knocked him off his horse. He stayed where he was, and then it happened just about like you said. I think he saw me in the barn, but he didn't tell the others."

I tied Boone to the rail in front of the farmhouse and took the girl inside. I told her to lie down while I dug the graves. "Can you do it… can you bury them between the garden and the creek?" She asked.

"Yes ma'am. I'll do that. You rest now."

The soil was loose and sandy and I had the four shallow graves dug in two hours. I wrapped the bodies in canvas. After they were lowered into the holes and covered, I fetched the girl. She put flowers from the garden on each of the graves.

Katherine Willis stood next to me and cried while I read a passage from my Bible. She was a touching sight as she stood, trembling, in her faded cotton dress. She looked like a lost and helpless child. I reckon that's just what she was. I stepped back and left her standing next to the graves for awhile before I said anything more.

"We've got a distance to ride, Ma'am," I told her, "Why don't you see if you can find some clothes that would be better suited for that?" Without saying anything, she went into the house. When she returned, she was wearing a pair of brown canvas pants, a checkered shirt, boots, and a dusty black hat. Everything was too big for her and it covered up her shape. She looked like a young boy wearing his father's clothes. I reckoned that was good.

I helped her up behind the saddle and we set out. The grey carried the girl and me easily, but I kept him at a walk or a slow jog for her comfort. The ride back to the cottonwood where I'd left the three men hanging took nearly two hours. Only the boy was still conscious when we arrived. The faces of the other two were discolored and their mouths were open. Motionless, they made no sound except for their shallow, raspy breathing.

All tolled it had been close to six hours since I'd hoisted them into the tree. I wondered how long a man could live hanging like that with a rope around his chest. I cut the boy down and rounded up the horses and the mule.

Shooting the two that were still hanging there crossed my mind, but I didn't do it. Nor did I concern myself with their discomfort or how long it would take them to die. I gave the boy some water and a few minutes to recover. With Katherine on the chestnut, the boy on the brown, and the mule and the bay following behind, the three of us rode north.

Chapter Four

Don't get fooled real often
Pretty careful that way
Gave the lad a big break
I'm sorry to say

The blonde kid rode slumped in the saddle and didn't say anything for the first few miles. He rode out front where I could keep an eye on him. I carried the only weapons except for a pistol I'd given to Katherine. I told her to keep it handy but out of sight. She slipped it into the waist band of her trousers and covered the handle with her shirt. Riding next to me, she never got more than a few feet from my side. Every time I looked in her direction she was looking my way, but she remained silent.

At the crest of a small knoll, I rode up next to the boy and looked into his face. He was obviously scared. "What's your name boy?"

"Lars, Lars Olson," he answered. "What are you going to do with me?"

"Why don't you tell me what happened back at that farm this morning, and then we'll talk about your future." He nodded.

"When we got there Red started talkin' about killin' the man and the boys and havin' fun with the woman. I said they should just take what they wanted and not hurt nobody. Joshua hit me and he… uh… he took my pistol. Said he'd kill me too if I didn't keep my nose out of their business. I saw the girl in the barn, but I didn't say nothin' about it to Red or Joshua."

"How old are you, Lars?"

"I'm near eighteen. I know I shoulda done somethin' to stop 'em, but I just froze. I was scared."

"How is it that you were ridin' with those two?"

"I… uh… I ran into 'em in Missouri 'bout a week ago. I was lookin' for work and they said they was gonna' have some horses that needed breakin'. Said they had a place up in Nebraska with a bunch of horses on it."

"Well Lars, Katherine, here,"…I looked in the girl's direction… "and the sign you boys left back at the farm told me about the same story you just did. You got nothin' comin' to you for what happened back there. When we get to town you and the girl can tell your story to the law. Don't tell 'em anything about me. Tell 'em where those fellas are hangin' in the tree and that you don't know who put 'em there. I'm gonna' skirt the town and keep headin' north. Is that agreeable with you?"

The boy smiled. He'd obviously been expecting a worse fate and was mighty relieved at what I'd said.

"You're going to leave me there? You're going to just leave me in Salina? Can't I go where…wherever you're going?" There was panic in the girl's voice.

"Folks there will take care of you, Ma'am. Nothin' good will come to either of us if you stay with me."

She looked at me for a few seconds but said nothing more. Her pleading eyes were blue and round and filling with tears. I couldn't help but feel her pain. At the same time, I was struck by how beautiful she looked. So much so I had trouble keeping my eyes off of her. Neither of those things changed anything, however. Allowing her to ride with me wouldn't be smart, and being smart kept me alive.

Now that he knew he wasn't going to be hanged or shot, the boy got a good bit more talkative. "They called you Crow. Back at your camp they called you Crow. Why is that?"

"When I was about your age," I told him, "I set out on my own. Got to El Paso and was lookin' for work. Told some boys I was a cowboy. They said I was too black to be a cowboy. Said I must be a crow… a crow with one bad wing. Those boys beat me up some and had a good laugh on me."

"Did you shoot 'em?"

"No, I ran. I ran, and then I jumped on this old grey and got the hell out of there."

"You just ran away?"

I nodded. "At the time, it looked like the best way to stay alive." There was more to the story, but I chose not to share it with young Lars.

A half mile outside of Salina, I wished the pair well, returned Lars' weapons to him, and turned the grey toward the north. The girl gave me a long, sad look as we parted. I felt something too, but I shook it off. I spurred Boone into a long-strided lope.

Staying off the roads, the grey gobbled up the uneven ground of the Kansas prairie in big bites. I wanted to get four or five miles north of town before making camp, and get out of the area altogether early in the morning. Four people had been shot dead and the two I left hanging in the tree might be dead by now too. The law might see fit to find a crime or two in all of that…something they could pin on a colored man. I didn't see any sense in waiting around to make it easy for 'em.

It was dark by the time I made camp in a mixed stand of Aspen and Birch next to a small stream. I hobbled Boone and turned him out to graze on the ankle deep grass that grew in the moist shade of the creek bottom. Antelope jerky and a left over sourdough biscuit passed as supper. I washed the sparse meal down with water from my canteen and refilled it from the clear, spring fed creek. Making no fire, I crawled into my bedroll. It was late June and the nights were short. Morning wasn't far away and I planned to be moving north again at first light.

Frogs were croaking and the crickets and coyotes joined the chorus with their noisy chirps and howls. Normally these familiar sounds would put me to sleep, but I lay awake for a long while and thought back on the day. The cruel brutality that had taken place at the Willis farm turned my gut. It brought to mind images of my own past. Images I'd been trying to outdistance for years.

Once I got my mind off the carnage, I realized there were some particulars of the outlaws' behavior that I didn't understand. Understanding people's behavior…white men's behavior…was important to me. More than any other thing, even more than my ability to shoot, it kept me alive.

Why had they given the kid's guns back to him? For that matter, why hadn't they killed him? Killing sure didn't bother them any. He was supposedly just riding along with them, and he'd seen the whole ugly thing. They'd killed an entire family, including two boys and a woman, yet they didn't kill him. It didn't make sense.

When I closed my eyes, I saw the girl's face as she stood over the graves of her family, and I felt real uneasy with the thought that I'd left her with that kid. I got out of my bedroll and saddled the grey.

Chapter Five

Just a sweet little girl
So pretty and nice
Guess he thought she'd make
The same mistake twice

"You know I seen you in the barn, but I didn't say nothin' about it to them other two. I reckon I saved your life."

The girl's lips curled into a sneer as she looked in the young man's direction. "You didn't do anything to stop them from killing my family. You ain't much of a hero the way I see it."

"Well he took my pistol from me when he whacked me." Her eyes narrowed as she responded to the statement. "No he didn't. I watched from the window. You had a pistol and a rifle. You either didn't want to stop them, or you didn't have the nerve to."

The boy didn't offer an argument to what she had said, and he was quiet for awhile as the pair continued their ride toward Salina. He had no need to try to convince her of anything. The way he saw it, he was holding all the cards. With the bridle reins in his left hand, his right drifted down to his side and came to rest on the handle of his revolver. Kate caught the movement out of the corner of her eye and thought about reaching for her gun, but fear got the better of her. She couldn't make herself do it.

Lars thought over his options and decided to sit tight for the moment. He could make his move on the girl anytime and it would be easy. He was so pleased with how things had unfolded in the last few hours that he couldn't stop smiling. He almost laughed out loud as he rode along. He'd come out of this mess smelling like a rose. It didn't matter that Kate had called him on his lie about what exactly had happened at the farm. Samuel was the dangerous one, and he'd bought his story completely. Believed it enough that he'd ridden off and left him with the girl. Left him to take her to the sheriff or do whatever he wanted with her.

In his mind he could picture Red and Joshua, red faced and unconscious, hanging from the cottonwood tree, and it made his smile broaden. He didn't feel much about Red one way or the other. It was the same ambivalence he had for most everyone. People just didn't matter to him. He'd grown up without caring about anyone but himself, and it was his way now. It went all the way to the core.

Joshua was actually his stepfather and the lone exception. The boy did have strong feelings for him. He hated him with every bone in his body. The thought of the lariat squeezing tightly around his chest and biting into his flesh brought him immense pleasure. Would the rope kill him, he wondered, or would it just keep him in agony until he died from a lack of water or food? Either way would be fine, but he liked the idea of the man suffering a slow death.

Joshua had taken up with Lars's mother when Lars was seven or eight years old. She was a whore working in a saloon in St. Louis. In those days Lars lived the life of a stray dog. He fended for himself by begging and scrounging for food and stealing whatever he could.

Joshua inherited a small farm in Missouri, and when he left to live on it, he took Lars and his mother along. What little work got done on the place was accomplished by the boy. When his mother and stepfather were drunk, which was most of the time, they pretty much ignored him. It was when Joshua was sober that Lars stayed clear of him, because that's when the beatings came, and they came without warning and for no apparent reason.

This kind of existence went on for six years until one day Lars walked into the cabin to find his mother lying on the floor. Her face was bloodied and most of her clothes were torn off. Her eyes were open and lifeless.

The boy looked down at her and felt nothing. Later that day he rode off with Joshua. He was never offered an explanation as to why the man had killed his mother and he never asked.

For the last four years they had been living on the trail, stealing horses, mostly, and a few cattle. Red had joined up with them maybe two years ago. The three of them got by stealing anything they could. As long as Joshua had money for whiskey, life was tolerable. He only got real mean when he was sober. His stepson did him one better…he was mean all the time.

Turning his attention back to Kate, he asked, "what are we gonna tell the law when we get to town?"

"We're going to tell them exactly what happened, except we'll leave Samuel out of it. Just like he asked us to."

He laughed. "Samuel? You mean that one handed nigger? I ain't gonna do what he told me to do. I got no reason to do that."

Young Katherine Willis shook her head in disgust. "He cut you down from that tree, when he could have left you there or even shot you, and he let you go free. You'd be dead now, or headed for jail, if he hadn't given you a break."

"Well, maybe he made a mistake when he done that. 'Cause I don't think I'm fixin to tell the law nothin'."

As he finished his statement, he drew his pistol from its holster and swung the muzzle her way. "We're gonna' camp here tonight, just you and me, and I'll decide what to do in the mornin'."

They rode into a thick stand of cottonwoods and dismounted. Katherine turned away from the boy. With the pistol in his hand, he walked toward her.

"I'm gonna have some fun with you tonight, darlin'. I was plannin' on sneakin away from the other two and comin' back to your farm for you tonight any ways. I wanted a turn with your momma too if they hadn't kilt her. That's why Joshua hit me. I guess the joke's on him and Red. They're probably dead by now from hangin' in that tree, an' you an' me…we're gonna have all the fun."

He walked up behind her, and took the pistol that was stuffed in the front of her trousers. His eyes and mind were on the girl as he carelessly tossed it into the tall grass. Kate watched it fall near the base of a tree. Pressing his gun against her back, he said; "Now take off your clothes… all of them."

Kate closed her eyes and fought hard to keep from crying. Only this morning she'd watched while her family had been murdered, and now she was going to be raped and probably killed. It would be better, she thought, to be dead. What did she have to live for anyway? She had felt some comfort when Samuel had been with her, but now he was gone and she felt so incredibly and hopelessly alone.

Her whole body was shaking just like it had been when she'd stood helpless in the barn and watched that horrible scene unfold. Somehow she had to calm herself and find a way out of this, and death looked like the way. She took a deep breath and let it out slowly. Somehow she had to find the courage and strength she needed to do it. She remembered her mother coming out of the house with the shotgun and being afraid to shoot it. Doing nothing wasn't an option…she couldn't let herself be the helpless little girl again.

Her mind raced… maybe she didn't have to die. For a moment she considered turning toward him and trying to grab his gun, or diving for the one he'd thrown in the grass. Then she thought about what Samuel had said about doing what you have to do to stay alive.

Or perhaps, she thought, she could use his advice to enable her to die on her own terms. She knew a couple of things for sure. She wasn't going to let Lars have his way with her, and in spite of how big and ruthless he was, she was smarter. Kate took another deep breath, set her jaw, and began to unbutton her shirt. Her hands were no longer shaking.

"That's right, Kate darlin', you do what I tell you and we're going to have us a good time, and maybe you won't get hurt. You just keep goin' til you got everything off that pretty little body of yours." He stood behind her, with the gun inches from her back as she did as he had instructed. When she was completely naked, she turned toward him and smiled.

The boy's eyes got big as he looked at the beautiful girl who stood before him. She made no attempt to cover herself, and she spoke first. "I've never done this before, Lars, have you?" He shook his head. "Well," she went on, "I reckon it's about time for both of us, then. Like you said, we can have us a real good time."

Kate took a step toward him. "If you turn that gun aside, I'll kiss you." She smiled again. "You wouldn't shoot a girl when she's kissing you would you Lars?" Standing on her toes, Kate took his left hand and put it around her waist. His right hand still held the pistol.

The boy had a foul smell about him, and she had to force herself to get close to him let alone kiss him on the lips. He froze up and made no response while she held the kiss for several seconds. She then stepped back a bit and looked up at his face with the smile still on hers. "Am I the only one who's going to be naked?"

The young man smiled nervously and stammered as he spoke. "Uhh…yeah, I reckon I need to get these off." He pointed toward his waist. "You do it for me."

Without saying anything, Kate unbuttoned his pants and shirt and dropped them to the ground. She helped him out of his one piece suit of long underwear. She tried to ignore how repulsive it was to touch it… stained from urine and perspiration and wreaking of body odor.

"Why don't we lie down in the grass over here, Lars, or do you cowboys do this standing up?" She took his hand and gently pulled him down into the tall green grass.

The pistol remained in his right hand as he lowered himself down on top of her. With her left hand she held him slightly off of her. "Go easy, Lars, I've never done this before." With her right hand she felt around in the grass for the Colt revolver.

A sudden chill went through her as her fingers felt the cold metal of the discarded hand gun. She pressed the muzzle against her temple and cocked the hammer.

Lars dropped his gun and reached out with his left hand. He got hold of her wrist and twisted it, but he twisted it the wrong way. When Kate squeezed the trigger, his shoulder was almost touching the muzzle. The bullet missed the bone, but plowed a deep furrow in the flesh. Lars cried out in pain and got to his feet. Bending and reaching for his own gun with his right hand, he saw Kate cock hers again. This time she wasn't pointing it at her own head.

His fingers were just inches from his gun when Kate's weapon spoke. Lars didn't feel the bullet pass through his body, only the searing flame of the burning black powder that belched from the barrel. A dark shadow of bewilderment fell over his face as he stepped back with his hands clasped over the wound in his belly. He looked at the blood on his hands like he didn't understand what had happened to him.

Kate got to her knees. She looked into his eyes as he stood not three feet from her. The Colt looked outsized in her small hands... hands that jumped with each shot as she emptied the gun into his midsection. The impact sent him staggering back against a tree, but, somehow, he remained on his feet.

With the smoking gun still pointed in his direction, she got to her feet, stepped back and stood there naked. She kept her eyes on him as she found cartridges and reloaded. She slipped a cartridge into five of the six chambers. She pulled the hammer back, and, for a moment, thought about shooting him five more times. Instead she eased the hammer onto the empty chamber and lowered the weapon.

Lars's eyes were wide and starting to glaze over, and his mouth hung open. Still trying to cover his wounds with his hands, he stood for a good ten seconds before falling to his knees. Soon he fell forward with his face in the dirt. He sucked some of the dusty Kansas prairie into his mouth with each raspy breath. His breathing gradually grew shallower, but it would be nearly half an hour before it stopped.

Kate found the boy's canteen and washed herself. She washed every part of her that had come into contact with him. She got dressed, stuffed the pistol back into her pants, mounted the chestnut mare, and began to ride away with the mule following behind.

She'd gone just a few yards when she jumped off the mare and walked back to where the dying man lay. She found his gun belt where he had dropped it and strapped it around her waist.

Lars had managed to roll over and his eyes were still open and they followed her, but he made no other movement. Her gaze lingered on his face for a few seconds, but she felt no compassion. The cold, hard expression that gripped her pretty face never softened.

She had been ready to die… ready to take her own life. It hadn't worked out that way, but she felt no great sense of relief. Nor did she feel any remorse for having killed the boy.

This morning she'd hidden in the barn and watched as her family had been shot down with neither cause nor mercy. If her mother had not hesitated to fire the shotgun, maybe things would have been different. It was a lesson young Kate had learned quickly and well. Never again would she let herself be in a defenseless position, and she wouldn't be afraid to shoot first. It was a lesson Lars had learned too late.

Chapter Six

Together once again
I know I shouldn't stay
I have the strength to leave her
If it doesn't slip away

I'd ridden no more than a mile when I heard the sound of hoof beats in the darkness. It sounded like a single horse or maybe two. Leaving the trail, I guided the grey into a stand of aspen and waited. The moonlight was bright and I recognized the chestnut mare and the mule from a good distance. The rider was plainly too small to be the blonde kid. I rode out onto the trail directly in front of them. The horse stopped so fast the mule ran into the back end of her.

"Kate, it's me, Samuel. Don't be afraid. It's me." I rode up close to her and got a look at her face. She didn't look like a sad and helpless girl any more. Her jaw was tight and her eyes were hard and steely.

"I ain't afraid," she said. I saw the gun belt around her waist and I took a minute to let it all sink in before I said anything more. "Where's the kid? Did you get to Salina and talk to the Sheriff?"

"No," she answered, "we didn't get to Salina, and he's dead. I killed him… shot him five times in the belly."

"He gave you reason?" I asked. The girl just nodded. I saw no point in asking for details, I had a pretty good picture of the situation.

"You bury him?"

"No," she responded.

"Where is he?"

"A couple miles south of town, just off the road in some trees."

The shock of what had happened to Kate had obviously hardened her and made her angry, at least for the present. Perhaps it was the only way she could survive the horrors that had been visited upon her. I knew something about that. I wondered how long the effect of it would last… for both of us.

There was now another white man lying dead on our back trail. Shot full of holes and lying on ground laced with the hoof prints of Kate's mare and the mule. I turned to her and spoke with urgency. "Let the mule go. We're riding north and we've got to put some ground between us and what happened here today. I reckon you're going to have to stay with me for a while."

She pulled the halter from the animal's head and looked my way. Her face had softened some. "I want to stay with you, Samuel."

We rode side by side, mostly at a fast lope, through the night. It was a couple hours after sunrise when we finally stopped next to a creek to rest…maybe catch some sleep… and water the horses. I figured we were close to fifteen miles north of Salina.

Soon after we'd set up our minimal camp, Kate pulled the pistol from the holster and studied it. She spun the cylinder several times and worked the hammer. "I want you to teach me how to shoot this thing really good, Samuel. I want to learn to shoot fast and straight."

I weighed her request in my mind for a bit. I thought about the day... what she'd been through and what she'd done. I figured it made sense to help her some.

"Don't worry so much about shootin' fast. There are two things that are important when it comes to shootin'. You gotta be accurate, and you can't be afraid to shoot...you can't do it out of fear, but a lot of times you have to shoot first. I think you might have a handle on that last part already."

Her eyes locked on mine as if to make sure I really meant what I'd just said.

I continued to look into her wide open blue eyes and nodded my assurance. "I'll help you, Kate. We'll rest here for a couple of hours and talk about shootin' later."

Though I was dog tired, I slept fitfully for the first hour. The sun was hot and bright, biting flies buzzed around my face, and I had an uneasy feeling. I covered my head with my blanket and after a while slept soundly, but only for a short while.

The report of a pistol rousted me out of my bedroll and onto my feet. It was followed by two more... one right after the other. The girl was nowhere in sight. With my pistol drawn and another hidden under my coat, I walked around the area of the camp looking for the source of the gunfire. It didn't take long.

She was standing at the edge of the creek, shooting at a beaver-cut stump on the other side. I could see no evidence that any of the shots had come close to the target.

"Ma'am, put that gun away," I told her, "We don't need to attract any attention. We'll get enough without trying. Don't shoot that thing unless I tell you to. Do you understand?"

She got a hurt look on her face and holstered the revolver. "I'm sorry. I just wanted to practice so I can protect myself. So I can help you protect us."

"Listen to me," I said, "the law will be investigating all of those…uh…those things that happened yesterday. They could be on our trail now. Gunshots will bring them down on us for sure. I don't think you understand, Kate, how much trouble could come our way. It's different for me. And you bein' with me makes it a whole lot worse."

"I'm really sorry… I" Her eyes were open wide again and looking into mine, and I shushed her up.

"It's OK, just try not to draw attention to us, and, like I said, I'll help you with your shootin' when the time is right."

She reached out and put her hand on my arm. Her eyes were wet with tears. I looked away from them and pulled free of her hand, but she grabbed my arm again; firmly this time. "You're going to let me stay with you then? Please, Samuel. I want to stay with you. I don't want you to leave me alone. Not ever."

I hesitated for a bit before answering. Being in her company made me feel good. Something I didn't like to admit, even to myself, but it did feel good to be with her. "I don't know…I don't think so…maybe for a while. I guess you'll have to stay with me until we get away from here. We need to saddle up and be gettin' out of here right now."

The chestnut loped along beside Boone at a smooth and steady pace for the next hour without showing any sign of tiring. She was a good mare; I'd known that from the first time I'd seen her. The girl sat a horse real well, too. That comforted me some. I liked that we'd put some miles between us and Salina without seeing anyone following us, but a chase was still a possibility.

Nobody was going to catch the grey, I knew that, and I was starting to like the mare's chances as well. She was tough, she moved real smooth and pretty, and the girl didn't weigh much. Didn't slow her down much at all. If she was going to be caught, it would take a hell of a horse and rider to do it.

The odds looked good to me. I always tried to be a step ahead and prepared to handle trouble. I knew trouble would come my way. It always had and it always would. Just had to get through it and come out the other side alive.

We rode north for another eight or ten miles, across rolling prairie, and then swung to the west. The terrain flattened out, and I could see for miles in all directions. I liked that. Except for the girl and me, the vast grassland appeared to be empty.

After we'd ridden west for a few more hours, we came upon a stream with a stand of Aspen lining its banks. There were a dozen or so prairie chickens roosting in the upper branches of one of them. The birds weren't alarmed by our presence or that of the horses, and we were able to ride up close. Confident there was no one nearby, I drew my revolver and fired twice. Two of the birds fell to the ground.

Kate dismounted and walked over to pick them up. "You shot their heads off. Both of their heads are shot right off. How did you do that? Can you teach me to do that?"

I nodded in response to her request. "Pick a small branch or leaf at the top of one of the trees and point at it with your finger. Point exactly at it; not just close, but exactly at it, and never look at your finger. Then do the same thing with another target and another and another. Always focus and concentrate on the target and never on your finger, and always pick a small target. After you've done that a hundred times, just using your finger, do it with your pistol. Don't shoot…just point. Do that every chance you get, and after a few days, we'll try some shootin'."

"Thank you. I'll do that. I'll work real hard at doin' that, Samuel."

Having ridden through the night and most of the day with little rest, and still feeling sure we were alone, I decided to make camp by the stream. The water was good and there was plenty of grass for the horses. I hobbled them and turned them out. Kate rubbed them down with prairie grass while they grazed.

I started a small fire with dry, beaver-cut branches I had found along the stream. I made coffee and began to prepare the birds for the pan, but the girl took over. She mixed up some sour dough and heated salt pork to grease the pan. While the biscuits were baking, she cut each bird in half and sprinkled the pieces with flour and salt. In a few more minutes they were fried to a golden brown and served with the warm biscuits. The meal tasted mighty good. It had been a long time since I'd eaten something I hadn't prepared myself.

The sun was low in the sky when we finished our meal. There was little breeze and the air had cooled dramatically. Some people, especially in the evening, find the prairie to be a place that's too open and lonesome and empty. I didn't feel that way at all. In fact I felt free and at home on the open prairie, and this evening was as pleasant as any I could remember.

I sat on a log and looped the sling around the steel sleeve on the end of my left arm. I'd found a rock, nearly as big as my head, and put it in the rawhide pocket of the device. Flexing and extending the arm at least a hundred times each, with a weight in the sling, was a routine I went through at least every evening and often in the morning as well. Since I was seventeen years old, I don't think I'd missed doing it on more than a dozen days.

Kate left her spot by the fire and sat down beside me. I got an uneasy feeling about having her so close, but when she leaned against me it felt good, and I kind of lost my focus. She reached around and put her hand on the upper part of my left arm. She stroked it up and down as I continued with my exercise. "You're strong, Samuel. Your arm is hard as a rock; it feels good," she said. "How did you lose your hand?"

The question caught me by surprise and brought my mind back to where it needed to be. I stood up and thought for a few seconds about whether or not I should answer. "They cut it off because I touched a white girl with it. And they would hang me if they saw you and me sitting together like that. You can't touch me anymore…don't touch me ever again. We shouldn't even be riding together. As soon as I can find a safe place for you, that's going to be over too."

She got the same lost and hurt look on her face she'd had the day I found her, and she turned away from me and ran toward the horses. In the shadows of the twilight, I could barely see her standing next to the chestnut mare, but I could plainly hear her sobbing. I breathed a heavy sigh and walked toward her. She turned away from me as I approached.

"Ma'am…Kate…It's just the way things are. It's not the way I want them to be, but it's the way things are in this country. It's not about you and me. It's about stayin' alive, Kate. It's about stayin' alive. That's what my life is about… Nothing else."

She turned toward me and looked into my eyes. Her gentle blue eyes were filled with tears and her lips were quivering. She looked vulnerable and beautiful at the same time. "I want to be your woman, Samuel. I don't care what color you are or what people think. I want to stay with you forever."

"That can't be Kate," I said, "It doesn't matter what you want or what I want. We can't hide from the rest of the world forever, and that's what it would take."

"Are you afraid of the white men? Is that why we'd have to hide?" She asked. "Men like the ones who killed my family." I looked at her and thought for a minute before responding.

"I'm not afraid of them hurting me or killing me, but I am afraid of losing…afraid of letting them best me and laugh about it…laugh at me and my daddy and my momma and my grandpa. I'm in a war I can't win, Kate. I can win little battles, and I can survive if I'm careful, and havin' you with me ain't bein' careful. It's as simple as that." She tried to say something, but I shushed her up, and the conversation was over.

After I'd laid my bedroll out on the ground, I went to the creek for some water. Kate looked confused as I poured the water on the fire and kicked dirt over the coals. "Can't we keep the fire going tonight? I'd feel safer with a fire."

"We're safer without it. Fire draws people to it. Havin' a fire ain't bein' careful." I looked at her as I spoke and saw she was afraid. Afraid of the dark, perhaps. I didn't know. I felt bad about what I'd said to her earlier, even though it needed to be said. "You'll be safe, Kate. I'll look after you."

For nearly nine years I'd been living by myself. From time to time I'd do some ranch work; working cattle, breaking colts and such, but mostly I lived on my own. It was a life I'd come to like, or at least accept, and it was a refuge. A refuge from a world and a past I wanted no part of. The presence of the girl seemed to be changing that.

The way Kate's life had recently been torn apart, and the similarity to what had happened to me as a child, was hard for me to face. It filled my mind with thoughts and memories that troubled me; took me out of that solitary refuge I had so carefully constructed. In spite of the deep sympathy I felt for her, and the attraction I was feeling but trying not to admit, I felt a need to escape. Sleep didn't come easy that night, and when it did come it was fitful and filled with dreams… chilling dreams.

*****

"Which hand did you touch that white girl with, boy?"

"I don't know suh, I didn't mean no harm. She dropped her purse."

I was struggling, but couldn't get free as they took me behind the store. With a grip like iron one of them held my right arm stretched out over the chopping block; the one they used for cutting the heads off the chickens.

I heard my Grandpa's voice. "He's only ten years old, boss. He didn't mean no harm, boss. Chop my hand off instead of the boy's. I shoulda been watchin' him closer."

"Which hand does he favor, old man?"

"Uhh… the left one. He favors the left one."

I heard the sickening, crunching sound of the axe and felt a sharp sensation of pain and then a foggy numbing feeling. I saw my left hand on the block and reached for it with my bloody stump. My stomach churned, and I threw up. "My hand, Grampa. Make 'em give me my hand back," I screamed.

I grabbed for my severed wrist and felt the cold steel sleeve that encased it. At the same time I felt Kate's hand on my shoulder.

"Samuel, wake up. It's alright, Samuel, you're having

a bad dream. It's alright." She wiped my brow with her bandana. I could feel the sweat running down my face and I felt a warm dampness all over my body.

The girl lifted the canvas cover of the bedroll and the blanket off of me. She continued to wipe my face and neck with the bandana. When I'd cooled off some, she lay down next to me and pulled the covers over us. I should have told her to get back into her own bedroll, but I didn't. Her body felt warm and soft next to mine. I didn't touch her, but I didn't ask her to leave either. I knew this wasn't smart. It was the kind of thing that might get me killed someday, but I didn't ask her to leave.

Chapter Seven

Woke up in Salina
And took him for a fool
Should have had a better story
For Sheriff Bob Poole

"Can you hear me? Can you hear me mister?" The doc put his hand on the man's shoulder and shook him roughly as he asked the question. His face and expansive forehead were badly burned from the sun. Protruding from between his scraggly black beard and mustache, were lips that were swollen and split.

"Yeah, yeah, I can hear ya." His voice was raspy and barely audible. "Where am I?"

"You're in Salina. I'm the doctor here. I'll get the Sheriff."

"What?" The man made an unsuccessful effort to sit up as he spoke. "No need to bother the Sheriff, Doc. The three of us will be on our way soon as we can."

"Well, you already bothered the Sheriff. He's the one that cut you down from that cottonwood you were hangin' in…and there ain't three of ya. It's just you and that red haired fella lyin' over there." The doc motioned with his head to a bed on the other side of the room. "Looks like he's comin' around too. Whoever hung you boys there had an imagination. Must have wanted you to die slow. You couldn't have lasted much longer, though. Both of you were near dead when he brought you in."

"How long was we hangin' there?"

"Don't know for sure," the doc responded. "Probably at least overnight. You both shit your pants at least once," he laughed, "figured you must have done that in the mornin'. I'll get the Sheriff, he's right outside, and he's the one wants to talk to you."

The patient got a puzzled look on his face. He was a little surprised by the doc's statement and attitude. "You a real doctor?"

The doc shrugged. "Close enough for Salina."

The black-haired one was in a sitting position, trying to get to his feet, when the Sheriff entered the room. He was a tall, well-built man, with a goatee and thick, sandy brown hair. "Relax, mister," he said, "you ain't goin' anywhere for a while. What's your name?"

"Uhh…Josh…uh, Joshua Smith."

"How about your partner? Who's he? Don't look like he's quite ready to talk yet."

"That's Red," the man came back, "Uh, Red…uhh…just Red, I guess." The Sheriff nodded and smiled.

"Doc says you mentioned a third guy. Who's that?"

"I uh, I don't remember," he answered.

The Sheriff took a step closer, his eyes narrowed and he looked squarely into the other man's face. "I got a jail cell just down the street that might help bring your memory back." Joshua Smith forced a smile.

"No need for that Sheriff. I'm just comin' around here. It's comin' back to me. He was a Swede kid. Name o' Lars, I think. Big, tall kid… blonde hair… maybe seventeen or eighteen years old."

Sheriff Bob Poole nodded. "Well, we found him. Shot dead. Shot in the belly at close range. Took so many rounds he was damned near cut in half. I reckon somebody must have been mad at him."

Joshua had to suppress a smile when he heard the kid was dead; stepson or not. Poole caught it, but didn't react.

Smith shook his head and spoke again. "That's a shame. He was a good kid. Nigger must have done it. He's the one hung us in the tree. Must have cut the boy down and shot him. Too bad…too bad. You find our livestock, Sheriff?"

"We found a bay gelding, and a sorrel mule," Poole answered.

"What about a mare? A liver chestnut mare, and a brown gelding. You find them?"

"No, we didn't," the Sheriff came back, "only found the two I told you about."

"Now tell me about this…uh…this nigra you say hung you up in that big cottonwood. Who is he? Do you know? And why'd he string you up like that?"

"It was that one-handed nigger. The one they call Crow. The one that's so good with a pistol. He's the one that done it to us."

"Yeah, I've heard of him," the Sheriff said, "and why do you suppose he did that to you boys?"

"Well, we was after him. We come upon a farm, east of where he left us hangin'…maybe six or eight miles."

"Everybody there was dead. A man, a woman, and two boys. Nigger took their mule, too. We followed the tracks. He was camped at that place where you found us, but he caught us off guard. He had his gun drawn and pointed at us before we could pull our weapons."

"He captured all three of you that way?" Poole asked. "Yeah he did, Sheriff. We ain't gun hands. We're just mustangers. Horses is our business."

"That farm, the one where you found the dead people, was it next to a creek?"

"Yeah, Sheriff, that's the one," Smith answered, "that nigger killed four people there. Killed 'em for a damned mule."

"And you found a man and his wife and two boys there… you didn't find a girl… a grown up, blonde-haired girl?"

Smith's face went slack and his eyes widened some. "Uhh…no…uh, we didn't find no girl. Just the woman."

"Did you bury the bodies, then?" Poole asked. Smith swallowed and took a breath before answering.

"No, Sheriff, we didn't. We figured we should get right on the trail of the nigger. We didn't want him to get too big of a head start on us."

Sheriff Bob Poole let the information sink in for a few seconds before saying anything further. "That Crow, the one that killed those folks, he rode six or eight miles and made camp?" The other man nodded. "And was he ridin' a big grey? A real rank, onry gelding with a jagged scar on his left shoulder?"

"Yeah, Sheriff. That's right… a mean lookin' sumbitch and that scar… you can't miss it."

Poole snapped a set of hand cuffs on Smith's wrists. "You're going to jail, mister. Some of what you told me might be true, but it ain't all true. I want to hear what your pardner's got to say when you ain't here to help him remember." Before he left with the prisoner, he cuffed Red's right arm to the bed frame.

Chapter Eight

Gave 'em a new day
Gave 'em one more dance
An' they killed every time
We gave 'em the chance

Joshua Smith and Red Wallace occupied the same cell in the Salina city jail. Smith poked Red in the ribs with his finger. "Wake up. Wake up you fat bastard."

Red's eyes opened and he put his arms up to protect himself as Smith continued to poke him. "I'm wakin' up for Crise sake. Leave me be for a minute." He swung his legs to the floor and sat on the wooden platform that served as a bed. "What the hell do you want?"

"What did you tell that Sheriff?"

"I don't remember. Hell, I was barely awake…like now."

Smith pushed him. "Did you say anything about that farm? Anything about what we done at that farm by the crick?"

"I don't think so. I told him the nigger hung us in the tree. You, me, and the kid." Red thought for a second. "Yeah, I think that's about all I told him."

Smith nodded. "Good. That's good. The kid's dead; got shot up real bad…got his guts tore up real bad. That's good too. He's the only one that seen what we done back there an' he ain't talkin'."

"Sheriff said somethin' about a growed up girl livin' at that farm. Do ya think she was there and we missed her?"

"I don't know," Red answered, "I sure didn't see nobody 'cept the four we got."

Smith stroked his whiskered chin while he thought for a minute. "If there was a girl there, maybe the nigger found her. Maybe he took her. He ain't gonna' come back and say nothin' to the law, but that girl might if she can get away from him."

He shook his head and sighed. "Besides, that ain't right at all… I mean a nigger havin' a young white girl like that, ya know? What's this world comin' to? We can't hardly let that be."

*****

Sunrise found Sheriff Bob Poole loping his roan gelding along the road that went east out of Salina. He'd made more than six miles already and was a third of the way to the Willis farm. The horse he rode was well known in the territory. More than sixteen hands high and powerfully built, he had a fluid, easy way of moving. There weren't many like him. He could run all day and into the night if he had to. Folks jokingly called him Railroad…said if you wanted to escape from the Sheriff and the big roan, you needed to take the train, because you weren't about to outrun them on a horse.

It was just past eight when he arrived at the little farm. The day was already getting warm. He was glad he'd left before dawn and gotten most of the ride out of the way while it was still cool.

The sign left from the day of the killings was getting old, but he was able to piece things together fairly well. He spent a fair bit of time where the bodies had fallen; between the house and the barn. Then he backtracked from the farm yard to the hills behind. The last thing he did was visit the spot by the creek where the Willis family was buried.

After he'd studied the sign to his satisfaction, the Sheriff spoke aloud. "Samuel Tucker, you're sure enough the one who put these people in the ground, but you didn't do the killin'. No sir…and you didn't shoot the Swede kid neither. I reckon young Kate's the one that done that. She's alive and she left here with you, but I reckon you've split up by now. Wouldn't be like you to do otherwise."

Poole was convinced the killers were the two men he had in jail. Proving that would be near impossible with the evidence he had, however. Tracks told him a lot, but that wouldn't be enough for a conviction in these parts. Especially with Smith and his partner claiming a black man did it. Kate Willis was the only hope for a witness to the crime. Finding her was going to have to be his number one priority. He hoped Judge Botsford would let him hold those two until he could get it done.

Poole swung into the saddle and hooked the roan with his right spur. On the first stride, he struck a lope that he kept up for the majority of the eighteen mile ride. In spite of his rapid pace, he arrived back in Salina a little late.

*****

The deputy walked across the room to the jail cell. He was a big, burly man with a pot belly and an unkempt appearance. On his belt buckle was an image of the confederate flag. "What do you boys want?" He got a grimace on his face and stepped back. "Geez, you guys stink."

Joshua Smith responded to his remark. "Well, Deputy, you might stink some too if you was left hangin' in a tree for a couple of days. You suppose you could fix us up with water and a tub so's we can clean up some?"

"I'd like to gents," he said, "I'd like to get some of the stink out of here, but that ain't part of the accommodations at this here fine hotel."

Smith made a show of looking at the Deputy's buckle. "I 'spect that means you fought for the South. Me an' Red, here, we done the same. Fought for state's rights and the freedom to do as we saw fit with the property we owned." The big deputy smiled. "Yeah, I reckon we were on the same side."

Smith went on. "You know what's happenin' right now while the Sheriff's holdin' us in this here jail? There's a nigger escapin'. A nigger that killed and robbed a whole family and stole a young white girl. We seen what he done, and we was after him when he beat us to the draw and hung us in that tree. He killed our partner, too. Killed a young white boy. He killed five white folks, stole a girl, and he's getting' away while we're sittin' in this damned jail… and we're the ones that was chasin' him."

"If that's true," the deputy said, "that's a damned shame. That ain't right at all, but I can't be lettin' you out of jail. Poole would hang me if I was to do such a thing."

"Well, knowin' what I just told you," Smith added, "and knowin' we were brothers in arms, couldn't you just show us a little respect and fix us up with a bath?" The deputy caught another whiff of the two and sighed. "Let me see what I can do, gents. Let me see what I can do."

*****

It was mid-afternoon when Poole entered his office. He nearly tripped over Deputy Mark Dupre's lifeless, naked body. There were red marks on his neck and his eyes were vacant and glassy. He'd apparently been strangled with a rope or a wire or something. The body was already feeling cool to the touch. The Sheriff figured he'd been killed sometime early in the morning.

The cell door was open and a wooden tub was inside. Water was all over the floor, apparently spilled from a couple of buckets that lay on their sides. One set of soiled clothes lay next to the body. Poole recognized them as the rank and filthy outfit Smith had been wearing.

Operating on a lawman's instinct, the Sheriff ran to the livery and was not surprised to find the proprietor lying in a pool of blood. His throat had been cut. The bay gelding was gone, and a couple of other horses were too. "We're gonna' have a lot of good reasons," Poole thought, "For hangin' these sons a bitches, and we ain't gonna' do it by the arm pits."

Bob Poole took a few minutes as he thought over his options. The two men had at least a five hour lead on him; probably more like seven. His own horse had covered nearly forty miles already today, and at a fast pace. Even the big roan needed some rest after a day like that. By the time he got his gear put together, and got on the trail, there'd be no more than a few hours of good tracking light left in the day. There was only one thing he could do. He'd strike out in the morning… on his own… just him and the roan. Confident in his ability, Poole figured he didn't need any help, and he sure as hell didn't need anybody slowin' him down.

Chapter Nine

Never thought love could get me
The truth has now hit me
A fairy tale it seems
Didn't end it or begin it
Woke up and I was in it
This dream I didn't dream

The girl and I had been traveling together for more than a week. I wasn't fooling myself; I knew it wasn't a good idea, but the thought of dropping her off somewhere wasn't sounding real good either. I had to admit that I'd come to like having her near me more every day.

Doing ordinary things, like making breakfast or taking care of the horses, was enjoyable when Kate was part of it. Life just felt better when she was around.

She liked to put her hands on me and hug me and I kept pulling away, but I wasn't as quick about it as I was at first. It wasn't scaring me as much as it had before. It wasn't bringing back the past…it should have, I reckon, but it wasn't.

After all of the years of living alone, I was surprised to feel this way…surprised to feel this attachment to another person…surprised to feel like I needed someone other than myself.

Like I said, I knew being with a white girl wasn't smart. It wasn't the kind of carefully thought out behavior that had served me so well all these years.

It didn't, however, mean I'd lost my wits altogether. I kept an eye on our back trail and had seen no sign we were being followed. We kept traveling in a northwesterly direction toward Colorado.

Initially we avoided roads and used cattle or game trails to cross the prairie, but after a few days, we cut a main wagon road and followed it west. We traveled at an easy pace; making maybe twenty miles a day.

The country was mostly empty, but when we came near a farm or anywhere that held some people, we separated. Kate rode ahead by a half mile or so, and when she got past the place she stopped to wait for me. She always made me promise I'd catch up with her and not leave her alone. In many ways she was a brave and capable woman, but she was clearly afraid of being left alone. Sometimes I had to prove to her that I could follow her tracks before she'd ride on ahead.

Kate was obsessed with the idea of learning to shoot well. She'd been real good about practicing pointing her finger and her pistol at targets of various kinds. After four days of that, I let her do some shooting. I didn't like telegraphing our position with the gunfire, but I'd picked an open spot where I could see trouble coming from a long way off.

Our horses were staying fresh and well fed on the grass of the creek and river bottoms where we usually camped. The mare was getting more fleshed out and more fit at the same time. She was proving to be an even better horse than I had thought when I first sized her up. I continued to like our chances of out running anyone who tried to chase us down. We might choose not to run, depending on the situation, but it was good to know we could run and run well if we had to.

I took Kate by the arm and walked her to within fifteen feet of a cottonwood stump. She flashed a warm and pretty smile. I hadn't been in the habit of touching her and the gesture was not lost on her. I returned the smile, even though I knew I could be heading for trouble. Trouble I might not be strong enough or quick enough to side step.

"That stump right there…" I started. "I can hit that, Samuel," she said, "it's so close." I smiled at her again.

"I reckon you can hit it. That knot about half way up and a little toward the left side…do you see that?" Her eyes grew a little wider.

"Yes, do you want me to hit that little thing?"

"No." I answered. "I don't really care what you hit right now; I only care about what you try to hit. That dark spot in the center of the knot… about the size of a pea… I want you to concentrate on that as hard as you can and shoot your pistol. Hold the pistol with both hands, relax, and squeeze the trigger gently. Other than that, don't even think about the gun and don't look at it. Go ahead. Take your time and shoot five rounds at that spot… not at the stump, not at the knot, but at the spot."

The Colt revolver looked over-sized in her small hands, but she approached her task with more confidence and resolve than one might have expected. It didn't come as a surprise to me. I'd come to know and understand her quite well in the short time we'd been together.

Small chunks of wood flew off the stump each time the pistol jumped. The sound of each shot was loud and intrusive as it echoed across the normally silent plains. I didn't like the noise, but I'd promised to teach her to shoot.

Except for the last one, each succeeding bullet penetrated the dead wood at a point closer to the tiny target. The hole from the fourth round was within an inch of the knot. "Was that good?" She asked. I nodded.

"That was good. You did real well, Kate."

"I can do better this time, watch."

"No," I said, "we're done for now. That revolver of yours will normally have five rounds in it. You need to learn to make them do the job. When you're using that thing for real, you don't get a practice round. Besides, we've made enough noise for one day." She gave me a pleading look, but I smiled at her and shook my head.

We mounted up and rode west. I wanted to get a few miles away from the spot where we'd done the shooting before making camp for the night. From a high point on the plain, I saw a long narrow stand of trees that I judged to be three or four miles away. In this country, trees like that usually meant a flowing stream.

The little creek was spring-fed with a good flow of clear, cold water. I gave it a quick look, turned the horses out to graze, and went about the task of setting up camp. Traveling as light as we were, there wasn't much to do, so Kate went off to explore the stream. After a few minutes, she came back with a big smile on her face. "Samuel," she said, "come with me."

She took hold of my left arm and led me toward the water. Kate was smart. There wasn't much that got past her. She knew I always kept my left arm, with the missing hand and the steel cap, to myself...out of sight for the most part. To show me that the disfigurement didn't matter to her, that she accepted me as I was, she made a point of touching it; even the steel cap on the end. She didn't have to say it, we were beginning to read each other pretty well, and I appreciated the gesture and the thought behind it. I no longer tried to keep it from her...didn't keep it stuffed in the pocket of my coat like I usually did when people were around.

She brought me to a spot where rocks and driftwood had formed a natural dam and a small pool. The edge of the pool was shady and the grass was deep and lush. I saw she had laid her bedroll out on the ground when she'd been here the first time.

Kate sat down, took off her boots and dangled her feet in the water, and motioned for me to sit next to her. I sat down beside her and she moved toward me so that our bodies were touching. I reached over and picked up her small, soft hand and held it in mine.

Without speaking, we sat there for a good long while, splashing our feet in the water, holding hands and smiling at each other. Any chance I had of resisting this girl… any chance of doing what my mind told me was the smart thing… disappeared like the ripples our toes made in the water.

I turned her way and put my hand around her shoulder. "You know, Kate…" I started, but she put her hands behind my head and pulled me on top of her as she sank back into the soft grass. The kiss we shared was long and warm and sweet.

Kate gently pushed me back. "This isn't right," I said. She cut me off again. "Look around you, Samuel," she said, "there's nothing but trees and grass and the water and maybe some trout. None of those things care about what color we are. I've never known a man who was as kind and decent," she smiled and stroked the muscle of my upper right arm; "and as strong and handsome as you are." She began unbuttoning her shirt, and gave me a look that told me I should do the same. I had no chance at all.

From the first day I'd met her, I'd found it hard to ignore

Kate's shape. I had taken notice of it many times, but when she stood naked by the creek that afternoon I had trouble believing a woman could be that beautiful. She stepped into the water and pulled me in with her. The pool was surprisingly deep. The water reached to the middle of my chest and nearly covered Kate's shoulders. Even in the icy cold water, her body and her soft breasts felt warm against my skin as I held her close to me.

We left the water and lay down on her bedroll. I thought I should say something, but, at the moment, I didn't feel real smart.

"We're getting your blanket all wet," was the best I could come up with.

"That's OK," She said, "We're going to sleep in yours tonight."

We made love by the edge of the little stream and again by the campfire later that night. The cold, harsh, unforgiving, solitary world I'd lived in for so long had changed forever. It was warmer, softer, happier…and a whole lot more dangerous.

Chapter Ten

With all that's gone wrong
In this young lady's world
Don't ever call her
A helpless little girl

"Hold up. Hold up a second. I want to look at them tracks. Two riders…they just came on to this road and it looks like they ain't too far ahead of us." Red dismounted and studied the hoof prints. "I'll be damned, Josh, one of 'em is that chestnut mare."

"Now how do you know that?" The other man asked.

"One horseshoe looks just about like every other one to me."

"I fit them shoes to that mare myself, and I filed my notch in the left front. And she toes in just a little on that one, too. It's her alright."

Joshua Smith thought for a few seconds. "You sure that's her?"

"You bet I'm sure," Red answered.

"Then I wonder," Smith said, "if we're followin' the nigger and that white girl."

"That could be, alright. I never got a good look at the tracks the nigger's grey made, but these here are from a big horse. We got no reason to follow 'em anymore, though.

What the girl saw an' what she might tell the law don't make a shittin' bit of difference now. They know damned well we killed the deputy and the other guy and stole these horses to boot. They could hang us three or four times if they had a mind to." The fat, red bearded one smiled and spit tobacco juice in the dirt as he finished his statement.

"Well, you're right about that," Smith said, "but that nigger's the one that strung us up in the tree, and I aim to kill him for that. I wouldn't mind amusin' myself with that girl neither, and, hell, we're goin' in the same direction anyway. We can get the mare back and add the big grey to our string, too. We can come out of this shit money ahead."

Red nodded his agreement to what his partner had just proposed. "Why not?"

*****

After an easy day of fifteen miles or so, Kate and I made a dry camp on a small knoll next to a draw that ran east to west. We'd watered the horses earlier that afternoon and filled our canteens and my big canvas water bag. It held enough to tide the horses over until the next day when we hoped to find a stream or water hole. I figured we had to be getting close to the Republican River, and I knew there'd be plenty of feeder streams nearby.

I loved being with Kate, but it still made me uneasy. If anybody found us together, trouble would surely follow. I picked our campsites more carefully than ever. I liked that I could see for several miles in all directions from this one.

The best grass around was in the bottom of the draw. I led the horses down there, put the hobbles on, and turned them out to graze. With the horses being down low like that, our camp didn't make much of a silhouette on the top of the knoll. I liked that, too.

For some reason, though, I was feeling a little more

edgy than usual today. Kate protested, but I didn't make a fire. There wasn't a hell of a lot of fuel available anyway… nothing but buffalo chips and sage.

When morning came, I gave in and made a small fire for making coffee and biscuits. Our supplies were running mighty low, and I was thinking about how we could replenish them when I noticed something off to the east. It was right on the edge of my vision, but there was definitely something there.

The image got bigger quickly, and I realized it was two riders clearing a rise with two more horses trailing behind them. Apparently they'd been sticking to the low ground to stay out of sight. It didn't look good. Our horses were still down in the draw, and couldn't be seen. At the moment, Kate was with them. That part was good.

I stood up and walked down to her as though I was paying no attention to the approaching horsemen.

"Kate," I said, "there are two fella's coming from the east. I want you to take your pistol and a rifle and hurry down the draw. See where it starts to curve off to the right? Stop there and stay out of sight, but watch those two as best you can."

"OK," she said, "but what should I do then?"

"It depends on what happens. Try to stay hidden and let me handle it, but do what you have to do to stay alive. If you have to shoot, don't be the second one to do it."

I kissed her on the cheek and started to walk back to the top of the knoll. Then I turned back and spoke to her again. "Kate, if you shoot, don't stop shooting until they're down and can't shoot back. Do you understand?" She nodded.

The riders kept coming. They were riding parallel to the draw at a gallop. When they were about a hundred and fifty yards out, they stopped and dismounted. Even from the distance, I recognized them as the two that I'd left hanging in the cottonwood. Seeing them alive surprised me. I reckoned they were no more than fifty feet from where Kate was hiding…maybe as little as thirty. It worried me some that they were that close.

One of them shouted. "Is that you, nigger? We're real happy to see you again. We still got bidness to take care of with you, boy. We didn't quite finish up with each other last time."

I watched them pull rifles from their scabbards. I remained standing, but inched back to where I could drop over the crest of the hill in a hurry. The slope wasn't much, but it would make me a little harder to hit. The only real cover was in the draw, and I didn't want to get them looking in Kate's direction. It was important that I keep their attention focused solely on me.

One of them hollered again. I assumed it was the black-haired one…the one who seemed to run the show. "Them pistols of yours ain't gonna' do you a hell of a lot of good at this range, boy. We gonna' have us a little turkey shoot… a little nigger shoot." He laughed and brought the rifle to his shoulder. I dropped to the ground, but kept my eyes on our visitors.

I was thinking I'd let them think they'd hit me with the rifle shots, and when they came up to check, I'd get them at close range with my pistols. That way they'd go right by Kate and she would stay out of it.

No more than a second separated the two shots. The echo sounded like it came from all around me.

When the bullets didn't kick up any dirt near me, I knew Kate had changed the plan. I watched both men stagger and turn toward the draw. They were still holding their rifles but not shouldering them. Four more shots came and the pair sank to their knees looking in Kate's direction.

Through the spy glass, I watched Kate climb out of the draw, reload her pistol, and walk toward the two fallen men. Still on their knees, they came face to face with the girl who had just killed them. At almost the same time, they fell forward, faces to the ground.

She was standing over them when I got there. I rolled them over. Each man had three holes in the center of his chest. Joshua had landed with his face in a fresh pile of cow or buffalo shit.

She was shaking and crying. I put my arm around her shoulders, but neither of us spoke for a while.

"You feelin' bad about doing what you did?"

"No…not at all. I'm just thinking about my family and how this maybe squares things in a small way, but it doesn't bring them back, does it? Nothing can bring them back, can it Samuel? I'm never going to see them again, am I?"

I shook my head. "No, Darlin', nothing can bring them back, and you won't see them again in this world. You did all you could, though, and you kept those men from ever hurting anyone again. It was the right thing to do, you were brave and you did some fine shootin'. I counted six shots, you didn't have the hammer sittin' on an empty chamber, did you?" She shook her head and said she didn't. "That was smart," I pulled her close to me and held her for a good long time.

The gunshots had no effect on the tired horses. All four stood quietly and munched on prairie grass within a few feet of the dead men. I quickly sized up the two that were saddled. The bay had a kind eye, looked to be a sensible horse, and he was stout. I took the lariat from his saddle and looped it around the feet of the black haired one. I got aboard, took a dally around the horn, and dragged the body to the edge of the draw and pushed it in. I did the same with the red haired guy.

The spring rains had washed a deep cut where the draw made the curve toward the north. I dropped both bodies, and all of their gear, into the cut. The bank was steep and sandy, and I broke enough soil loose to pretty well cover everything up.

It wasn't a perfect job, but it wasn't like I was burying my own kin, either. If the rain washed the dirt away and the coyotes and other scavengers got a bite to eat, that would be just fine. Hell, they were both plenty fat.

We broke camp and saddled our horses. I took the tack off the other four horses and turned them loose. Kate asked me why I didn't keep them. "Can't prove I didn't steal 'em, Kate. In this country I'm guilty unless I can prove otherwise. Remember that. Things ain't the same for me."

Kate was quiet as we resumed our ride west. I looked her way. "It's finished now, you know. You got all three of the men who killed your family. Do you still want to keep that gun?"

She nodded. "What happened to me at the farm that day… where I watched and couldn't do anything… that's never going to happen again."

We rode in silence for the first few miles and then Kate turned toward me. I could see tears in her eyes.

"How did this happen, Samuel? All my life I never hurt anyone… never fought with my brothers… never even slapped anyone. Now I've killed three men. How can this be? How can life turn around so quickly and so completely?"

I said I didn't know…but I did.

Chapter Eleven

If we're caught together
It might spell the end
Is this swift pursuer
A foe or a friend

I felt more at ease after burying the two outlaws. That business had taken a good share of the morning, but I saw no need to hurry.

By late afternoon we reached the Republican. We were about fifteen miles from where we'd planted those two, and I figured that was far enough. I built a fire and Kate fried up some Prairie Chickens she'd shot. I smiled when I saw that the head had been cleanly shot off of each bird. The girl learned quickly.

The sun was just starting to disappear below the western horizon when we'd finished cleaning up after supper. I sat down on a log. Kate sat next to me and took my hand.

"Can I ask you some questions, Samuel?" I smiled at her.

"Is there any way I could stop you from doing something you wanted to do?" I countered.

She playfully elbowed me in the ribs. "I mean some personal questions. Questions about your past… things you haven't told me about." I nodded.

"I guess that would be alright."

"How did you get to be so smart? You speak and read better than anyone I've ever known, but you never talk about going to school. How did that happen?" She turned toward me and those big, soft, blue eyes of hers begged for an answer.

I squeezed her hand and thought for a minute.

"Remember the other day when we sat with our feet in the pool and splashed and laughed?"

Kate blushed. "Yes, I don't think I'll ever forget that day." I laughed too.

"I won't forget it either, but I'm talking about when we were just playing in the water. That's the first time I can remember… uh …playing… since I was ten years old… since before those men cut off my hand. I spent nearly all of my time after that day preparing myself for the future. Preparing myself to survive and never be the victim of men like that again, and to maybe one day settle the score. I guess you understand that better than most." I squeezed her little hand again.

"I learned to ride and shoot and fight and I made myself strong, and more than anything I worked on my education… I wanted to be smarter than those who would do me wrong."

"My grandpa taught me that those were the things I needed to do. He was illiterate, like most former slaves, but he got a kind old white woman to help me with my reading and numbers and such. She had books on any subject you could think of, and she let me read all of them. When I wasn't working in the fields, I was studying."

"Grandpa taught me to pick my battles… taught me that it was sometimes better to run or look the other way and be alive to fight another day. My daddy didn't do it that way. He stood up to the white men when he had no chance of winning, and they hanged him."

I hesitated for a bit and then took a folded up piece of paper from a leather pouch I had in my coat pocket.

"My Grandpa is a wise and special man. He gave me this, too. These are the names of the two men who cut off my hand, and this one was with them when they hanged my father."

My voice was shaking some, but I went on. "I'll finish that someday just like you did with those men this morning."

Kate and I sat for awhile, holding hands and not speaking, but I wanted to tell her more.

"There were two men at a ranch in Texas who helped me, too. Henry and Luke…a colored man and a white man. They helped me with my studies and showed me how to make this arm into something I could use. It was all shriveled up and weak, and they made the first sling and showed me how to exercise it. Luke made the steel cap for the end of it, too. Instead of letting it hang at my side like a piece of rope, I can use it. I can use it as a weapon if I need to. I've hit a few men with it, Kate." I looked at her and smiled. "But I never had to hit any of 'em more than once."

"So that's it. I've spent the last sixteen or so years working on getting smart and strong and ready for the trouble I know is coming. Trouble, and surviving it, has been my whole focus. Until you came along, I really didn't think about enjoying life. I never played or loved and I rarely laughed… until you made me splash my feet in that water… until you made me fall in love with you."

Kate rolled off the log and pulled me down on top of her. "I think," she said, "we need to get you caught up on some of that loving and playing."

The night was clear and the stars were as bright and

numerous as only the high plains or mountains can show them to be. The light they gave off was enough that I could clearly see Kate's soft, feminine form. I never got tired of looking at her. I marveled at her beauty, and I marveled at how deep my love for her had become.

We lay in my bedroll, looked at the sky, laughed, and made love deep into the night. I can't imagine a man feeling any better or more complete than I did that night. My sleep was as deep and peaceful as I can ever remember it being.

The sun had already cleared the eastern horizon when I got up and set about the job of getting the fire going and making coffee. Kate was sound asleep.

We'd finished with our coffee, biscuits, and the left over prairie chicken and were breaking camp when I noticed a movement far off to the east.

I pulled my glass from my saddle bags and took a closer look. "We need to get movin', Kate," I said, "we got another visitor coming… the prairie's gettin' crowded. He's far enough off, though. I expect we can keep ahead of him and then lose him when we get the chance."

"Do you think he's following us?" She asked.

"Probably not. We're a long way from Salina. They'd have to want somebody pretty bad to come this far, and there's only one of 'em. It doesn't make sense that they'd send just one. Still, there's no reason to wait here and find out."

We struck a fast lope and headed off to the northwest across open prairie. By abandoning the road, I knew we'd find out in a hurry if the rider was following us or not.

After a quarter of an hour, I looked back and saw he'd left the road, too, and was following the same course we had taken. I was surprised to see he'd gained some ground on us. The pace we'd been riding should have been fast enough to maintain our lead.

Kate and the chestnut mare were right next to me. She liked to ride so that our knees were nearly touching. I looked her way. "We need to move a little faster," I said. She nodded, and we both leaned forward slightly and touched our horse's flanks with our heels. Even at a gallop, the mare stayed beside Boone like she was glued to him.

We continued at that pace for another quarter of an hour or better. As we crested a rise, I signaled for Kate to hold up. I reined in the grey and glassed our pursuer. He had gained additional ground on us, and, through my old army spy glass, I could now make him out more clearly.

I dismounted and started to pull the saddle from Boone. "What are you doing?" Kate almost shouted. "He's going to be here in no time at all, and we're in the open."

I smiled at her. "Don't worry about it, Darlin', and please don't shoot him when he gets here."

Seeing how fast he'd been gaining on us had me puzzled at first. An ordinary horse and rider shouldn't have been able to do that. When I glassed them for the second time and could make out the big roan and the way his rider sat in the saddle, I understood.

With only the one hand, I still had more than enough fingers to count the men I considered to be my friends. Bob Poole was at the top of that very short list. Kate looked at me with a wide eyed, puzzled expression. I smiled at her and kept reminding her not to shoot.

When he was close enough, Poole shouted. "Hey Sammy. Is that big grey horse of yours gettin' old, or did he surrender because he knew he couldn't out run Roanie?"

"No, that wasn't it," I told him, "I recognized you, Bob, and I knew you'd run that horse into the ground and kill him before you ever caught us. I just asked old Boone to show you some mercy, that's all."

Kate was astonished. "You know Bob Poole, the Sheriff in Salina, Samuel?" I nodded. "Known him for years, Kate, but I had no idea he was the law in Salina. We would have played this whole thing a lot different right from the start if I'd known that." She laughed.

"I guess I could have told you the Sheriff's name… but you could have asked as well."

Poole dismounted and turned the roan out to graze before he said anything more. Then he walked up to me with a big grin on his face and held out his hand. He was a good half a head taller than me and I looked up at him, returned the smile, and took the hand that was offered.

He turned toward Kate. "I'm sorry about your family, Ma'am. They were good folks. Mighty good folks." Kate choked up some as she thanked him for his condolences.

Poole went on. "Well at least it looks like you squared up with those boys that done it. I found where you put 'em in the ditch."

"You need to have us tell you how that happened, Bob?" I asked.

"No," he said, "those two escaped from jail, killed my deputy, killed old Howard at the livery, and stole two horses. And that's all on top of what they done to Kate's family. If you'd skinned 'em alive I wouldn't have any questions for you."

"How about I get a fire goin', Bob, and make us some coffee?" Poole nodded at the suggestion.

"Sounds good. You did a lot of hard ridin' you probably wouldn't have had to do, Sammy."

"I 'spect so," I answered, "but I didn't know you were the one wearin' that thing in Salina." I pointed at the star on his chest.

"When did that happen?"

"It's been near three years now," Poole answered. "Left Texas, came straight to Kansas and got this job right off."

"That's a good ride," I said with a smile. "You must have been on the trail for a week or better. Made that same ride once on the grey… took me almost a full day."

The Sheriff laughed. "Someday," he said, "we're gonna' have us a little race and put that discussion to bed."

I nodded in his direction. "Someday we will."

The three of us decided stay right there and make a dry camp for the night. We didn't have a lot of water left, but I reckoned it would be enough to get the three of us and the horses by 'til the next day when we'd get back to the Republican. After supper we sat around the fire and talked.

"Where are you planning to go Sammy?" Poole asked.

"I don't know. We were just heading west, trying to get away from Salina, and get Kate somewhere safe. I didn't like my chances back there when all of the bodies started showin' up."

"Well, there's no reason not to go back there now. We know who did all of the killin' and those two are fixin to feed the coyotes and buzzards any time now."

"The family farm belongs to you now, Kate. I'll bet we could find somebody to help you run it. And Sam," he went on, "I'll be needin' a new deputy. I think you'd do just fine."

The suggestion caught me off guard. "Are you serious? I've never heard of such a thing," I told him.

"Yeah, I'm serious and I think we should go back there and see if we can't make that work."

Poole had made no comment about Kate and I being

together nor had he asked any questions. Nonetheless, I knew he understood and accepted our relationship. Men like him were rare in this country. I understood what he had in mind when he continued the conversation about heading back to Salina.

"You know, Sammy," he said, "You workin' and livin' in town and Kate bein' close by on the farm might be a good arrangement. It might be the only way you can really do it. We need to find the right people to help her with the farm, but I've got an idea about that." I looked at him and nodded and he knew I was following his line of thinking.

"Me bein' a deputy in Salina," I said, "how's that going to set with the folks there? Seems to me like that would be a problem."

Bob Poole thought for a minute and looked into my eyes when he finally responded. "That could be, Sam, but if they don't know anything about you and Kate, it might work. You… that is Bad Wing Crow… has quite a reputation in this part of the country. Folks might like the idea of having a deputy with your legendary skill with a gun. The fact that you got the men who killed Dupre and Howard and the Willis family is good too. That will sit well with the locals. I think we can work this thing out."

I hadn't told Bob who had really shot those three outlaws, and, for the time being at least, I planned to leave it that way. I didn't figure telling the story would do Kate any good as fragile as she was in the aftermath of all that had happened. It was her story to tell if she wanted it told. If she chose not to, it wouldn't matter much to the already overblown reputation of Bad Wing Crow.

Kate did want to know how Bob and I had gotten to be friends and she wouldn't stop asking questions until she knew the whole story…

Chapter Twelve

Busted A Ranch, 1878

He went off all alone
It worked out in the end
Spoiled the day for two cowboys
And met his best friend

Luke Hopkins stood back at a distance of a hundred yards from the river and counted the shots. After the fifth one, he began to walk toward the young man who had done the shooting.

"Hold your fire, gunslinger, I come in peace." Samuel Tucker turned around and greeted his boss with a wide smile. "You gettin' that shootin' figured out, Sam?" The rancher asked.

"I believe I am Luke. These pistols you gave me shoot mighty nice, and that way of shootin' you showed me sure works. I appreciate you doin' that for me."

The lad already had a way of looking a man straight in the eyes as he spoke. Luke liked that and took some credit for it.

Hopkins put his hand on the boy's shoulder and squeezed the firm and well defined muscles. "You ain't a skinny kid any more, Sam. You're growin' into a fine young man. I need to keep you around here. Remember a few years back when you was fixin' to leave and I kept you here by givin' you the grey?"

Sam nodded. "I sure do. If you'd known how good he was going to be, would you have still done it?"

"I don't know, Sammy." Luke laughed. "Yeah, I reckon I would have. You made that horse what he is today. None of the other cowboys on this place could have done as well. You're about as good a hand with a horse as I've ever seen."

"I suppose you think," the boy said, "that givin' me these Colts and the shootin' lessons is what kept me here for the last two years."

The older man gave him a playful shove. "That's exactly what I think, Sammy, and it was the right thing to do. Now I want a close up look at some of that fancy shootin'. Let's see you hit that branch that's sticking out from that dead tree over there. The one on the left about head high."

"I usually only take five shots when I practice and try to make 'em all count. A wise man taught me that. Said I wouldn't be gettin' a practice round if I was shootin' for real." The boy delivered the answer with a grin.

"I know that," Luke responded, "but a wise man is asking you to make an exception in this case and give him a demonstration."

Without further discussion, the boy cracked off five more shots. No more than a second separated any of them. Each time he pulled the trigger, an inch long section from the end of the branch flew into the air.

Luke Hopkins shook his head. "I might have got you started on this, but you've got a gift for shootin' that didn't come from me. I've never seen a man who could do what you just did, son. Never seen one before and don't expect to see another."

The pair turned away from the muddy ribbon of water folks called the Pecos River and began walking back toward the ranch.

"You know, Luke, I appreciate everything you've done for me." The boy spoke in a soft and serious voice. "You and Henry have treated me like I was your own son."

The big man put his hand back on the boy's shoulder. "That's how I think of you, Sammy. I couldn't be more proud of you if you were my son, and I know Henry would say the same thing."

There was a long silence before Luke said what he'd been thinking for some time. "You're fixin' to leave, aren't you?"

"Yeah, I am." The young man answered. "Before winter, I plan on ridin' out. Got some things I want to do."

"It don't sound like I'm gonna' be able to change your mind this time." Sam looked at his boss and shook his head.

"No sir, not this time…a couple more months and I'm movin' on. I'm grown up now, Luke…got some business to take care of. Got to get ready to handle it when the time comes."

Later that evening Luke and Henry sat on the front porch of the ranch house, drank coffee and smoked their pipes. "The boy told you he was leavin', didn't he?" Henry's question was really a statement.

"Yeah, he did. How long have you known?"

"I've known for a good while, but he didn't say nothin' about it until last night."

Luke looked to his friend. "We been ridin' together and workin' together since before the war was over, Henry, and we ain't never run into anybody like that kid. He ain't got but one hand, and he's barely growed up, but there isn't another man on this place who can come close to matchin' him. I believe he could take over this ranch right now." Henry nodded his agreement.

"Well, he ain't leavin' just yet, boss, so there's no sense in cryin' about it now."

"God damn it, Henry, quit callin' me boss."

The next morning found Sam Tucker riding the far western edge of the Busted A looking for a half dozen head of horses that had apparently wandered off during the night. At first he didn't pay close attention to the tracks the missing animals had left, but when he got to the soft ground next to a water hole, something caught his eye.

Six horses had gotten out of the corral, but there were eight sets of tracks. It put him on edge. For a minute, he thought about turning back and getting more men, but then decided to go on alone. He was confident in his ability to handle the situation, and he didn't want the horses and whoever was driving them to get any more of a lead than they already had.

As the trail led the young man further and further from the ranch headquarters, he became increasingly vigilant. He checked to see that both pistols, the one on his hip and the one inside his coat, were loaded.

Each time he crested a hill, he dismounted and crouched low until he'd viewed the ground ahead with his spy glass. He didn't want to make himself an easy target by being silhouetted on the skyline.

He stopped to think about the task he'd set out to accomplish. It was nearing midday; warm and sunny and the smell of sage and prairie grass was sweet and strong. Riding the west Texas prairie would have been pleasant on a day like this, but he was facing a test, and he needed to focus his attention on getting it right. The horses he was following never deviated from their course. They were heading due west and they didn't stop to graze. If there had been any doubt before, it was now very obvious they were being driven and not wandering on their own.

The prairie flattened out and stretched all the way to the western horizon. It was bordered to the north by a steep ridge. He felt sure the horses would be herded completely across the immense flat and probably to the road that leads to the little town of Pecos.

He left the trail, crossed the ridge, and loped the grey along the far side. He was riding parallel to the route the horses were taking, but unless they crossed to his side of the ridge, there was no way the men driving the horses would spot him. If he moved quickly, he should be able to catch up and get ahead of them without being seen.

The grass was short from cattle grazing on it, and Samuel saw that the footing was good. He gave Boone a loose rein and he took it as an invitation to stretch out. The young cowboy and his mount moved as one and ate up big chunks of prairie with each long and fluid stride.

For nearly an hour they maintained the brisk pace without letting up. At the end of that time they had covered close to fifteen miles, and the powerful grey gelding had barely broken a sweat. The horse had been his partner for over two years now, and Samuel had long been aware of his amazing strength and stamina, but he appreciated it more and more as time passed and the bond between them grew.

When they reached a small notch in the ridge, the boy rode most of the way to the top and reined in. He left Boone ground tied and walked ahead to look around. Looking a mile or so back to the east, he saw the six stolen horses and the two riders.

The cut in the ridge turned into a deep draw that ran down the south side and met the flat prairie below. If he hurried, he thought he could get the grey into the cover of the draw without being seen and wait at its mouth until the riders and horses approached. He remounted, kept to the lowest ground and lay flat on the saddle until he was in position. As he waited, he worked on developing an idea for what to do next.

When they were within a quarter mile, he rode slowly out of the draw and into the path of the riders. As young men often do, he'd wondered how he'd hold up in a situation like this. So far he was pleased with himself and how it was going. He felt little fear and he was confident… confident in his ability to face these two, whoever they might be. And he was very confident in his ability to use his guns.

The Pecos road was no more than a good rifle shot behind him.

He wrapped the reins around the horn of his saddle and waited. His arms were folded in front of his chest with his hand inside his coat holding the pistol holstered there. He made sure the pistol on his hip was in plain sight of the two men.

The two salty looking thieves made no effort to dodge the single horseman who blocked their path. They didn't stop until the horses they were herding were even with Samuel. One of the men was skinny with long sandy brown hair and crooked, tobacco stained teeth. The other was huskier with dark hair and a walrus mustache. Neither of them was a kid; they looked to be somewhere in their thirties.

It was the dark haired one who spoke. "What brings you out here, boy? If you're lookin' fer some cotton to pick you need to go back east of here." Both men laughed at the remark.

Samuel smiled. "No sir," he said, "I ain't in the cotton pickin' business. I'm lookin' for a couple of horse thieves. Looks to me like I found 'em."

"You might have found 'em, nigger boy, but if your figurin' on doin' somethin' about it, you done bit off more than you're gonna' be able to chew." The skinny one was doing the talking now. "We're gonna' add that big grey horse of yours to our string and leave your black ass out here for the buzzards. They'll eat most anything."

The rustlers started to laugh again, but stopped when they saw a rider approach from the road. He'd come from the north, so the ridge had kept him hidden from view until he was almost upon them. Using only light leg pressure on the horse's flank, Samuel positioned the grey so he could keep an eye on the rustlers as well as the approaching rider.

Up until now, Samuel had figured the odds were in his favor, but that could change depending on whose side this new guy was on.

He second guessed himself for a moment…maybe he shouldn't have taken out after these horse thieves all by himself, but it was too late now. His only option was to handle it on his own. He backed Boone up a few more steps to make it easier to keep all three riders in his field of vision.

The third man was young, tall, and he sat easy in the saddle as he trotted his big roan gelding up next to Samuel and Boone.

A glance in his direction told young Tucker he wasn't cut from the same cloth as the horse thieves. He pushed his duster aside revealing the silver star pinned to his vest. "Afternoon, gents," he said, "what brings the three of you out this way?"

"Well damn, we're mighty glad to see you Sheriff," the dark haired one said, "we caught this here nigger kid with these stolen horses. Took 'em from the ranch 'bout a half day's ride back to the east."

The lawman nodded. "The Busted A…I know the place. You boys work there?" Before they could answer, Samuel tried to say something, but the lawman held up his hand to shush him up.

"Uh…yes sir…uh Sheriff," the skinny one said, "We just started ridin' for that outfit this month."

"So old Pete Miller took you boys on as cowhands, huh?"

"That's right. We're working for Pete, and he sent us out to catch this here nigger that run off with these horses." The skinny one liked the way this was going and smiled as he did the talking.

The Sheriff turned to Samuel. "I'd like you to show me your left hand, son. You can keep the right one on that hog leg you've got inside your duster if it makes you more comfortable."

The boy moved his arm out to his side showing the steel-capped stump. "Luke told me about you, son. Says you're the best hand he's had since he started the place. Is Pete Miller still doin' the cookin' for Luke and Henry?"

Samuel smiled as he spoke, but he kept his eyes on the dark haired cowboy. "Yes he is, Sheriff, you can't hardly eat most of it, but he's still doin' it."

His expression grew more serious as he continued. "That fella on the bay just took hold of his pistol."

The words of warning had barely been spoken when the man brought the hand gun up and swung it toward the Sheriff. As he pulled the hammer back, his partner drew his piece as well. The Sheriff brought his up at the same time. None of the three got off a single shot.

The Colt jumped twice in Samuel's hand and both outlaws toppled from their horses.

The lawman holstered his piece, looked with raised

eyebrows at the young man, but he didn't speak. He nudged the roan forward until he could look at the faces of the two fallen horse thieves.

Each of them had a small hole in the center of his forehead. The back side of each man's head was pretty well blown away, and what was left rested in a growing pool of blood.

"Bob Poole," the lawman said, as he rode up next to the grey and extended his hand.

"Samuel…uh…Sammy Tucker," the boy appeared shaken as he stated his name and took the hand of the Sheriff. "I…uh…I… never killed nobody before, I can't believe I did that."

"You did what you had to do, son, and I'm not sure I'd be alive right now if you hadn't." Poole stroked the whiskers on his chin and shook his head as he spoke. "I'm not at all sure I believe what I just saw either, but I'm mighty glad you did it. Don't be worryin' about it."

"How 'bout we bury these assholes right here," he went on, "and I'll help you get the horses back to the ranch. You may as well keep the two those fellas were ridin'." Poole looked in the direction of the dead outlaws. "They ain't gonna' be needin' 'em. Maybe we can even get to the ranch in time to enjoy some of Pete's fine cookin'."

Samuel's brow got furrowed up and he squinted as he addressed Poole. "We're gonna' just bury 'em here, Sheriff? Don't we have to take 'em in to a judge or a court or somethin'?"

Poole smiled. "If they were alive I guess we'd do that, but there ain't a hell of a lot they'd be tellin' the judge as dead as they are. A man's behavior can cause him some serious hardship, son. It can cause him to lose some of his rights, and the way I see it these two gave up their right to a fair trial when they pulled iron on us."

He looked again at the hole in the forehead of each of the rustlers and shook his head. "Gave up their right to breathe, too."

"How we gonna' bury 'em in this hard ground? We got nothin' to dig with"

"We'll drag 'em back into that draw and pile rocks on top of 'em," Poole answered, "and we ain't gonna' say any words over 'em neither. It ain't like we're buryin' anybody real special. Sons-a-bitches stole horses and tried to shoot us. Coverin' 'em with rocks is a sight more than they'd have done for us."

Samuel nodded. He'd seen so-called justice meted out swiftly before. This was the first time he'd seen it done fairly, and it was the first time he'd been on this side of it.

Still shaken and feeling sick to his stomach, he covered his feelings. "I reckon you're right, Sheriff…we may as well pile rocks on top of these assholes and be done with 'em."

Poole laughed. "You catch on real fast, son."

Samuel and the Sheriff took their time driving the horses back to the Busted A. It was around four in the afternoon when they closed the corral gate behind the eight head. Luke and Henry were leaning against the corral waiting. They both greeted the Sheriff before Henry turned his attention to Samuel.

"Got a couple of questions for you, son. How come you went out there alone and how come you come back with two more horses than got run off?"

"Well, sir, I reckoned I should try to catch 'em as quick as I could without wastin' time comin' back here for help. And I felt like I could probably handle it alone."

Bob Poole fielded the second question. "These horses

belonged to the two hombres that stole your six. They both gave up ridin' just this mornin'. Your man here saw to that. I reckon he saved my hide when he did it too."

Henry tried to hide his smile as he nodded in response to the Sheriff's statement. Luke addressed Samuel. "You did a fine job Sammy…mighty fine job, but next time something like this happens, come back and get help. You understand?"

The young cowboy nodded. "Yes sir, I do."

"Well, don't forget." Henry added. "We didn't know there were rustlers involved until we looked at the tracks down by the river just an hour ago, or we'd have come after you. By that time we could see the dust you was kickin' up on your way back."

*****

That late September morning came too soon for Henry and Luke's liking. The hot summer weather hadn't abated much in the Pecos River country, and Sammy was in the saddle as the first hints of daylight began to wash away the night. He wanted to get some miles behind him before it became unbearably hot.

Luke and Henry leaned against the gate and watched as the boy became an ever smaller shadow on the western horizon.

"Wasn't nothin' we could have done, was there Henry?"

"No there wasn't nothin'. We both tried, but I knew two years ago we'd never get him to stay. There's a gentle little boy inside that young cowboy, Luke. A little boy who felt more pain and had more taken from him in the first ten years of his life than most of us ever have. It ain't that he wants to leave us behind…he's tryin' to leave all that behind…where he's been, what he's lost, and even who he is. I believe he thinks he can be somebody else, somebody who won't feel that little boy's pain."

Luke nodded. "I reckon he's going to spend a lot of his life alone, Henry, runnin' from something he can't escape. Can't help thinkin' he'd be better off goin' back to Arkansas and facin' up to all that…uhh…all that history he has back there."

"Maybe so, Luke, and I reckon he might someday. Then again, you lost your wife and son, and I lost my wife in the war. When was the last time you or I went back to Georgia?

Chapter Thirteen

Salina

The best days of my life
Were an illusion it seems
Old Jim made me face it
I let go of the dream

Bob Poole and I accompanied Kate to her family's farm. It wasn't hard to see she was uneasy with the idea of staying there, but she didn't object. Poole told her about the couple he had in mind to help her run the place. Said he'd talk to them and let her know what came of it.

He had already arranged for a woman from a neighboring place to stay with her for the time being. That woman was there when the three of us arrived. I had previously promised Kate I'd spend some time with her as soon as I could. I sure couldn't do that in the presence of the neighbor lady, so Bob and I mounted up to ride off toward Salina. Just a quick "good bye Ma'am" to Kate and I was gone.

A whole lot of thoughts began to swirl through my head as we rode out of the farmyard. This was the place where Kate's family had been murdered just a few weeks earlier. Going back there had to be bringing back horrible memories and feelings to her. Leaving her there and riding away felt awful…like I was abandoning her when she needed me the most… but there was no way I could keep her with me or even stay with her at the farm.

The reality of what I'd gotten into with her was beginning to sink in. While we were alone out on the prairie I'd been able to sort of look the other way, but now the truth was hard to ignore. I didn't speak to Bob for the first few miles, and knowing what was on my mind, he chose to let it be as well. The horses were responsible for finally breaking the silence and gloom.

It was as though Boone and Bob's big roan had heard the speculation about which of them was faster. When we left the farm, we started out side by side at a smooth, collected lope, but neither horse was happy with that. Both of them wanted to be in the lead, and we had to continually hold them in. After fighting them for a good while, we let them pick up the pace until we were at a gallop.

Boone stood an inch under sixteen hands at the withers and had a round and muscular body. The roan was another three inches taller and built leaner. He ran almost effortlessly with long and fluid strides. Both horses had endurance, but one look and you could see one was a distance runner and one a sprinter.

We were still side by side as we approached a stretch of road that was straight and level for better than a quarter of a mile. Bob looked at me and smiled. I turned his way and nodded. "How about to those trees up there by the base of the hill, Sheriff," I suggested. Poole nodded his acceptance, put some slack in his reins and lightly hooked the roan with his spurs. They got the jump on me and Boone.

Poole and his horse had better than a two length lead by the time I loosened the reins. The grey leapt forward at full speed with no further urging from me. In less than a hundred yards we were side by side again and I made sure we stayed that way until we were three quarters of the way to the trees that marked the end of the race. At that point,

I touched Boone's flanks with both spurs and he surged ahead and kept opening up the lead to the end.

It took us nearly another quarter mile to get the horses settled down enough that we could talk. "I didn't really think we could beat you in a short sprint like that," Poole said, "and I know you were playing with us. Now how'd you like to try it all the way to Salina?"

I shook my head and laughed. "No thanks," I answered, "Boone could never keep up with that long legged boy of yours for that distance, but he'd probably kill himself tryin'."

It was nearly dark when we rode into town. The few folks who were up and about turned their heads and looked at us as we rode by. I suppose we were an unusual and somewhat imposing looking pair as we trotted up Main Street on the two big geldings.

We took both horses to the livery and then walked to Bob's office. He pinned a deputy's badge to my shirt, had me swear to uphold the law, and just that fast I was a lawman. "We'll talk to the mayor and city council tomorrow and get their blessing." He said. I slept that night on a cot in the office.

It was close to noon the next day when Bob and I walked into the church where the mayor and council were gathered. The mayor was a big, bald-headed man with a heavy southern accent…Arkansas or Mississippi I guessed. Neither of those possibilities gave me a good feeling. He was also the local judge. "What's the reason for you callin' this here meetin', Sheriff?" He asked.

Poole took time to make eye contact with all present before he spoke. "Mr. Mayor, gentlemen, I'd like you to meet Samuel Tucker. He was attacked by the two escapees I was trackin' and he killed 'em both. As you know, they were the pair that massacred the Willis family and killed Deputy Mark Dupre and Howard Albertson. After I met up with Mr. Tucker, we found Kate Willis and took her back to the farm. She was about a half day behind me trailin' the same two fellas." Bob was revising the story to meet the requirements of the present situation.

Mayor Jack Botsford nodded, scratched his whiskered chin, and addressed me directly. "I've heard some about you, Tucker. Folks call you Crow, don't they?" I nodded, and the mayor went on. "Heard mighty tall stories about your shootin'. Are those all true?"

"It depends on what you heard, sir," I answered, "I can shoot some."

Bob Poole jumped back in to the discussion. "I've known Samuel for better than seven years. He got me out of a spot down in Texas that I might not have survived on my own. Did it with some shootin' like I'd never seen before, and he wasn't but nineteen or twenty years old at the time."

"If he'd have been a deputy ten days ago, and in charge of those two prisoners, Dupre and Albertson would still be alive right now. I'd bet my life on that. So I made him my deputy today. Since he ain't exactly…uh…white, there may be some folks who don't like it. I'm askin' you gentlemen to back me up."

One of the councilmen spoke up. "If we did that, Bob, I'm afraid we'd have trouble. I don't think the town's folk would take kindly to havin' a nigra for a deputy…takin' orders from him and such."

Poole responded in a soft but steady voice. "We already have trouble in Salina on a regular basis, Percy, and I'm the one who handles it. You boys can either approve of my new deputy and back me up with the people of Salina, or you can handle the trouble yourself until you find a new Sheriff.

Those are the choices you have, gentlemen."

Botsford smiled. "No reason to get excited just yet, Bob. How 'bout we go out back and see some of that shootin' this boy's so famous for while we think about this for just a little bit."

We walked to the empty street behind the church. The mayor pulled an apple out of his coat pocket. "Set this out at a comfortable distance and let's see you put a bullet through it." He tossed the apple in my direction. I batted it into the air with the steel cap on my left arm.

It was close to fifteen feet above me when I shot and blew it into little pieces that showered down on the mayor and council members.

The mayor looked toward the four councilmen as he brushed fragments of apple from his jacket. "I don't think any of us are going to object to Mr. Tucker being our new deputy Sheriff, are we?" Nobody did.

*****

Jim Davis was a colored man in his mid-forties. He worked at the livery, cleaning stalls, feeding the stock, and taking care of the blacksmith work. He was a big, sturdy man with a medium to dark complexion. Not too different in color from me.

His wife, Nettie, was some ten years younger and she worked as a maid at the hotel. The tone of her skin was much lighter. Not much darker than that of a lot of white people.

Bob Poole introduced me to Jim and Nettie. Though we had a nice long talk, I didn't say anything about my relationship with Kate. Bob explained her situation and said that she needed help. Coming from farm families in Mississippi, life in Salina was not proving to be what they were looking for. They jumped at the opportunity to work

Kate's farm in exchange for a place to live and a share of the crop.

For the most part, folks in Salina accepted me well. Many of them, in their ignorance, still used the word "nigger", but they tried not to be derogatory about it, as contradictory as that may seem. I guess they thought of me as "their nigger" as opposed to all those other niggers out there. In any case I appreciated the generally kind treatment.

Instead of calling me by my given name, they referred to me as 'Crow'. To many of them, I was a legend. I was flat out amazed at some of the stories they'd heard about the notorious Bad Wing Crow and the dozens of men he'd killed.

In truth, I'd backed quite a few men down, and had some fist fights, but after the two horse thieves in Texas, I'd been involved in only three more gunfights. The fist fights, without exception, ended quickly. I had, after all, a five pound piece of pipe on the end of my left arm, and I wasn't all that bad with my right.

Those boys in El Paso, the ones who stuck me with the Bad Wing Crow handle, had fallen victim to the pipe when I came back to town to square up with them. Two of the three men who had faced up to me with a gun were drunken cowboys who were in over their heads. I shot each of them in the shoulder as he tried to draw his weapon, and they both survived.

The third was a gun hand; sober and calm and knowing exactly what he was doing. Men like him and me were few and far between. There were never all that many gunfighters in the country anyway, and the number of encounters each of us had is exaggerated as well.

My face off with this guy was the real thing, however. Neither of us had any illusions about the other backing down or getting rattled and making a mistake. Most times a gunfight is a test of resolve and courage, but that wasn't the case here, and we both knew it. If either of us felt any fear, it was under control and only served to make us sharper. Fear would not be a factor in the outcome. This was a test of speed, accuracy and execution…nothing more. The man who was more skilled would live and the other would die. Our eyes told that story as plainly as if it had been written on the wall.

I can still see his unflinching, unblinking eyes as he pulled the big Colt revolver from his left hip in one smooth and easy motion. A motion that was just the tiniest fraction of a second too late. The cold expression on his face barely changed even after I'd put a bullet through the center of his chest.

Mortally wounded, and with an unsteady hand, he squeezed off two rounds that went wild. Knowing he was dead, he was hoping to take me with him. To make sure he didn't get lucky with his desperate shots, I put him down with a bullet to his forehead.

He'd showed no fear of death. Killing me was all that mattered to him, and it was a sobering thought to realize I was just like him in that respect. I believe I would have acted the same way in his place. It gave me a chilling feeling to realize that was the kind of man I'd become…the kind of man gentle, innocent, little Sammy Tucker had become.

However, things had changed some now. I knew I could still act calmly in the face of death. I still didn't fear death, but now I was afraid to stop living. There was a reason for that, and I decided to ride out to the little farm by the creek and see her. It had been nearly two weeks since Poole and I had left her there, and the neighbor lady had gone home. Jim and Nettie Davis had moved in the day after Bob had made them the offer. They were working, side by side, in the vegetable garden as I approached the farmyard.

Seeing two colored folks working the soil in the sweltering Kansas sun brought me back to my childhood days in Arkansas. The memories of those times carried with them a curious mixture of emotions; the warmth of home and family; of my parents and grandpa, and the horror of the things that happened to us there. I thought of how the fear I'd felt as a boy, from the acts of cruelty that had been visited upon me and my family, had been slowly replaced over the years…replaced by the deep and burning anger I carried inside me today.

That anger was my constant companion and with it was the resolve to someday go back and fulfill the pact my grandfather and I had made so long ago. To go back and have my day…to go back and settle up. Somehow I'd always been able to control that anger and keep it inside… able to wait and not let it out until the time was right. Until the day my grandpa had spoken of came around.

I guess it was these thoughts that caused me to keep my eyes fixed on the Davis's as I rode by. Nettie looked up, and at first she seemed puzzled by the blank stare on my face, but then she gave me a broad smile and a wave. The greeting brought my mind back to the present and I returned the wave and managed to force a smile of my own.

Jim's eyes turned my way for a second or two, but he remained silent and made no gesture. His failure to acknowledge my arrival meant something and I knew it. I don't let things like that get by me.

I was still wondering what was bothering Jim as I rode Boone into the corral, but I'd no sooner pulled the saddle and turned around, and Kate was on me. With happy tears in her eyes and that big pretty smile, she jumped up, wrapped her arms around my neck and hung there with her feet off the ground. For the time being I forgot all about

Jim Davis.

Kate wasn't heavy…maybe a hundred and twenty pounds…but she was nonetheless a lot of girl to have hanging from my neck. Especially since she was hugging me so tightly I could barely breathe. "Kate, darlin'," I said, "I'm happy to see you too, but you're going to have to ease up a bit or you're going to pull my head right off."

She let go, slid to the ground, and took a step back. That wonderful smile didn't change even as she spoke. "Samuel, I'm so glad you came. I've been watching for you every day and hoping you'd come. I've never missed someone so much in my life." Then she added; "I've never loved someone so much in my life."

I pulled her toward me, wrapped my arms tightly around her, buried my face in her soft blonde hair, and deeply inhaled her sweet and warm scent with each breath. "Nor have I, Kate. I've never loved anyone nearly this much…not nearly this much."

Those words were no exaggeration. The solitary existence that had been mine for the past several years had been totally devoid of anything close to love for another human being. There had been nothing in my life that had given me anything remotely resembling the special, magical feelings that took control of me when I was with Kate.

Jim Davis hardly spoke when the four of us had supper together that evening, but I was so wrapped up in Kate, I paid him little mind. After supper, we saddled Boone and the chestnut mare and she and I went for a ride along the creek.

We were reminded of our time on the prairie west of Salina. We talked about our dip in the creek and our first night in each other's arms. I was reliving those days when Kate smiled, turned her horse around and galloped back toward the farm. I knew what she was thinking, and I had no quarrel with it. I stayed just a stride behind her.

That night was the first we'd spent together in a real bed. It was different. The nights together on the prairie were wonderful, but this felt more legitimate…like she was my wife. We talked about that and whether there might ever be a possibility of making that happen.

When morning came, I knew the dream had to end for now and I had to get back to Salina, but it was the last thing I wanted to do.

After a cup of coffee and some warm biscuits and bacon, I headed out to the corral to saddle the grey. Jim Davis was waiting for me when I got there. He looked big and menacing. With his shirt sleeves rolled up his heavily muscled arms and massive hands showed like weapons. His expression was dark and somber. I hoped he hadn't come to fight.

I caught Boone and began brushing him while I waited for the other man to say what was on his mind. It didn't take long for the morning silence to be broken by his deep, resonant voice.

"We don't know each other real well, Tucker, but I got somethin' needs sayin', and you're the one needs to hear it."

For a minute or so I didn't respond. After I had the saddle in place and the girth snugged up, I turned my head in his direction and our eyes met.

His eyes made it plain that I was going to hear what he had to say whether I wanted to or not. And I didn't want to. I knew what it was going to be about, and worse yet, I knew he was going to be right. It was something I didn't want to face. My life had been all about looking at situations rationally and making calm and thoughtful decisions. Like I said before, that's what kept me alive, and now I'd strayed from that path onto a much more dangerous one.

"I knew about you and Miss Kate the first time you, me, and the Sheriff talked, Samuel. Nettie figured it out the first day we were here on the farm, even though I hadn't said anything about it. How long do you reckon it's gonna' take the white folks in Salina to catch on? It will happen for sure and it will happen fast."

I tried to ignore the truth of his remarks by shutting off the conversation with a show of strength. "I've survived on my own in this country for a lot of years without any advice from the likes of you, Davis. I can handle anybody who might call me out because he disapproves of my behavior."

I let my eyes drift down to the revolver holstered on my right hip to emphasize my words. Even to me, my response felt thin and desperate.

Davis didn't let it slide. "The white folks around here told me all about Mr. Bad Wing Crow, the gun fighter… the pistolero." He smiled at his own characterization of me and my reputation, and then he went on. "But I know something about Samuel Tucker, too, and I know you ain't gonna' use that gun on me, and I ain't scared. I ran into some folks from back in Arkansas, and I know who you are and where you came from. I also know they hung your daddy and how you lost your hand and why."

I got a sick feeling in my stomach and my head sank to my chest. I could even feel my eyes moistening some. Jim Davis wasn't going to let go. He was going to make me face the reality I didn't want to face. The reality I'd been pretending didn't exist; the reality that my love for Kate and the euphoria and fantasy of it allowed me to ignore.

His expression as well as his voice softened as he went on. "Samuel," he said, "I know, and you know, that lynchings and such can still happen to a colored man if certain white men think he might have stepped out of line. You and me may not see anything wrong with you bein' with Kate, but white folks ain't gonna' like it at all, and they'll make it into somethin' they can hang you for. You'll be gone then, just like your daddy. They will have bested you…laughed at you hangin' from a tree. They'll hang a sign on you. Somethin' about Bad Wing Crow, the nigger gun fighter who molested a white girl."

"You see, Samuel, most all white folks think us colored men are animals. They think we are all wantin' nothin' more than to have our way with white women, and they are scared of that… they are real scared.

Now I believe there are some colored men who are like that, and I know, back at the plantations, there was white men aplenty who would leave their wives to spend time in the cabins with the slave girls. The difference is they can do what they want to the colored girls and nothin' happens to 'em, but they hang us if they even think we're wantin' a white woman. That's just the way it is."

Davis took a break to let his words sink in, but they already had. I hated what he was saying, but I couldn't fight it. I wanted it to end and I wanted a place to hide from it, but he went on and hit me with the final thrust of his argument.

"And what happens to Kate, Samuel? What will folks say about her and how will they treat her after they've finished with you? I don't have to answer those questions for you, Samuel. You're a smart boy. You know the answers as well as I do."

I put my foot in the stirrup and swung into the saddle. As I turned Boone toward the gate, Jim Davis spoke to me in a gentle voice. "I'm just tryin' to be your friend, Samuel Tucker."

He stepped forward and took my hand in his and held it in a firm grip. I nodded, took a deep breath and responded in little more than a whisper. "I know you are, and I know the words you just spoke are true, and I know I have to accept all of that for Kate and for me."

"There is one other thing I need you to believe and understand, though. I love Kate for who she is and not for what color she is. If I could somehow turn her into a colored woman I would do it this minute." Pulling my hand from his, I held it up. "And I would let them cut this one off to make that happen."

*****

I played Deputy Sheriff for a couple of days after getting back to Salina, but I knew I couldn't make it work much longer. Jim Davis had opened my eyes to the fact I couldn't continue my relationship with Kate without the white folks finding out, and I knew he was right about what would happen when they did. There was nothing I could do about it. This was the last straw, and I was all stirred up inside.

The anger that had boiled inside of me for so long had now grown too big and too hot to contain. I hated this world I was living in. A world that allowed everyone else to be with the woman he loved, but not me. I had let myself be fooled for a while, but the dream was over and I knew I had to leave. I had to leave now. Seeing Kate one last time would have just made it harder…maybe impossible.

I explained things to Bob Poole as I handed him my badge. I'm sure he'd seen it coming. He made no attempt to get me to stay. "Don't do anything stupid, Sammy," he said, "and send for me when you do." I asked him to talk to Kate and try to make her understand.

I saddled the grey, but before I mounted I took the small piece of paper from my saddle bag. I read the names of

Robert Coolidge, Buster Coolidge and James Howard aloud. When I got to the edge of Salina, I turned southeast toward Arkansas. This might not have been the way my grandpa had pictured it, but I wasn't going to wait any longer for that day of reckoning to come. It was going to come real soon.

Chapter Fourteen

Finally headin' back home
Doin' whatever I can
To see that they pay
For a little boy's hand

I traveled at an easy pace as I began my journey to Arkansas. I didn't want to use up my horse and I needed time to think. The business I had down that way had to be done right. When it was over, I didn't necessarily have to be alive, but there were three men down around Pine Bluff who had to be dead.

Twenty miles was about the most I made in any one day. At that rate I figured it would take the better part of a month to get to Pine Bluff. Last I heard my grandpa was still share croppin' just east of there. I expected to see him in late August or early September. It had been a long time, and I hoped to find him alive and well.

After ten days on the trail, I rode into Wichita. I was ready for some good food, maybe some whiskey, and sleepin' on something other than the hard ground. First thing I did was take Boone to the livery. He was in need of a change of pace and a little comfort as much as I was.

A colored man, said his name was Peter, was running the place, and he promised to take care of him like he was his own. I asked him if he did the shoein' around there as well, and he said he did.

"Good, he needs a new set. Those he's got on have worn mighty thin. Leave as much heel and as little toe as you can get away with when you trim him up."

He glanced at Boone's feet. "I see what ya mean," he laughed, "them feet get any longer and he'll be walkin' like a duck." I liked the man and felt confident about leaving my horse with him. That was about the last thing that went well for me in Wichita.

I went to the hotel and walked up to the front desk. It was manned by a big fellow with long sideburns and a fringe of black curly hair on an otherwise bald head. His eyes were small, cold and dark, and set deep in a pock marked face. He wore a white shirt with a dirty, frayed collar and large, yellow perspiration stains under the arms. I reckon he would have smelled as bad as he looked were it not for the stub of a cigar that hung from his lips. The heavy, blue smoke wasn't pleasant, but it shielded me some from the rank body odor of this foul character.

He spoke without looking up from the desk. "You ain't expectin' to get a room, are you boy?" I took a shallow breath and forced a smile…figured I'd take a few seconds, slow myself down, and maintain control.

"Yes, sir," I answered, "that's what I had in mind." He flashed a condescending smile and looked me up and down before speaking again.

"We don't rent our regular rooms to niggers, boy. We got a storeroom out back. You can lay your bedroll out on the floor." His smile broadened. "We let that one go for the same price as our hotel rooms…fifty cents a night. If that don't suit you, I hear the straw down at the livery is nice and soft. That's where the animals sleep."

I tensed up some. My tolerance for that type of remark,

or any kind of affront for that matter, had grown thin.

I looked around the lobby and saw it was empty except for the clerk and me. I put my hand on the edge of my duster and pulled it back to expose the revolver holstered on my right hip.

His eyes followed the movement, came to rest on the big Colt, and his smile faded. For close to a minute, I held his attention with an icy stare and didn't speak. I wanted to watch him sweat.

Had Boone been re-shod and tied at the hitching rail in front, I would have seriously considered drawing the weapon and pistol whipping him. Things had changed of late, and I wasn't of a mind to be as careful as had been my habit in the past. As it was, though, I didn't like my chances of getting out of town alive if I buffaloed him. No matter how angry and reckless I was feeling, I couldn't ignore that…besides, I had work to do in Arkansas.

Reluctantly, I moved my hand a few inches and scratched my ribs. "This place makes me itchy. Must be bugs in here. Stinks too. I reckon I'll bunk at the livery." I let the duster fall back over the Colt and walked out of the place.

Earlier, on my way from the livery, I'd seen a café about a half block from the hotel and across the main street. I went there now hoping to have better luck finding a good meal than I'd had trying to get a decent place to sleep.

A Chinaman was sitting on a bench in front of the place. Though I didn't ask, he told me I'd have to go around to the alley and enter through the back door. Maybe, he said, they'd let me eat in the kitchen.

I didn't know if the Chinaman owned the place, worked there, or was just the guy who herded colored folks around to the alley. It made no difference. About all I cared about was getting something to eat and getting out of Wichita as soon as I could.

The alley was piled high with trash and it reeked of human waste thrown out of chamber pots from second story windows.

As I approached the café, two large, nearly black rats scurried under the wooden steps that led to the kitchen door. A third one remained on the stoop feeding on something. My presence didn't seem to faze him.

"Perhaps," I thought, "he, not the Chinaman, is the owner of the place." After taking a few more steps, I could make out what it was he was feeding on. It was another rat that I imagined had passed away from eating something unhealthy at the café.

Turning around and ignoring my hunger for the time being suddenly seemed like the thing to do. Maybe Peter, back at the livery, would be able to help me out with some grub.

My experience had been that saloons in this part of the country were more tolerant of people like me than were the restaurants and hotels. I supposed it was because white women, except for the ones who worked upstairs, generally were not present or even allowed. The girls upstairs might be any color…white, black, brown, red, yellow…didn't seem to make any difference. They might have interested me before I knew Kate, but not anymore. A glass or two of whiskey sounded damned good, though.

There were two saloons in town. The one I entered was called The Trails End. It was a typical cattle town saloon; smoky, noisy, spittoons scattered about the dirty wooden floor, and, with nightfall approaching, it was about two thirds full of patrons.

There were a few local businessmen present, but most were cowhands, and for the most part they were heeled and rough lookin'. I noticed one guy who might have been a half breed or a Mexican, but I was the only one who was obviously not white. None of this surprised me. The sign out front was the only thing that distinguished this Kansas whiskey hole from the dozens of others I'd visited over the years, and I knew what to expect.

I put my money on the bar, asked for a drink, and the man poured it without making a fuss. I thanked him…even called him "Sir". The liquor went down warm, sweet and easy, and nobody was bothering me.

When I'd first come in I'd noticed a lot of eyes turned my way, but they'd apparently lost interest, and I was no longer drawing any special attention. I liked that. Maybe my luck was changing.

The bartender had just poured my second drink when one of the girls, a pretty little red head, walked up to the bar, and leaned her body in close to mine. As she looked up at me, she batted her eyes and smiled. Her low-cut dress was blue and made from some kind of shiny fabric that fit her body snugly. Her breasts were round and pushed up and they looked like they were trying to burst out like the bubbles in a coffee percolator. She wore enough perfume to make my eyes water.

"I love hombres like you," she whispered, "maybe you'd like to go upstairs with me?"

I noticed that many of the cowboys in the place were, once again, looking my way. It seemed a little strange to me that this woman, and not one of the darker skinned ones, had picked me out. I pushed the remainder of the money that was sitting on the bar toward the bartender, and stepped away from her. I made a show of raising my arms over my head and I spoke loudly. "This is all the cash I've got, ma'am. Can't even buy you a drink."

She looked at someone across the room, shrugged, and moved on down the bar to another prospect. Maybe her love for me had simply faded as quickly as it had developed, but something told me it was time to take another, more careful, look at the faces in the saloon.

In a little while the front door swung open and the livery man came through. He looked nervous and shuffled over to me with his chin pressed down on his chest. I guess he was trying to look like a non-threatening, humble black man.

I moved over to make a space for him at the bar and ordered him a whiskey. He was hesitant, but took it when I insisted.

After a quick swallow he began to talk in a hushed but hurried way. "I put shoes on your gelding, and I saddled him and brung him here. He's tied out front." I nodded and waited for him to further explain.

"There's talk 'bout you havin' words with the man at the hotel. That's Foster…he's the mayor… mayor of Wichita. Talk is he's plannin' on gettin' even with you for what you said. We best get out of town now."

For a moment I was speechless…not because I was surprised Foster was after me, but because I couldn't believe any town could have elected a man like him as their mayor.

I let that thought slide and returned to what Peter had said about leaving Wichita. I raised my eyebrows and looked squarely into his face. "We?" I asked. "What do you mean, we best get out of town."

Peter's eyes narrowed as he returned my stare. He was serious about what he was proposing. "You're headed to Arkansas. I got kin down that way an' I'm tired of this place. You've seen what it's like. I'm plannin' on ridin' with you. My horse is tied next to yours. Let's go now."

Peter nervously looked around the room and sighed.

"He's here. That's him over there and he's got a couple of fellas with him."

"I know," I said, "I saw them earlier. I'm pretty sure he sent a saloon girl over here a few minutes ago. Maybe tryin' to set me up for something they could turn into a hangin' offense."

"What are we gonna do now?" He asked.

"I'm going to finish my whiskey and see what they do."

We didn't have to wait long. In the mirror behind the bar, I watched Mayor Foster and the two tough looking cowboys walk confidently across the room. Foster was standing directly behind me when he spoke.

"You feel like talking big now, nigger?" Still watching him in the mirror, I saw the same sneering smile he'd had on his face at the hotel. Up until now I'd kept my left arm stuffed in the pocket of my duster. I didn't want to advertise who I was.

It was time to show my cards. I drank the last swallow of whiskey, set the glass on the bar and backhanded him across the face with the steel-encased stub I'd been hiding.

In almost the same motion, I pulled the revolver from the cross draw holster under the left side of my duster. I held the gun on the two cowboys. Neither of them made a move to pull their iron. They stood where they were, big eyed, and stared at Foster.

He was unconscious at my feet with a steady flow of blood coming from the gash above his left eye. His face was in the bright red puddle that had formed on the floor, and his breath made little ripples in it. I'd hit him plenty hard, but his breathing told me I hadn't killed him. Perhaps, I thought, I should have hit him a little harder.

The other men in the place were all facing me now, but

none of them went for their weapon. I turned to the wide-eyed livery man. "Peter, my friend, I think you're right. It is time we got out of Wichita." We backed out the front door, mounted, and rode out of town at a gallop.

After a mile or so we slowed the pace some and Peter rode his horse up close. "You hit the mayor right upside the head. They gonna chase after us for sure, now. What'd you go an do that for? An' how come we're ridin' west if we're goin' to Arkansas? What we gonna' do if they catch us?"

The barrage of questions made me smile. "I hit him because he had it coming, and since I knew they would come after us, and I didn't want them to know we're going toward Arkansas, we're going to ride west for a while. We're going to let them catch us, too, so we can pick the spot where we meet. You're going to stay clear and I'm going to take care of them. I'll hurt 'em or kill 'em if I have to."

Peter looked at me in disbelief. Closing both eyes, he shook his head. He appeared to be trying to speak but evidently couldn't find the words he needed.

We rode hard for another few miles until there were just minutes of daylight left. Just enough light to see what we were doing. I had Peter build a good sized fire in a thick stand of trees, tie the horses forty feet from it and stay with them. I ran back in the direction we had come from, for a distance of some two hundred yards, and hid in the brush at the top of the hill.

Less than ten minutes had passed since we'd dismounted, and, that quickly, we had things set up like I wanted them to be. The moon was full and well above the eastern horizon. I liked the level of light it provided. I figured our pursuers would be along soon, and I was almost certain they'd stop here when they saw our camp. The hill was the first place from which the fire would be visible to anyone coming from the east. Because I'd waited until sunset, it wasn't likely the smoke would be seen from a distance.

Within a few minutes four riders approached and stopped where I had expected them to…right in front of where I was hidden. The moon shone brightly on them while I was shaded by the trees and tall brush.

I listened to them make plans to surround the camp and kill us both. There was no talk of taking us back to Wichita alive. That didn't come as a shock to me. They were confident, laughed, and talked tough. I was disappointed, but not surprised, that Mayor Foster was not one of them. He'd taken a pretty good blow to the head. Hitting guys with my steel "hand" wasn't really fair, but it sure was effective.

When Peter and I rode off to the west some thirty minutes later, three of the men were hanging from a couple of those big Kansas Cottonwood trees that come in so handy. Their lariats were around their chests and under their arms. We let their horses go and started them back toward Wichita. The fourth guy had a nasty bullet wound in his right shoulder and we let him ride off.

I could have killed him, I guess, and maybe I should have, but while I was pretty good at being a gunfighter, I wasn't much of an executioner. I gave him a break he really didn't deserve. He was planning to kill me, but I didn't kill him.

Someday, maybe, that sort of weakness would be my undoing. When the wounded man and the horses made it to town, folks would come out and find the other three. I figured they'd still be alive.

The incredulous look was back on Peter's face. I knew he was wondering how he'd gotten himself into this and probably also wondering who in the hell I was.

We made plain tracks in a westerly direction until we came to a well-traveled road. After a bit, we split off one at a time, stayed on hard ground, and swung to the southeast.

Having seen me hit Foster with the iron cap on my left arm, I knew the folks in Wichita would figure out who I was. The posse I left hanging in the tree might tip them off to my identity as well. I knew word of my hanging those other three near Salina, in the same fashion, had spread around the territory. I also knew there was no way anyone was going to find our trail and follow us to Arkansas.

Finding our way cross country in the dark wasn't easy, so we stopped when we'd put four or five miles between us and the spot where we'd left the road. We hobbled the horses, laid out our bedrolls but made no fire. Peter hardly spoke a word. It wasn't until morning and we were back on the trail that he hit me with all of the questions he'd been saving up.

"Samuel Tucker, huh?" He cocked his head and squinted as he spoke. "I heard one of them fellas you hung in the tree call you Crow. Are you that gunfighter they call…uh… Bad…uh…Bad ass Crow?"?

" Bad Wing," I said, "they call me Bad Wing Crow." I held up my left arm. "This is the bad wing they're talkin' about."

His face was serious, he nodded his head several times, and then a smile broke across it. "So old Peter here's travelin' in some mighty fast company."

I looked his way and returned the smile. "Not as fast as my reputation would have you think, my friend."

"If you ain't that fast," he countered, "how'd you get all four of them boys rounded up last night without getting' shot your own sef?"

"Well," I answered, "when I stood up and told them to drop their guns, one of them had his pistol already drawn and another was drinking from his canteen. I shot the one in the shoulder as he started to swing his pistol in my direction, shot the canteen out of the other one's hand, and said "the name's Crow, gentlemen, Bad Wing Crow…next shot's gonna' be in the middle of somebody's forehead."

"If they'd gone for their iron, I doubt if I could have shot all three before they got me, but they must have believed all the things they'd heard about me, and they didn't put it to the test. I suppose they knew I'd have probably killed one or two of them. Men lose their nerve at times like that. They know somebody's going to die, but they don't know who, and they sure don't want to be the one."

"Should I be callin' you Crow then?"

"No, call me Sammy. I only use that other name when I want to shake somebody's confidence. When they gave it to me they were makin' fun of me. Now, when they hear it, they shit in their pants."

Chapter Fifteen

The rock of my life
Too much time had gone by
A flood of emotions
For the old man and I

Peter, his last name was Kraemer, and I got along well. I never asked him his age, but guessed him to be pushing fifty. He was compact, stood about five foot seven and weighed a hundred and eighty or so. Strong from his work as a blacksmith, he was smart too. We got to know each other well, and, as men commonly do on the trail, we became good friends quickly.

He told me about his early years as a slave, his family being broken up during the war, and his struggle to get along in the west in more recent years. It wasn't much different from the stories of thousands of other black individuals and families of the time. I told him my story as well, except for the part about my personal involvement with Kate. I thought about it for a long time, but I did tell him why I was going back to Arkansas.

As we drew near to Pine Bluff, I tried to convince him to leave me so he could stay clear of the trouble that was coming. I may as well have been talking to a stump. "Sammy," he gestured with his hands continuously now as he spoke, "what they done to you…what they done to your daddy…what they done to me…they done that to all of us.

You understand? All of us." I nodded.

"When you have your day, old Peter's gonna' be there. He gonna' be part of it. Old Peter's gonna' have a piece of this pie and he's gonna' enjoy every bite, and don't try to tell me no different. You understand?"

I nodded again, and he went on with an ever widening grin on his face. "You see, I'm gonna' find the apples we're after and help pick 'em…maybe slice 'em up some… an' then Mr. Bad Wing Crow…he's gonna' bake us a pie that's gonna' be the best thing anybody's tasted in more'n a hundred years."

We were both quiet for a while. I understood all too well what the man had said, and I had no desire to argue with him. Already I was beginning to see ways where he might be of help. He could play the humble, frightened, downtrodden colored man when it served his purpose, but he was plenty savvy, and he was nobody's fool. And he wasn't at all frightened. When trouble came, and I knew it would, he'd be a strong and reliable ally…one who wouldn't let me down.

As though he'd been reading my thoughts, Peter turned to me and started in again. His eyes were becoming moist.

"Yeah, Sammy, I been shufflin' my feet, hangin' my head, sayin' yes suh, and no suh, and kissin' white men's asses for a damn long time. A damn long time, an' I'm plumb sick of it."

His eyes had a sparkle to them even while they were still a bit red and wet with tears. "Now things are different. Now I'm ridin' with Bad Wing Crow, an' we got business to take care of. Me an' old Bad Wing, we in this shit together. We in this shit together right to the end."

I smiled in his direction. "Yeah, Mr. Kraemer, I guess we are, and I'm glad to have you with me."

We skirted Pine Bluff and headed east. It was a hot, sticky day. I stayed out of sight while Peter approached a couple of men in a wagon loaded with fire wood. It was pulled by a team of mules that were sweaty and covered with dust.

"Howdy, gents. Sure is a warm one, ain't it? Name's Peter Kraemer. I was wonderin' if you'd know of a fella name of Tucker…Harold Tucker. An older fella. Believe he's been croppin' around here for a good long while."

The men were tough and wiry…working men whose dark skin was weathered and toughened from long days in the Arkansas sun. Like the mules, the dust from the road coated their moist skin and their clothes as well. They were silent for a moment, before one of them nodded, wiped his brow, and spoke up.

"Sho, we know him. Everybody 'round here knows old Tuckah. His place be the first one down that cross road… on the right-hand side. But he ain't croppin' no mo. He owns his eighty acres his ownsef. Yes suh, he's one darky that owns his place his ownsef."

"What y'all want with him? Ain't bringin' no trouble are ya?" He squinted and looked real serious. "Tuckah, he a friend of ours. You got a problem wif old Tuckah an you got a problem wif us, too. You understand?"

"Yes I do, and no suh, I ain't bringin' no trouble. No trouble at all. Got a message for him from another old friend of his…fella I ran into up in Kansas, that's all."

"Thas fine," the man said, "Tuckah be at his place right now, workin' in the garden. Done drove by der a few minutes ago."

The excitement that hit me when Peter pointed to the house and told me grandpa was there right now, on a farm he owned, about knocked me off my horse.

During the long ride from Kansas I had never hurried,

just took my time. Now I couldn't get there fast enough. I hooked Boone with a spur and he lurched into a gallop. Peter did his best to keep up, but his horse had no chance of matching the speed of the big grey.

Grandpa heard the hoof beats and walked from the garden to the front gate to see what was going on. He saw Peter riding hard some two hundred yards behind me as I came to a stop in front of the little house. At first, he didn't recognize me.

"Somebody chasin' you young fella? Why you stoppin'…" and then his old face lit up. "Sammy! Lord Almighty, Sammy, you come back!" He walked toward me and looked again at Peter. "You want me to get the shotgun, Sammy?"

"No," I said, "he's my friend. His horse ain't quite as fast as mine, that's all."

Grandpa opened the gate and stood there waiting for me to dismount. I stayed in the saddle for a minute and looked at him. Nearly seventy-five years old, he was still straight and strong. His eyes were bright and clear and his smile was broad and warm. A smile that hadn't changed in all the years and instantly made me feel like I was home. I took my bandana from around my neck and wiped the sweat from my face and a few tears from my eyes. We'd been apart a long time, and I couldn't believe I was seeing him right up close.

I jumped from the saddle and dropped the reins to the ground. I could feel myself shaking as I walked toward him…felt like I was made of jelly. My mouth opened and closed but I couldn't make the words come out. The old man took a couple of quick steps toward me, put his hands on my shoulders, pulled me toward him and wrapped me up in his powerful arms.

"Sammy… Sammy boy, I love ya. I knew you'd come

back, Sammy. This here's my place. Ain't share croppin' no more…this place belongs to me."

"I heard that, Grandpa, good for you. Good for you."

He stepped back, opened my duster and looked at the two revolvers I had strapped to my body. Then he took hold of my left arm and examined the steel sleeve. "You got some new equipment." He nodded as he slowly said the words. "Yes, suh, Sammy you got some weapons, don't ya?"

"Yeah, Grandpa, I do. Where I've been and how I've been livin' I needed 'em…and they've served me well. I'll tell you some about that later."

"It's good to see you, Grandpa. There have been times when I thought I never would." I shook my head, snuffed my nose, and wiped away a couple more tears. "You look good Grandpa."

His smile broadened and he got a twinkle in his eye. "I always been good lookin', Sammy. I believe that's where you got it from."

By this time, Peter had arrived and dismounted. He stood quietly next to his panting horse while Grandpa and I talked. I motioned for him to join us.

"Grandpa, I'd like you to meet my good friend Peter Kraemer. I believe the day we talked about so long ago is comin' soon. When that day comes, Peter's gonna' be part of it." Grandpa looked at me with a questioning eye, I nodded to him, and that's all it took to assure him that Peter could be trusted.

"Peter," he said, as he held out his big right hand, "I'm Harold Tucker, an' I'm pleased to meet you."

"Your grandson done told me plenty about you, sir, and I'm mighty glad to make your acquaintance." They shook hands.

"Let's all go inside," the old man said, "I got somethin' that'll wash the dust out of yer whistles. Best batch of corn liquor I ever made. Just might be the best batch anybody's ever made." He laughed at his own boast, put a big arm around each of our shoulders and ushered us into the house.

The shades were drawn and the house was dark and fairly cool inside. Certainly it was much cooler than it was outside in the hot afternoon sun. It wasn't big; just a main room, a bedroom, and a small store room in the back. Though I'd never been in the house before, it had a familiar feel and smell to it. Like the places we'd lived when I was a boy, this one was sparsely furnished, clean, and everything was in its place.

I noticed a shelf filled with books and pointed toward them. "Are those yours, Grandpa?" He smiled proudly. "Yes they are mine. Done learned how to read. Can read pretty good now. Figured if I made you learn, I ought to do it my own self. That same old woman that helped you taught me."

I had tears in my eyes again as I looked at him and nodded my approval. "That's good Grandpa, that's real good. I'm proud of you for doin' that." His face told me he was proud as well. If I'm not mistaken, there were tears starting to form in his eyes, and I think that's why he changed the subject.

"Sit right here boys," he motioned us to the kitchen table, "and I'll get some of that good whiskey. We got some celebratin' to take care of." He set three glasses on the table and got a gallon jug from the store room. I'd learned a thing or two about Grandpa's corn liquor before I'd left home. When my glass was one third full, I stopped him from pouring any more. Peter allowed him to fill his glass nearly to the brim. We all three held up our drinks and clinked the glasses together before tasting the clear liquid. It was indeed excellent quality; smooth, sweet and it warmed the insides all the way down.

Initially, the conversation involved getting Grandpa caught up on where I'd been and what I'd done in the ten or so years since I'd left home. Peter, beginning to feel no pain, volunteered more than enough information. He told how I'd acquired a reputation as a gun hand and was known quite widely by the name of Bad Wing Crow.

Grandpa's face contorted into a scowl when he heard that, but he didn't say anything. I hadn't expected him to be real enthused and would have preferred if Peter had not brought the subject up. Peter, however, was enjoying his drink more with every sip, and his tongue was well oiled up and loose. It seemed like a good time to change the topic of conversation to the business I'd come for.

I took a gulp of the liquor and held it in my mouth for several seconds and gathered my thoughts before swallowing it. I took a breath, turned my eyes toward my grandfather, and came right to the point.

"Most of what Peter said about me is true, and I think you know what I'm here to do, Grandpa. I'm well equipped to take care of this. It's best, I think, if you stay out of it. Peter and I can handle it fine, but I need you to tell me what you know about the Coolidge brothers and Howard. Are they still in Pine Bluff?"

Grandpa took a swig of his drink and held it in his mouth just like I had…maybe that's where I got it. Then he stared at his glass and nodded his head repeatedly until I was beginning to think he wasn't going to answer. When he finally spoke, his eyes were narrowed and steady, and he had a dead serious look on his face.

"All three of them boys are still in the area. James Howard

has a freight hauling business headquartered in Pine Bluff. Hauls stuff to all of the towns around the area. Them two boys you ran into on the road were workin' for him.

Robert Coolidge owns a big farm south of town…has maybe a dozen share croppers on it. Keeps his croppers poor, tired and in debt. He actually owns most of this section my place is on too. All that cotton you seen when you rode in is his.

Buster owns one of the saloons in town, and he's drunk most every day. He carries a pistol, like you do, and when he's sober, he's pretty good with it. Buster's the meanest of the three, but nobody around here messes with any of 'em."

"As far as me stayin' out of it," the old man went on, "you can forget that idea altogether, Sammy. That was my son they hung, and I was there when they cut off your hand. There was nothin' I could have done at the time without gettin' more of us killed, but I ain't forgot none of it, and I been waitin' a long time for this day."

I knew there was no point in trying to talk him out of being involved. "Alright," I said, "but it isn't going to be today. We have to plan this out and do it right. I'm going to kill those three and I don't want anyone else to get hurt. You can help, Grandpa, but nobody but we three can know about it, and I'm gonna do the killin'."

Grandpa nodded. "We will talk about that later."

I was about to let the discussion rest when one last question occurred to me. "Grandpa?"

"Yes, Sammy."

"Which one of those three swung the axe… which one cut off my hand?" The old man hesitated. For the better part of two decades he'd been trying to drive that horrible scene from his mind, and he'd not discussed the details with anyone.

"I guess there's no reason not to tell you," his answer came in a subdued voice and his eyes moistened as he revisited that moment, "Robert held your arm down on the block and Buster swung the axe. I knew you favored your right hand, but I told them you favored your left. That's why they took the one they did."

It was as hard for me to hear the story as it was for grandpa to tell it. I felt a chill run down my spine and a sick, helpless feeling settled in my gut. It was just like those dreams I kept having.

Peter was too drunk to participate in the conversation and didn't seem to understand what we were talking about. He took the last swallow from his glass and pushed it toward my grandfather to fill it again. I put my hand over it and shook my head. Peter started to protest, but couldn't form the words. Soon his head was on the table and he was out cold.

Grandpa laughed. "Let's talk about this some more in the morning. We'll drink coffee instead of this stuff."

Grandpa and I carried Peter to the sofa, laid him out, and covered him with a blanket. He was totally limp and his slow, rhythmic breathing never varied. I got the spare mattress from the storeroom and laid it on the floor. It felt better than the cold, hard ground to which I was accustomed. Being in my grandfather's house felt good, too, and I slept well.

It was noon before Peter had sobered up enough to involve himself in the planning of what we'd come to Arkansas to do. Early into the discussion it was clear to me that we didn't have enough information to develop a plan we could successfully carry out unless we were very lucky. I didn't like counting on luck.

I also didn't like the idea of these three being killed right after two new colored men arrived in town…especially since one of them was me. It didn't seem likely that I could keep my identity hidden for very long if I stayed around. Surely, if folks figured out who I was, I would be the main suspect in the killings. In these parts that meant a lynching.

We decided Peter should try to get a job with Howard's freighting company. Grandpa would see what he could do to get closer to Robert Coolidge's farming operation. I would head back west for three or four months. We'd figure out what to do with Buster when I got back. He was the one who carried a pistol. All I'd have to do is get him alone.

Chapter Sixteen

What had felt so right
Now seemed a mistake
How much more trouble
Could a young girl take

Jim Davis pushed back from the table and wiped his mouth with his napkin. "Mighty fine breakfast Netttie… Miss Kate. Ought to hold me good for bringin' in that corn crop."

"I'll drive the wagon for you today, Jim. One more cup of coffee and I should be feelin' ready to go." Kate volunteered.

"Why don't you just tidy up in here, honey, and let me and Jim work in the field. It's gonna' be a warm one today and you haven't been feelin' well." As she made the suggestion, Nettie Davis gestured with her hands for Kate to stay seated.

"Oh, no I…" Kate started, but the other woman shushed her. "Please, Miss Kate, I'd really rather work outside today and you should stay out of the sun. You can busy yourself in the house today."

When the mule was harnessed and hitched to the wagon, Nettie took the lines and Jim sat next to her on the wooden seat and breathed deeply of the fresh morning air. The sun was bright in the eastern sky and it had already drunk up most of the heavy dew from the night before. There was no breeze and no doubt at all that it would be a warm, dry day.

Neither of them spoke. It wasn't until they had reached the corn field that Jim turned to his wife. "You were a might bossy with young Kate this mornin', Net. Maybe that poor girl didn't want to stay in the house all day. Maybe she wanted to work outside."

"This ain't gonna' be no kind of day for her to be out here. She's got no business doin' this kind of work in the hot sun. Least wise if what I'm thinkin' is right."

"Just what is it you're thinkin', Net? She's been doin' hard outside work all summer, an' she's been just fine. She works just as hard as you and I do."

"She's a good worker alright," Nettie responded, "but you ain't been payin' close attention to her lately."

Nettie looked at her husband for several seconds as she weighed what she was about to say. "If I ain't mistaken, Jim, that girl's with child."

Jim's jaw dropped nearly to his chest and he sighed deeply. "Good Lord," he said, "that ain't good…that ain't good at all. That child ain't gonna' be…uh…it ain't gonna' be white. Folks around here won't take to that. No sir, they won't take to that at all. What's Miss Kate gonna' do?"

Nettie gave her husband a look. "You mean what are we going to do, don't you?" She went on. "We're just going to have to help her, Jim. That's what we got to do, but first I have to talk to her and make sure."

"Uhh…what do you want me to do?" The woman smiled and took her husband's hand. "Why don't you just act like you don't know nothin' about it? Just play dumb."

The man nodded, and gently squeezed her hand. "That's

what I was hopin' you'd say. That sounds like just the right job for me," he laughed, "playin' dumb."

The Davis's worked steady all day picking corn from the twenty acre field. Nettie drove the wagon while Jim went row by row chopping the ears off of the stalks and throwing them into the wagon. The man and his wife kept up a steady banter as they worked, and sometimes, like in the slave days, they sang some of the old songs. Songs that had been passed on for generations and still hadn't been put on a sheet of paper. It made the day pass quickly and made the hard work tolerable.

They saw Kate several times while they worked. She brought cool water out to the field for them, and at noon they came in for the lunch she'd prepared.

It wasn't until after supper that Nettie broached the subject that had been on her mind throughout the day. When the kitchen was cleaned up, she suggested they step outside. The heat of the September afternoon had subsided and the evening breeze was soft and pleasant in their faces as they walked down toward the creek. The air had the smell and feel of early fall.

Though Nettie was only ten years older than Kate, a mother/daughter type of relationship had developed between them over the past few months. Nettie had a kind, nurturing personality, and with the loss of her family, Kate needed some comfort. Samuel's leaving left another big hole in her life and in her heart. It was a lot for a young girl to handle in such a short time. She was very grateful for the presence of Jim, but at this time in her life, she was closer to Nettie than she was to any other person.

Kate stopped when they came to the graves of her parents and two brothers. Both women stared at the wooden markers in silence until Nettie put her hand on Kate's shoulder and ushered her toward the creek.

They stood on the bank and watched the water flow by for a minute or two before Nettie spoke up.

"Kate, darlin', I've seen how you been feelin' the last month or so; 'specially in the mornin'. Unless I'm mistaken, you haven't had your monthly lately either. Am I right?"

Kate's eyes teared up some and she snuffled through her nose before answering in a soft and trembling voice. "You're right, Nettie. I've been feelin' poorly and it's been three months. I'm with child, I know it, but I don't know what I'm going to do. I wish Sammy would come back." She wrapped her arms around the other woman, laid her head on her shoulder, and sobbed.

"He can't come back, honey. You know he would if he could, but he just can't. I'll help you, though. Jim and I will help you. We'll help you get through this…you and your baby. There's nothing Sammy could do. It would be worse for you and the child if he was here. If folks knew you and him was together, if they knew you had a child together, I'm afraid of what would happen. It would be bad for both of you, and it would be bad for the baby."

Kate stepped back, took a deep breath to compose herself, and looked straight into her friend's eyes. "What can I do? Where can the baby and I go where folks will leave us be?"

Nettie put her arm around the younger woman's shoulder. "I don't think there's anywhere in this country you could go, but you don't have to go nowhere, dear. I've been thinkin' about it for some time now, and I know what we can do. We got everything we need right here.

We'll make folks think the child is mine and Jim's. I ain't much darker than you are, and I bet folks would believe it.

We don't get many visitors out this way…usually nobody but Sheriff Poole, and we can trust him. If anybody else comes, once you start showin', we'll keep you out of sight.

Of course you won't be able to go into town then neither. If need be, I'll make myself look like I'm the one that's with child."

"When it's time for the baby to come, I can help with that, too. I've helped with the birthin' before. It will be fine, honey, just fine."

Kate hugged Nettie, laid her head on her shoulder again, and sobbed as she whispered her feelings. "Thanks, Nettie. Thanks for helpin' me. You and Jim are the best friends I've got. God, I wish Sammy was here. He said he loved me, and now I'm going to have his baby and he's gone."

"Sammy does love you, honey. He loves you very much. That's why he had to leave."

Chapter Seventeen

Made a deal with old Tucker
Couldn't do him no harm
He'd find out much later
About buyin' the farm

My grandfather tied his big brown mule to the hitching rail and began harnessing him. He talked to the massive beast like he was a person. "Brownie, we got us some business to get started on today… some business I been waitin' to take care of for a long time. You ready to help old Harold out, Brownie?"

When the mule was harnessed and hitched to the wagon, Grandpa settled into the seat and turned the rig toward Pine Bluff. The old man was deep in thought as he drove the four miles of narrow, dusty road.

There'd been no rain at all for more than two weeks and things were drying up. The grass in the old country cemetery was long and brown. It crunched under his feet as he walked to his son's grave.

He bent down and brushed the leaves and debris from the head stone. Tears filled his eyes as he read the words carved into the granite; James Tucker 1839-1864. "I'm here, Jimmy. I think you know there was nothin' I could have done to stop 'em when they did this to you. I would'a traded places with you if I could, but there was nothin' I could have done without gettin' you and me both killed and leavin' little Sammy with nobody. But I'm sorry about what happened, and I never forgot."

"I never forgot what they did to the boy neither. Sammy's grown up now into a fine young man, a real fine young man. You'd be proud of him, I know you would, and him and me, we gonna' take care of this now. We gonna' get some justice for you…we gonna set things right. Your boy don't need no lookin' after no more. He can take care of himself just fine. He can take care of himself no matter what becomes of me."

Wiping his eyes with his kerchief, he got back aboard the old wagon and turned it toward the south. The wood-spoked wheels rolled across another two miles of dirt road before they came to the Coolidge plantation and squeaked up the lane that led to the house. The grounds were green and well groomed. A young colored man was trimming shrubs and there were two more unloading a hay wagon at the barn.

The scene made Grandpa sigh. He was looking at clear evidence that things here weren't all that different from the slave days. All of the folks working in the fields he'd passed along the way were colored. They were called share croppers now, not slaves, but the work was the same and the pay wasn't much better. The rights they had won as a result of the war were words on paper and little else. A white man could still do about anything he wanted to a colored man.

He tied the mule to the rail behind the house and walked to the door. A woman servant came to the door and greeted him. "Mr. Tucker, good mornin'. What brings you out this way this mornin'?"

"I'd like to speak with Mr. Coolidge if he's not too busy, Margie. You might tell him it's about the eighty acres I own next to that big piece he has northeast of here a few miles."

The woman nodded. "Wait right here, Mr. Tucker, an' I'll see if I can fetch him."

Robert Coolidge was a tall, well-built man in his early fifties. He had a cigar in his mouth and a glass of bourbon in his hand as he came to the back door. His arrogance and impatience were apparent before he'd said a single word. "What is it you want, Tucker?

"Well, suh, it's about the piece a land I own next to where you got yo big section a cotton."

"What about it?"

"Well, Suh, I be gettin' on in years and farmin' on my own is gettin' real hard on me. I was thinkin' maybe I could work for you here, doin' somethin' a might easier, and your workers could farm my place."

"Now, why would I want to farm your land? You wantin' me to be your share cropper?" The white man laughed.

"No Suh, I wasn't thinkin' that way at all, but I was thinkin' maybe we could make a agreement for you to buy my place. I'd give you a real good price on it if you went an' gave me a job an' let me stay in my house for maybe another five years. Unless, maybe I wanted to leave sooner. You wouldn't have to pay for the land until I moved off of it. There's a real good well on the place, you know."

"What kind of work were you thinking of doing, and how much would you want for the land?"

"I was thinkin' I might be your driver an' just do jobs around here…no more field work. You know, just the kind of jobs an old man can handle."

Coolidge nodded. "And the price of the land?"

"Around ten dollars an acre…I was thinkin' that would be about right…about eight hundred dollars. An' I was thinkin' you'd pay me twenty-five cents a day for workin' an' I don't need to get any part of the crop from my land neither."

Coolidge spoke through a barely suppressed smile. "You don't want any money down on the land?"

"No Suh, I don't. We can just write up a paper sayin' after five years, if you gives me eight hundred dollars, the land is yours. An' it will say you can farm it for nothin' as long as you payin' me to work at your place."

"That sounds fair enough, Tucker. Drivin' the family around and some other light work around here will be fine. I'll have the papers drawn up and you can start working here as soon as tomorrow if you'd like."

"I can read and write now, Suh. If you don't mind, I can get the paper ready for us both to sign."

"Very well, if that's how you want to do it."

"I'm a little surprised you came to me with this idea, Tucker. There ain't no bad blood between us, anymore?"

The old man shook his head. "You the one who owns the land next to mine and it just made sense, that's all. The bad times was a long time ago, Suh, and there ain't no sense draggin' em up again. A lot of bad things happened durin' the war an' after. We jes got to let them things go, Suh."

At seven the next morning Grandpa was at the Coolidge place ready for work and that's the way it was every morning. He was never late and he did everything asked of him, with a smile on his face, until he went home at five in the afternoon.

Coolidge approached him just before quitting time on a Tuesday afternoon after he'd been on the job for three weeks or so. "Poker night starts tomorrow, Tucker. I want you to drive me to the saloon in town. We'll leave here at six and it will be midnight or so before we leave to come back. You can sleep here in one of the cabins so you won't have to drive all the way back to your place."

"Thank you, Suh." The old man responded. "Will we be doin' that every Wednesday?"

"Yes we will. We don't play in the summer, but we'll be goin' now every week until the first of May."

The old man's ever present smile grew wider. "Since we goin' to town, I'll spend some time tomorrow cleanin' and oilin' harness and gettin' them horses of yours all brushed and shined up, if you don't mind, Suh."

"That's a fine idea. Clean 'em up good."

Grandpa started at two the next afternoon getting everything ready. He did the harnesses first and draped them over the hitching rail to let the oil dry in the sun. Next, he washed down the carriage and cleaned the seats with saddle soap. That too, he let dry in the sun.

The matched pair of black carriage horses was the last thing he tended to. He bathed them, put blacking on their hooves, and brushed them until their coats and long manes and tails shone brightly. By five forty-five they were hitched to the carriage, nervous, and eager to go. Grandpa stood in front of them holding the lines to keep them settled down until Coolidge came out and got in the carriage. He smiled when he saw the fine looking outfit, but made no comment.

The horses continued to be fresh and frisky, and they trotted out at a good clip. It took little more than half an hour to make the five mile trip to Pine Bluff.

The rig immediately in front of them, when they pulled up in front of the saloon, belonged to James Howard. As Howard got out of the carriage he turned to his driver. "Take this outfit to the livery, Kraemer, and come back here by eleven thirty."

When Coolidge and Howard were both in the saloon, old Harold Tucker clucked to the team and followed Pete Kraemer to the livery.

With the two teams unhitched and turned out in a corral, Grandpa pulled a jug of corn liquor out from under the seat of Coolidge's carriage and a deck of cards from his pocket. The two men sat on bales of straw, drank, played gin, and talked for the next five hours.

"Old Howard and Coolidge got us two steppin' and fetchin' for 'em just like we was their slaves, Harold. Just like the old days." Pete made the observation with a wry smile on his face.

Grandpa nodded in agreement. "Yes, suh, but we're steppin' and fetchin' right where we want to be, son. Right where we want to be."

"How we gonna' get word to your grandson about what we got set up?"

"Sammy should be in Fort Smith by now, I told him I'd write to him there. He's gonna' check the post office every week or so."

This same routine was repeated by the four men every Wednesday for the next two months. Each night Harold and Peter had a good time, but made sure they got a little less drunk than their bosses.

Chapter Eighteen

Spent years all alone
Kept others at bay
Then things started changin'
Changin' faster each day

It took me two weeks to traverse the two hundred miles from Pine Bluff to Fort Smith. For the most part I followed the Arkansas River but detoured from it occasionally to avoid the towns. I camped along the way and lived on rabbits and quail and the few basics I carried in my saddle bags. Some days I made thirty miles and some I didn't travel at all. Boone had plenty of time to rest and graze. I didn't want to wear him down and I wanted to give Grandpa and Pete plenty of time to get close to Coolidge and Howard. Most importantly, I didn't want things to happen too soon after Pete's arrival in Pine Bluff. I had a lot of reasons to take my time.

Maybe I wouldn't have had to travel so far, but I wanted to be sure I was well out of the picture. Fort Smith was beyond the area that Howard's freight company served. When the three men died, I didn't want anyone to suddenly remember seeing a one-handed colored man anywhere near Pine Bluff. Many of the people in that town…maybe all of them… knew the story of my hand being cut off and who did it. They didn't talk about it, but they knew and they remembered.

The situation I was in left me with a lot of free time and I spent too much of it thinking about Kate. Sometimes I wished I'd never let her get close to me. When we'd started out I had been clear about that, and had the best of intentions, but I'd caved in without really much of a fight. Not a good show of strength and resolve by the notorious Bad Wing Crow.

I realized, of course, if I'd kept my distance from her I would have missed the most wonderful time of my life, and the only time when I'd known the love of a woman. It was also the only time I'd ever given my love to a woman. It was all new territory for me, and, except for the pain I felt, it hardly seemed real.

It was real, though, and how it had ended weighed heavily on my mind. I'd left Kate. She had no family, she was scared and shaken by what had happened to them, and she loved me…and I had left her. I knew Poole and the Davis's would look out for her. I had no doubts about that, but I still knew I'd hurt her and let her down.

I could see her face. I didn't even have to close my eyes, and I could see her face with those big blue eyes flooded with tears. That's how she'd looked the last time I saw her, and that picture kept coming into my mind time after time. Beyond that, I just plain missed her, and it tore me up when I thought I would never see her again. That thought was so painful I fought to keep it out of my mind, but, like the picture of her face, it kept coming back.

I knew there hadn't been any other good options. At this time and in this country there was nothing else I could have done. There was no other way I could protect her from the things people would say and do to her if they knew about us. There was no reason to think that would change any time soon…maybe it never would. What a sick damned country.

Certainly, if folks found out, I'd be in more danger of being harmed physically than she, but I didn't spend a lot of time worrying about that. The only thing that scared me some was the prospect of being hanged. That had to do with the dreams I still had about them lynching my father. They might well kill me some day, but I'd make damned sure they wouldn't hang me.

I'd been dwelling on Kate and me for too long and it was wearing me down. I had to move on and find something else to occupy my mind. I needed to take it off the subject and escape the hollow, empty feeling that was threatening to take me over completely. When I arrived in Fort Smith, I was hoping it would offer the distraction I needed. It was like most of the other river towns I'd seen, the streets were mostly dirt, and except for right after a rain, everything was dusty. It was busy with goods of all kinds constantly being loaded on and off of boats and wagons. Nobody seemed to pay much attention to me as I rode down Main Street. Any looks that came my way appeared to be directed at Boone. The big grey horse did tend to attract attention.

When I got to the part of town that held the stock yards and stables, I started asking folks if they knew of anyone who had horses to break or train. A man at a livery stable mentioned a fellow by the name of Mason…said he was bringing mustangs, and other miscellaneous mares, in from the adjacent Indian Territory, Oklahoma Territory, and Texas. He was crossing them with Thoroughbred studs, and selling the foals to the Army. I decided to look him up.

Mason's place fronted the river, west of town, right on the Arkansas/Indian territory border. It was one of the prettiest spots and one of the nicest ranches I'd ever seen.

When I rode into the place, I saw a cowboy trying to saddle a young horse in one of the corrals. There was another fellow standing at the rail watching. He was a dark haired man with sort of an olive complexion. He was just about my size and shape; lean and of average height. I guessed his age to be somewhere close to forty.

I introduced myself. Before he said anything he looked me over carefully. He looked good and hard at my left arm, and didn't try to hide what he was doing. Then he smiled and said he was Bill Mason, owner of the ranch.

As we started to talk, I looked from time to time at the cowboy. It was plain to see he was having no luck with the bronc. From the way he was going about things, I knew his luck wasn't about to change.

"I heard you've got quite a few colts that need breakin'."

"Well, you heard right," he answered, "got a hundred three and four year old's to start right now. I'm sorry, but I don't reckon its work a one-handed man can do."

I glanced again in the direction of the young cowboy in the corral. He was still carrying the saddle. The colt had pulled away from him and he was trying to catch it while it trotted around the corral, with his head high, dragging the lasso.

"Suppose I show what I can do with that colt right there, Mr. Mason." The man nodded. "Go ahead. There's five bucks in it for you if you can lope him around this corral before supper time." He laughed as though to say there was no way I'd ever get that done.

The colt was a dark bay, tall and rangy, with a Roman nose. He wasn't the least bit pretty, but he was straight legged, short backed, and he looked like he could grow into being a functional and sturdy saddle horse.

I rode Boone into the corral and threw my loop around the colt's neck. I stayed mounted and ponied him around the corral; kept him right along the rail. He resisted at first, but I worked with him until he came along willingly. In no more than ten minutes he was following me around like a puppy dog.

Next, I dallied my rope around the saddle horn and backed Boone up until it was snug. He braced up and the young horse pulled back hard. He may as well have tried to move a mountain. The grey knew what he was doing and had him outweighed by a good four hundred pounds.

I dismounted, picked up the saddle and walked up to the colt. For a minute or so I petted him and let him sniff the saddle and pad. He seemed to relax pretty quickly. After touching him with the saddle and pad on both sides, letting him get the feel of them against his body, I put them on his back and lightly snugged up the girth. The cowboy gave me a headstall with a braided rawhide bosal attached. I slipped it on the colt's head and removed the lasso from his neck.

With the girth tightened the rest of the way, I put some weight in the stirrups…first with my hand and then my foot. I didn't mount until I'd stepped part way up, with my left foot in the stirrup, four or five times. When I finally swung all the way into the saddle, the colt just stood there and didn't seem to be bothered in the least about having me on his back. It was becoming apparent that this horse had a pretty good head on his shoulders and wasn't going to be much of a problem.

I took my time with him and tried to not give him any reason to act up. It wasn't that I didn't think I could stay on him if he got rank. No, I always figured, if you could keep a horse from ever learning he can buck, you were ahead of the game, and you'd get a better mount that way. Once he finds out he can buck, there's a good chance he'll try it sometime later when he's under pressure, and that can become a bad habit, especially for an army horse.

Within thirty minutes of when I first rode into the corral,

I was loping him around the rail. Once he knew I wasn't going to hurt him, and knew what I wanted, he never refused me a single time, and he never offered to buck.

There was something different about Mason that I couldn't put my finger on, but he seemed to be a good natured and friendly sort. He had a broad smile on his face when he handed me my five dollars.

"You got a job, son, if you still want it. I didn't mean no offense when I made the remark about your hand." I smiled back at him. "No offense taken. It was a fair enough question to ask. That's why I figured a demonstration was in order." He nodded. "That was a pretty damn good demonstration; well worth the price."

Bill Mason got twenty-five to thirty dollars a head from the army. I didn't argue when he said he couldn't really afford to pay five dollars for every colt I gentled. We settled on two dollars, and I still made more money in a week than a regular ranch hand made in a month.

I worked with each horse for a week, rode him five times, and then handed him off to one of the other cowboys. The real rank ones I put a couple of extra rides on, but that was only about one out of every dozen. Mason's studs were all pretty good-minded, and that showed up in most of their offspring. The ones that had some ugly in them got it from their mommas.

Most weeks I broke eight to ten colts well enough that most any cowboy could finish them up to the army specifications. Both Mason and I were pleased with how the arrangement was working out.

Though the boss spoke with a deep, southern accent, he didn't have the same attitude toward colored folks that most white people had. He treated me with the respect he would afford any other person. That's what was different about him…the thing I had sensed earlier.

Quite often, in the evening, he'd invite me to sit outside and have a drink and talk. He was an educated man and we had some good conversations. I looked him in the eye and related to him as an equal, and if I disagreed with him, I told him so. He had no problem with any of that. On one of those occasions he surprised the hell out of me with what he had to say. It was then that I began to understand about him being different from most white men.

"You're one of the Tuckers from down around Pine Bluff, aren't you Sam?" I thought for a minute before cautiously nodding my head. The conversation was turning in a direction that was counter to my intention of lying low in Fort Smith

"And, unless I miss my guess, you're the boy who got his hand cut off down there in the late sixties. I was livin' there at the time, and I heard about it… it was an awful thing they did."

I nodded again, and Mason went on. "You're also the one folks call Bad Wing Crow, aren't you? I mean folks out west of here."

This time I shook my head as I answered. "You know more about me than I usually want folks to know, Bill… way more. How did you come by all of that…uh… information?"

"Well, like I said, I lived in Pine Bluff when they did that to you…the Coolidges and Howard. Everybody in town knew. They just didn't talk about it…didn't talk about what they did to your daddy either. Over the last five or six years, when I've been in Texas and the territories buyin' horses, I started hearin' about Bad Wing Crow. I just now put the two together."

"You're pretty good at figurin' things out." I said.

Mason stayed on the subject. "Those three boys never paid for what they did. They never paid a nickel and they never spent a minute in jail. The Sheriff knew all about it and I don't believe he ever even spoke to them. Unless he slapped 'em on the back and congratulated them for it."

My jaw tightened at his last remark, I was wondering where he was going with this, but before I could ask, he answered the question for me.

"There's a very special reason why all of this interests me, Sam…besides you and me bein' friends. The Coolidge boys and I have the same grandfather."

"What?" I blurted the word out. "What did you say?"

Bill smiled and nodded. "My grandmother was a slave girl who worked in the Warren Coolidge's mansion. She was fairly light-skinned, real pretty, and old man Coolidge took a likin' to her. She had a daughter by him when she was just fifteen years old. That happened a lot in those days. The owners considered slaves no more than animals, but didn't mind bedding down with the pretty young girls. Coolidge sold the little girl, his own daughter, to a cotton grower named Mason when she was ten. That's where I came from. Mason used my mother just like Coolidge had done to my grandmother. Ernest Mason; he was my Daddy."

Too obviously, I guess, I began studying his face looking for indications of his African heritage. He laughed out loud. "It's there, Sammy boy, and I'm not ashamed of it. In fact I'm proud of it. It's the Coolidge and Mason blood I wish I didn't have. I've been passin' all these years just because it makes life and business a whole lot easier."

I nodded. "Yeah, I've done some things just to get by myself at times. Times when the odds were stacked against me."

"From the things I heard out west," Mason said, "you stood up against some tough odds plenty of times as well. You're figurin' on standin' up to Howard and the Coolidges someday soon, aren't you?"

Not knowing how I wanted to respond, I sat there and looked at him. He poured me another three fingers of brandy and a like amount for himself.

"You don't have to worry about me, Sam." He assured me. "I'd like to see those three get what's coming to them. I'd include my own father in that group as well, but he died shortly after the war. He treated me like any of his other slave kids…my own father, and I was his slave. I was his slave until I was twenty years old…until he had to free me." Bill's voice broke as he said those last words.

He hesitated, closed his eyes, and got a grip on his emotions. "The worst part, Sam; the worst part was the way those men, Mason, Coolidge, and hundreds or even thousands of others, treated women… women like my mother and grandmother. They used them, made babies with them, and treated them like animals. And even today, all these years after emancipation, they can do anything they want to a colored woman and get away with it."

I took a drink of brandy and let the warm sweet liquid slosh around in my mouth while I let the things he'd just told me sink in. "Well," I said, "there are three of them who aren't going to continue to get away with what they did to me and my family, because I am figurin' on standing up to those boys real soon. You don't have a mind to be part of it, do you?"

"You're damned right I do."

I still didn't have a plan for how we would take care of the Coolidges and Howard, although I had thought quite a bit about how their last moments of life might be. The last moments of Buster Coolidge were of particular interest. How we'd get to that depended a lot on how Grandpa and Pete were doing back in Pine Bluff.

What part Bill Mason might play was certainly an unknown, but it was easy to see how having a "white man" in on the deal might come in handy. We didn't go any further with the discussion that evening, but we had an understanding, and I was mighty glad I'd stumbled on to this new friend.

My friendship with Bill grew and deepened day by day. We were again having a drink in the evening, after I'd been at his ranch for about five weeks, when he brought up something else. It was a subject that caught me completely off guard.

"What do you know about your mother, Sam?" I looked at him in silence for a bit, wondering why he'd asked the question. Had he been most anyone else I would have told him to mind his own business. I hadn't seen my mother since I was four or five years old and I liked to keep my fading memories of her to myself. I was possessive of them and didn't want to share them with anyone. The memories were all I had of her and I fought to keep them alive. I treasured them.

Bill kept looking into my eyes, waiting for an answer. "Well," I said, "she got sold off after they hanged my Daddy, and we never saw her again. They didn't sell me with her because she fought back when the boss told Buster he could have his way with her…go to the cabins as they called it. It was to settle a poker debt."

"My Daddy fought them too, and that's what got him hanged. They hanged her husband, took her only child from her, and sold her. That was her punishment for fighting against being raped. Two years later someone told Grandpa she'd gotten sick and died, and we never heard anything more."

Mason put his hand on my shoulder. "Sam, I don't think she's dead." The words made me feel like I'd been hit in the belly with a wagon tongue. My head sank to my knees and I started to shake. After a couple of deep breaths, I was able to speak. "What do you mean…what are you talking about? We always thought…"

He held his hand up to quiet and calm me down and went on. "My mother lives in the middle of Oklahoma Territory. She, like quite a few other former slaves, is married to a Cherokee Indian. They have a small ranch there on the North Canadian River. I see them when I go out that way to buy horses. She knows a colored woman out that way who sort of let it slip that she came from the Pine Bluff area. She doesn't use the name, Tucker, and doesn't talk about her past, but I think she's your mother, Lizzie."

"You see, Sammy, I met your momma when we were both kids. She was a couple of years older than me, but I thought she was pretty, and I remembered her. Last time I was in Oklahoma my mother pointed this woman out to me. We saw her in town. She was a distance away, but I'm pretty sure it's her. We didn't talk, and I didn't tell my mother I recognized her, but I'm almost sure it's her."

My drink fell out of my trembling hand and I made no effort to recover it. Tears ran freely down my cheeks. I had neither words nor the ability to speak them.

Chapter Nineteen

A young Cherokee lad
Straight and strong as a tree
And I'll find out why
He looks so much like me

The possibility of my mother being alive was almost overwhelming. I tried to tell myself it was impossible and to not let my hopes get too high. Yet I could think of nothing else, and I knew I had to set everything aside, go to Oklahoma Territory, and find out. It meant close to another two hundred mile ride, each way, but I had to do it.

I'd lost my mother and father at the same time. I was somewhere between four and five years old when it happened and it felt like my world had ended.

My grandfather did a good job of looking after me, and he began to fill the hole left by the loss of my father, but nothing ever came close to replacing Momma. For three or four years after she left, I often woke up at night crying and calling for her. After they cut off my hand, it started again.

Even now I sometimes have dreams about her being auctioned off and led away. The boss brought me to the auction and I still have a clear picture of that terrible day in my mind. He brought me there, I suppose, to punish my momma even more. Punish her by letting her see me, hear me cry, and call for her.

I asked Bill to send a telegram to my grandfather. We'd worked out a code of sorts before I'd left Pine Bluff so as to not give any clues as to what we were about, and to be sure no one knew of my presence in that area. The telegram read like this:

Mr. Tucker, Schedule has changed. Must travel west before coming for the mules I've purchased. Expect to be delayed by about four weeks. You may continue working the animals as though you still owned them. Mr. Samuel

I took the ferry across the river and followed the road that ran parallel to the north bank. I wasn't aware of exactly when I crossed the line into Indian Territory, but I knew the border was only a short distance from Fort Smith.

Traveling at a deliberate pace was not an option this time. Every ounce of me wanted to get to the North Canadian as quickly as possible. Fortunately I had the horse to do it, but even on old Boone it would take a solid week. Longer if we ran into bad weather or trouble of some other kind.

We had to cross Indian Territory from east to west and then ride into the middle of what was now unofficially called Oklahoma Territory. It was land that had been ceded to the Cherokee when they were forced to leave their homes in the southeast, but had now been taken back and opened to white settlement.

The ranch that Bill's mother and her husband owned was bordered on the north by the North Canadian River and by two smaller tributaries on the east and west.

If I took a course that was just north of due west, I figured I would hit the North Canadian. My plan was to cross over and follow along the southwest bank until I found the ranch or someone who knew where it was. I wasn't worried about getting lost…Boone and I had found our way with less information on many occasions. I had the names of Bill's mother and stepfather. Bill had assured me his mother would help me find the woman...the woman whom he believed to be my mother.

Once again I found myself on a solitary journey with nothing to do but think. And now I had another thing on my mind that was troubling and burdensome. Kate and my momma were the two most important women in my life... the only two I'd ever loved, and they'd both been taken from me. Stolen, really...stolen in different ways and at much different times, but stolen nonetheless.

Solitude is not the friend of a man burdened with troubles and haunted by his past. I'd spent too much time alone in my life and had begun to accommodate to it. Then those short, wonderful weeks with Kate came along in glaring contrast to the life I'd been living. My return to a solitary existence made me more morose, introspective and resentful than I had been in many years.

And now the possibility of my mother still being alive... the possibility of finding her. In my mind, I went over and over the possible outcomes of this quest. Was she alive? Would I find her if she was? Would I recognize her if I did find her? Was my memory of her intact?

The question of memory was a big one. As a small boy I'd already been exposed to the defeated and hopeless attitude that slavery instills in so many of its victims... that resignation to accept whatever fate brings your way. I guess some of it must have rubbed off on me in spite of the defiance I'd seen in my father and the quiet, calculating resilience of my grandfather.

I had held out no hope, as a child, of ever seeing my mother again. I didn't allow myself that hope, I suppose, because it would have been more painful to hope and suffer the almost inevitable disappointment than to simply resign myself to never seeing her again.

Her memory, however, was a different matter. That was something even a little slave boy might be able to hang on to if he tried, and I clung to it and worked at it.

I would repeat little phrases I could remember her saying and I would mimic her speech pattern, inflections, and accent. Things like; "Sammy, darlin', would you fetch your momma's apron, please?" She would ask me to do that sort of thing because she knew I took pride in helping and being useful.

We had no pictures of her, so I would frequently try to draw her likeness thinking it would help me keep the image of her fresh in my mind. When I had finished a sketch I would show it to Grandpa and ask, "does this look like my momma?" Invariably his response was something like; "yes indeed, Sammy, that looks exactly like her…exactly like her."

I couldn't free myself of these thoughts and memories as I endured the hot, steamy, ride across the rugged and varied terrain of the territories.

The big grey gelding was a wonder. With ears forward, he willingly and swiftly covered the unforgiving country. Bold and powerful, he was a smart horse at the same time; avoiding badger holes, cactus and even rattlesnakes without any guidance from me. I thought back to that day at the Busted A when Luke had given him to me. Even though I was just a kid at the time, I had a good feeling about the horse. On that first day I had a feeling he might be something special, and time and time again he'd proven me right.

Boone was more than a horse…he was a friend. It had been ten years now, and, over that span of time, he'd been my best friend…the only friendship that had lasted…the only one that was there day after day and year after year. I had friends like Bob Poole and now Pete Kraemer and Bill

Mason, but the time I spent alone far outweighed the time when I was in the company of another person. Maybe, I thought, that was a sad commentary on my life. The solitary life of a one-handed slave boy who almost never let himself get close to another human being.

Kate was the major exception, but she was a bright spot in my life that had quickly disappeared. Like a shooting star that burns brilliantly for an instant, then leaves the night sky seeming darker than ever before, and leaves us wondering where it went.

And now I faced the prospect of finding my mother…the hopeful, and horribly frightening prospect of finding my mother. As I reflected on my dismal history with human relationships, the frightening side of the picture began to dominate the hopeful side.

For the first time I was beginning to understand Bad Wing Crow. How he'd come to be and why he'd chosen the life he'd been living. Sammy Tucker had been a frightened, heartbroken and damaged little boy. His life had been torn apart. Except for his grandfather, everyone he loved…everyone who protected him…had been taken from him. His life and heart had been broken beyond repair and it had all happened in Pine Bluff, Arkansas.

I didn't understand it at the time, but I knew I had to get out of there and become a different person. I had to bury little Sammy Tucker and the sorrow that wouldn't let go of him.

When I was just short of my sixteenth birthday, I said goodbye to Grandpa and headed out into the world. I never asked for the name they gave me and I almost never used it, but I did become Bad Wing Crow. I replaced abandonment with voluntary solitude, vulnerability with toughness, and fear with anger. I did it because I wasn't strong enough to be Sammy Tucker.

Then I met Kate and the armor of Bad Wing Crow cracked and crumbled a bit, and some of the old feelings were exposed.

The news of my mother caused more of the same. Now I almost wished I could turn the clock back. Turn it back to before I'd met Kate and before Bill Mason had told me about my mother. Back to my life on the trail where the only danger I faced was that brought my way by the angry white men I ran into from time to time. Men like the three who had killed Kate's family…men who brought danger, but not the kind that scared me…not the kind that made me hurt inside.

But I couldn't go back, and, scared as I was, I don't suppose I would have if I could have. I guess that meant little Sammy Tucker, the five year old boy who lost his momma, and the ten year old who lost his hand, was still somewhere deep inside this rough character I'd become.

*****

Boone and I pressed on toward the North Canadian River. It was late in the afternoon when we reached the northeast shore. It was a bit smaller than I expected it to be and not as muddy. The current wasn't real swift, the bottom was mostly sand and gravel, and the banks weren't too steep. I had no trouble finding a place to ford, and Boone easily picked his way across to the southwest bank without having to swim at all. By lifting my feet up out of the stirrups, I was even able to keep my boots dry.

There were small flocks of ducks landing on the water all up and down the slowly flowing stream. I watched a dozen or so fat, tasty looking Mallards set their wings and settle in behind a tall, thick clump of cattails not far from the game trail Boone and I were following. "Horse," I said, "while you're eating grass for supper, I believe I'll be enjoying roast duck."

Wrapping the reins around a small aspen, I left my mount and sneaked up to the bank under cover of brush and cattails. I was hunkered down in the weeds for only a few minutes when a big green headed drake swam my way. Very slowly I parted the weeds enough to get a clear shot.

When the Colt revolver barked, it caused the duck to float with the current, while his detached head sank to the bottom. A .44 caliber slug will do that to a duck. This time I couldn't avoid getting my boots wet as I ran downstream and waded out to retrieve my supper.

I made camp right there and roasted the duck while Boone grazed. For this time of year, the grass was still quite green, and the big horse enjoyed his supper as much as I did mine. I roasted the fat Mallard slowly so it stayed juicy and the skin got crispy. Even the dry biscuits I had tasted good when I used them to sop up the juice. It was a simple yet satisfying meal; much better than most I'd had in my years on the trail.

I didn't get into my bedroll until the sun had been down for two or three hours. The sky was clear and the stars seemed brighter and more numerous than usual. It occurred to me that perhaps they were shining down on my momma at this very time and she might not be so far away. I thought of Kate, too, and how the same stars would be looking down on her at the little farm in Kansas. Those thoughts got me all wound up and even made a tear drop or two run down my cheek. I suspected I would get little sleep this night and my suspicion turned out to be right.

The water in the North Canadian was every bit as cold as one would expect it to be on an October morning, but it felt good to bathe in it nonetheless, and the chill woke me up. I drank a few cups of coffee and ate two dry, stale biscuits. The first bite of biscuit made me seriously consider shooting another duck, but I decided that would take more time than I wanted to spend.

Anxious to get on with my quest, I saddled Boone and started my ride along the river to the Northwest. A fairly well used two track trail followed this side of the river. Since the trail had obviously been made by wagons, it wouldn't be long, I expected, before I would come to a ranch or farm.

Little more than a mile from where I'd camped, I crossed a small creek. Another quarter mile down the trail I spotted a man plowing a field with a pair of sorrel mules. He was in the middle of the small patch of ground turning over rich bottom land soil that was black as coal. The pattern of his plowing told me he would come along side me, within four rods of the trail, on his next pass. Remaining mounted, I waited until he was nearly even with me before I spoke.

"Gettin' a jump on spring time, I see." The man stopped the team, looked my way and smiled. "Yes, I am, and if this here river don't flood too bad come spring I'll have an easy time gettin' the crop in."

"Can we talk for a minute?" I asked. I dismounted, pulled the bridle off Boone so he could graze more easily and began to walk in his direction.

"We can if you'll bring that canteen with you and share a bit of your water. I forgot to bring any with me this mornin' and I'm gettin' mighty dry."

Nodding, I grabbed the canteen off the saddle and left Boone to chomp on the deep lush grass at the edge of the field.

When I got close enough to get a good look at his face, I saw the farmer was little more than a boy…maybe seventeen or eighteen years old. With long, thick, straight black hair and dark skin, I assumed he was Cherokee. That was somewhat of a relief since I figured an Indian was a lot less likely than a white man to give me any grief. With all of the emotional turmoil I'd been going through I knew I would have little tolerance for anyone who chose to mess with me…especially a white man.

I handed him the canteen and waited while he took a deep drink. He wiped his lips with the back of his hand, thanked me, and gave the canteen back.

"You ain't afraid that big horse is gonna' run off on ya?"

The kid flashed another big smile as he looked in Boone's direction. His teeth were wide, even, and looked very white in contrast to his coffee colored complexion. With prominent cheek bones, a square jaw, and a straight, fairly broad nose, he had a handsome if rather uncommon looking face…a face beaded with sweat and smudged with dirt from the field. I waited as he wiped it clean with his bandana before responding to his question.

"No," that old boy's got nowhere to go except where I'm goin'. He's my pardner."

"Looks like a mighty good one."

I nodded in response to his comment and offered my hand. About the same height as me, the kid was raw boned and muscular. The strength of his grip impressed me as I shook his wide, calloused hand.

I must have been anxious, because I stated my business without introducing myself. "You wouldn't happen to know some folks by the name of Pascal, would you…Jack and Sarah Pascal? I've been told they have a place somewhere near here."

"I would indeed. This here field I'm plowin' belongs to them. I work for Jack when I ain't needed on our place. They're good friends of mine…me and my folks. You got business with them?"

"Yeah, I'm lookin' for someone and I've been told Jack and Sarah might know where I can find her."

"Well," he said, "Jack and Sarah's place is just a half mile up river, on this side, but they ain't there…went in to town for a couple of days. Who is it you're lookin' for? Maybe I can help."

Normally I would have played it closer to the vest and not divulged my business to a stranger, but, for some reason, I took an immediate liking to this kid and felt like I could trust him. What the hell, I thought, might as well just say it.

"I'm lookin' for my mother. Haven't seen her since I was five years old. Heard she was livin' in this country. Her name was Lizzie Tucker, but I don't think she goes by that now. She's a colored woman, kind of light to medium complexion, and she was real pretty as a young girl. I guess she'd be about forty-three or forty-four years old now. She used to live in Arkansas, near Pine Bluff, back before the war was over. She left…got…uhh…sold off…just before it ended."

The young man's eyes narrowed for just a second, and then opened wide again, accompanied by an even wider grin. "I didn't catch your name," he said, "Mine's Johnny Black Fox."

"I'm sorry," I responded, "I'm Samuel Tucker."

"Well, Mr. Tucker, I'm gonna' unhitch these mules, leave the plow right here, and ride one of 'em back to our place. You ought to come with me."

"Why should I do that, Johnny," I asked, "do you know her?"

"I just might, Mr. Samuel Tucker, and you and me just might be brothers."

Johnny Black Fox rode one of the big draft mules bareback while I ponied the other one with the lead rope dallied around my saddle horn. The kid was balanced and he sat the mule well in spite of not having a saddle. We moved along at a brisk pace.

What he'd said about us maybe being brothers had my head spinning and full of questions. I felt like my heart was trying to beat its way out of my chest and my hand was shaking. In spite of all the questions I had, I was unable to speak. Johnny was quiet at first, too, but after a half mile or so he looked my way and started talking, and he seemed to have a pretty good idea of what was going through my mind.

"My daddy is Joe Black Fox. He's a full blooded Cherokee. He was just a young 'un when they took the family farm away down in Mississippi and marched all our people here. All of 'em that didn't die along the way that is. My Grandma was one of the hundreds, maybe thousands that died along the trail. They called it the Trail of Tears."

"My Grandpa staked out a land claim here and started farmin' on the place we're goin' to right now. Grandpa died not long after the war. He died protectin' the place from some southern boys that didn't want to admit they'd been beat. My Daddy killed two of 'em and run the rest off."

"It wasn't long after Daddy took over this farm that a colored woman showed up lookin' for work…field work, house work, whatever she could get. Daddy hired her and married her two months later. She's my momma. That's why I don't look exactly like a regular Indian. Momma's name is Lizzie Black Fox now, but she went by Lizzie Wilson before Daddy married her".

"One time, when some folks came through here…folks from Arkansas…I heard her ask 'em if they knew any Tuckers in the Pine Bluff area. She seemed real interested.

I believe she's forty-four now and fits the description you gave me…and she's still pretty." The kid laughed, "That's why I'm so good lookin', and that's why I'm thinkin' we might be brothers."

I was overwhelmed, shaken, and buoyed all at the same time by the things Johnny had said. I chewed on it for a few minutes while I silently stared at the saddle horn. This can't be, I told myself…the first person I run into in Oklahoma Territory is my half-brother and he's leading me to my mother. It can't be.

Out of the corner of my eye I saw him looking at me. I turned my head to meet his gaze. Then it struck me. I realized why I'd felt so comfortable with him from the start. He looks like me. He has different hair and he looks like an Indian, but he also looks like me. Maybe this can be, I thought, maybe this can be true.

I guess Johnny read the recognition in my eyes, because he nodded and reached over and touched my left arm. "What happened to your hand, brother?"

Chapter Twenty

Pine Bluff, Arkansas 1863

A loving wife and mother
Worst day she ever had
Lost her husband and baby
Can things remain this bad

The day was hotter and stickier than anyone who hasn't been in Arkansas in late July could likely imagine. Dust from the road, kicked up each time a horse drawn rig went by, coated the sweat covered faces of everyone present.

"Six hundred dollahs? Hell, this here boy is worth four times that much if he is worth a nickel. Look at him. He is strong as a mule and barely twenty-five years old. Don't be worried about what Lincoln's gonna do, we gonna win this war and you gonna be able to work that boy for another forty years."

The man being sold, lot number six, stood on the auction block with his head bowed and his face devoid of expression. He was of medium height with a sturdy build. Wearing no shoes and trousers that came only to the middle of his calves, he was shirtless so as to show the powerful muscles of his arms and shoulders. His wrists and ankles were shackled.

Though the auctioneer tried every trick he knew to elicit more money, he could get no more than the six hundred dollar bid. Resigned to whatever fate might befall him, the black man cared not whether he had been sold for ten thousand dollars or fifty cents. Showing no reaction or emotion, he shuffled off the block to join his new owner.

"Mr. Walker done stole that young buck, but now we're comin' to lot number seven…the one I know you boys have been waitin' for. Yes sir, somethin' a little different is comin' up on the block right now. Just look at this right here… uhh…ain't she somethin' special."

"I reckon I don't have to tell you boys all the benefits you might realize from buyin' this here young girl. She's as clean an' as fine lookin' a nigger girl as you are ever gonna' see, and she can make more. That one standin' right there…see that little nigger boy right there…she made that one an' she can make more like him. You win the bid on this one an it's like gettin' maybe six or seven niggers for the price of one an' maybe a whole lot of fun doin' it."

Young Lizzie Tucker was all fixed up and scrubbed up for the event. She wore a close fitting red cotton dress, slit up the side to display her long shapely legs, and her black hair reflected the sunlight like a mirror. Everything was calculated to increase her selling price, and it seemed to be working.

Everyone present, except for the little boy, looked only at her body…as though they were buying a calf or a mule… and she was, indeed, pleasing to the eye. Had they seen her as a person, had they looked into her eyes and glimpsed her humanity, they would have seen something quite different. But that's not how things worked at slave auctions. They saw her only as a piece of flesh.

Her head was bowed, the left side of her face red and swollen, and tears ran freely down her cheeks. She made no eye contact with the auctioneer nor with any of the bidders. Her gaze was locked on the confused, frightened little boy who stood next to her master, Henry McGregor. She mouthed the words; "I love you," over and over again. The boy said "Momma" a few times and cried.

The despair she felt was so deep she didn't feel alive. In the last three days she'd been raped repeatedly by Buster and Robert Coolidge. She'd seen her husband hanged for trying to protect her and now she was being sold like an animal…sold to some other white man who would use her for his own pleasure. And, worse than anything, she knew she was seeing her only child for the last time.

Amos Walker, the Texan who had bought the young man for six hundred dollars, made his way to the front of the rather sparse group of bidders. He was a small man standing around five feet seven and weighing no more than a hundred and forty pounds. His appearance actually bordered on being comical, with an oversized head, a thick crop of curly brown hair and a set of mutton chop sideburns dominating his angular, rat-like face.

As the auctioneer had predicted, the bidding for the beautiful slave girl was fast and spirited. Amos was bidder number sixteen and each time someone made a bid he immediately held his card high and raised it by ten dollars. In the end he won out by paying an amazing three thousand and fifty dollars.

The auctioneer slapped him on the back and said, "Enjoy her son. You paid a handsome price but you got yourself a fine one right there. Enjoy her."

As her new owner led her off to his wagon, Lizzie kept her head turned toward the boy and kept telling him she loved him. The boy reached out with both hands and tried to go to her, but McGregor, with a firm grip on his shirt collar, held him back.

When she was seated in the wagon and shackled, Buster Coolidge walked up and said something to her. She fell to the floor and sobbed.

*****

Upon arriving at the Walker plantation in east Texas, Lizzie was shown to her room on the top floor of the main house by Maggie, the colored woman who was in charge of the domestic servants. She was told her duties would involve cleaning, serving meals and working in the gardens.

The room was large, well furnished, and had a balcony overlooking the grounds on the west side of the mansion. Lizzie was overwhelmed. "Is this just for me? Who else is gonna be here with me? I ain't the only one gonna be sleepin' here, am I?"

Maggie sighed. "Yes, darlin', this room is yours. It was mine, but now it's yours, an' I am glad to let you have it. I am so glad to let you have it."

Maggie Brown descended the stairs to find her mistress, Helen Walker, waiting for her below. Mrs. Walker was a short, heavy set, rather plain looking woman in her mid-forties. She cracked a wide smile when Maggie approached. "You, feel bad about losing the room to the new girl, Maggie?"

Maggie returned the smile. "No, Miss Helen, I surely do not. In fact I thanked God as I walked down each of them steps."

"I'm happy for you, dear…I only wish I could get a new bedroom." With that, the two women shared a warm hug.

Maggie and Helen had an unusual relationship. Helen was the mistress and Maggie was the slave, and each woman had two children fathered by Helen's husband, Amos. Yet they were best friends. The only thing they ever disagreed about was which of them despised Amos more.

"I'm feelin' bad for that poor girl," Maggie said, "Knowin'

what she's got comin' to her from Mr. Amos, an' all. She seems like such a sweet thing and she's been through some real hard times already…been abused, lost her man and her little boy…real hard times."

Helen looked squarely into Maggie's eyes. "I wish there was some way we could persuade Amos to just leave her alone."

"I do too, but what could we do? We got no hold on him. He is done with us, Miss Helen…we got nothin' he wants now. Not now that he went and bought her."

A full minute passed before Mrs. Walker responded. "You know about those people who help runaways get up north, don't you?" Maggie's face showed her surprise at the question. "Can you find out who they are and ask about getting Lizzie to them?"

The colored woman's eyes got wide. "I reckon I could, but surely not before Mr. Amos gets to her. What would Mr. Amos do if he found out we did such a thing?"

Helen was silent again for a bit. When she did speak the look on her face left little doubt about how serious she was. "We're just gonna' have to see that Mr. Amos never does find out."

That evening, Maggie laid a thin, black nightgown on Lizzie's bed. "Put this on after your bath, honey. Mr. Amos will be comin' up to see you in an hour, maybe less."

Lizzie's eyes closed and began to tear up. Then she looked desperately at the other woman, silently pleading for help. Maggie sighed, deeply, and touched her shoulder. "Don't you worry, honey, jes' don't put up a fight an' it will be over soon enough. You gonna be alright."

Amos was clearly eager to become acquainted with his new purchase. With a bounce in his step, he approached Lizzie's room no more than thirty minutes after Maggie had left. His thick lips were contorted into a crooked smile and looked more out of place than usual on his rodent-like face.

Wearing the black nightgown, Lizzie was beautiful except for the frightened look on her face. A face that spoke of how hopeless, and powerless she felt. She was sitting on the bed across the room from the doorway when Amos arrived wearing his blue silk robe. She turned toward him but her expression didn't change as he spoke. "Say there Darlin'. Are you ready to get to know Master Amos?"

His sick smile broadened as he untied the belt, let the robe fall open, and began walking toward her. She closed her eyes and turned away from the sight of his scrawny naked body. In moments he would be touching her, lying on top of her and forcing his way into her. The thought of it made her feel so sick she was sure she was going to vomit. She fought to hold it back. Surely she would be beaten…or worse… if she threw up in his presence.

The sound made her look up. It wasn't real loud, but it was sharp; like the noise that would be made by striking a large stone with an axe handle. Lizzie's jaw went slack, her eyes opened wide, and she gasped. Amos crumpled to the floor.

*****

There was a large, very ugly and rank, hammer-headed black mule on the Walker plantation. He was called Handsome as sort of a joke. His mean disposition and unattractive appearance matched perfectly. Uncommonly strong, he could pull a plow all day, but it took two brave men to get him harnessed and hitched up.

Come morning, Amos was found, by one of the slaves, lying in the dirt and manure on the floor of Handsome's stall. Nobody could figure out why he'd gone in there alone, but they weren't surprised that the mule had kicked and trampled him to death.

The next day, Lizzie was in a covered wagon on her way to Oklahoma Territory. Maggie could have gone with her, but chose to stay at the Walker plantation with her friend, Helen, and the children. She baked a chocolate cake which she, Helen, and all four children enjoyed with their afternoon tea.

Neither Helen nor Maggie was able to weep convincingly at Amos' funeral, but they both made a sincere effort.

Chapter Twenty-One

Oklahoma Territory

How could I be here now
Living on the brink
Of a dream I feared to dream
A thought I feared to think

The farmstead sat on a flat piece of ground just above the flood plain of the North Canadian and slightly below the rolling prairie. The rich ground was all bottom land. Over the centuries, the river had widened the swath of fertile soil as it cut its bed and the wide valley ever deeper into the earth.

There was a barn, a couple of sheds, corrals, a garden plot, and a small frame house. None of the buildings were painted, but the place looked neat and well maintained. Out behind the house were a soddy and a tiny log cabin that must have been the main residences each in their own time. Testimonials, I thought, to all the hard work the Black Fox family had done over the years, and a visible history of their pioneering life.

I remained mounted while Johnny slid down from the back of the big mule and climbed the steps of the wooden porch. Boone pawed the ground nervously. He'd obviously picked up on how anxious and wound up I was. You don't get stuff like that past a horse. I swear Boone knows my mood and what I'm thinking better than I do.

The morning had warmed considerably and the front door was open. Johnny shouted. "Momma, come out here please, I got somebody you need to see."

The voice I heard from inside the house caused my eyes to flood with tears. "Johnny, what you doin' back here so soon? You're supposed to be plowin' the Pascal's field and I know you can't be done already."

My momma…I knew it the minute I heard her voice…came to the door, and she looked just like the picture I had of her in my mind. Still slender and pretty, the only change from my memory of her was a few gray hairs sprinkled among the black ones. She wore a long blue dress and an apron, and that was familiar as well.

She glanced in my direction and said, "my goodness, I ain't dressed for company, Johnny."

When she looked my way again she noticed the tears running down my cheeks. Looking back to Johnny, she asked, "what's wrong? Is this young man alright?"

Johnny Black Fox gestured in my direction with his open hand. "Momma, I'd like you to meet Sammy Tucker."

She took a few steps toward me. Her big brown eyes got even bigger and locked on mine. "My God, is it really you Sammy? Is this really my baby?"

My response came slowly. It was with great effort that I was able to choke out the words. "Yes, Momma, it's me."

I dismounted and my knees buckled as soon as my feet touched the ground. Had I not had a hold of the saddle horn I'm sure I would have collapsed in a heap right under my horse.

Momma closed the last few steps separating us and wrapped her arms around my neck. We were both sobbing and she kept repeating, "Sammy my baby…Sammy my baby boy."

I held her tightly to me. I guess I was afraid she'd get away if I didn't…afraid this moment would turn into a dream and she'd be gone. I tried to talk, but it was a good long while before I could speak even a single word. Finally I was able to say "Momma", and once I got it out, I kept saying it over and over again.

This was the moment I'd been longing for since I was a small boy, but a moment I'd never really let myself believe would happen. Even as Johnny and I were riding toward the farm, and he was telling me about her, I didn't completely count on her being my mother. There was too much at stake. If it hadn't proven to be true it would have been like losing her all over again…like opening the wound I'd been trying to heal for more than twenty years.

I was only five years old when she was taken from me, and she was a young mother in her early twenties. This reunion was between those two people…not between a tough young man with a reputation as a gun hand and a middle aged woman.

The feelings that were present when that little boy and his momma were torn apart came back. They came back instantly and they were raw and undiminished. Bad Wing Crow was nowhere to be seen.

I gently put my hand and my stub of an arm on my mother's shoulders and pushed her back so I could see her face. I found I could speak if I breathed deeply and slowed things down.

"Momma, I never thought I'd see you again…I never let myself believe it. I never stopped missing you…never stopped loving you."

We looked into each other's eyes for a bit and we both smiled, and the smiles broke into laughter…the relief and all the pent up feelings just turned into laughter.

"Sammy darlin'" she said, "I never stopped missin' and lovin' you neither. I would have come back to Pine Bluff to find you after we were freed, but Buster Coolidge told me they'd kill me and you both if I ever came back. After what they done to your daddy, I knew he meant it and I was too afraid, but I thought about you every day…every day since they took me away."

I looked up and saw a sturdy, raw boned Indian man standing next to Johnny. He smiled. "Little Sammy Tucker, and unless I've missed my guess, Mr. Bad Wing Crow."

I noted, but wasn't surprised by how well-spoken he was. I did my best to put a coherent response together. "And you…uhh…you must be Mr. Joe Black Fox. Evidently you've heard some of the stories about me…they ain't all true."

"Yes I have, but I had no idea the famous one handed gun fighter was my Lizzie's missing little boy."

With that he flashed a big smile and walked down the wooden steps toward me. When I offered my hand, he brushed it aside and wrapped his thick arms around me in a powerful bear hug. "I'm glad to have you here, son, and I can't tell you how much your mother has longed for this day to come."

"I know," I said, "I've done the same."

When Joe released his vise-like hold on me, I stepped back, caught my breath, and took a good look at him. His skin was no lighter than Johnny's, but it had more of a copper color to it. He had thick, black, shoulder length hair that reflected the morning sun. His face was angular and chiseled, and his arms and shoulders were powerful and seemed outsized for his five foot six inch frame. Clearly he was a man only a fool would take lightly.

Joe's eyes were his most striking feature and they said a lot about him. They were large, nearly black, and they were honest and kind. His eyes told me he was a good man. I looked directly into them for several seconds and then spoke again. "I'm glad to meet you, Joe, and I'm glad my mother found you."

"I'm glad she found me too," Joe said, "it was the best day of my life. Let's all go inside."

Joe, Johnny, and I sat at the kitchen table while Momma brought coffee and some freshly baked cookies. She asked if I'd like some eggs and bacon or some biscuits…she couldn't seem to stop offering to get things for me. I said, "Momma, please sit down here next to me."

I pulled an empty chair right next to the one I was sitting on and patted it with my hand. As soon as she was seated she wrapped her arms around my neck and started softly sobbing. I hugged her back and then pried her arms loose and smiled at her. "Momma, we got some talkin' to do."

Sitting at that little wooden table, I felt like I had a family again. I told them everything that had happened in the last twenty years of my life. I told them how I'd lost my hand, how Luke had made the steel sleeve for my arm, and I even told them about Kate. I felt no need to use the cautious, guarded approach that had become my usual way. Being open and trusting like that felt really good. For too long I'd lived on edge without trusting anyone.

My momma seemed to tense up when I talked about the understanding Grandpa and I had come to years ago…the understanding that we would, one day, have our day and square things up with the Coolidge's and Howard. That day, I said, was close at hand, and that's why I'd soon be heading back to Pine Bluff.

Joe and Johnny took an interest in this venture and

asked questions. I told them about the roles I thought Pete Kraemer, Bill Mason and Grandpa would play in it. It was when Johnny volunteered to be part of the operation that Momma stepped in.

"Those three men did awful things," she said. "They hung your daddy, they abused me and sold me off, and they cut off your hand…they cut off a poor little boy's hand."

She paused for a bit and looked from me to Johnny. "Now you're fixin' to hurt them anyway you can and kill them? You thinkin' about hangin' them? Will that bring your Daddy back? Will that bring your hand back? No, Sammy, it won't…but it might make you a little less than you are now…maybe a little bit like them."

When she'd finished having her say, Momma got up and walked to the stove and pretended to be busy with something. Things got real quiet for a bit. I was surprised to hear the things she had said.

Nobody had suffered more at the hands of those three white men than she had. They had taken her husband, her dignity, her home, and her only child from her. I thought she'd be full of anger and want to even things up.

In my mind, my desire to square things up was for her, perhaps, more so than it was for me or my father or anyone. Hearing her speak out against my plan and imply I should turn the other cheek was the last thing I had expected from her.

The hush was broken when Joe decided it was time for him to weigh in on the subject. "You know Lizzie, I understand what you're saying about not letting those kind of people drag us down to their level, and I understand the value of forgivin'. But doesn't that work better…doesn't it make more sense when those who've done you wrong apologize and change their ways?"

"Back in the early days when my people were in the south, the white man told us to quit livin' our way and to become farmers, and that's what we did. They took the land that had been our country…our home for centuries and gave us back little pieces of it so we could be farmers. We went along with it. We didn't fight, we didn't make a fuss, and we did our best. Eventually some of us even had plantations, and, I'm ashamed to say, some of us even had slaves…we did what they told us to do…we tried to be white…we even went to their churches."

"Then they decided they wanted our farms. They wanted all of what had once been Cherokee country. So they just took our farms and our homes from us and marched us out here. They herded us like we were cattle, only, unlike cattle, they didn't care how many head they lost along the way. And I haven't seen them change or apologize to this day. Now, if they decided to run us all out of the Territory and on to some reservation somewhere else, they'd do it."

"I can't ask Samuel to show those men any mercy. Not when he knows who did all those things to your family and he knows where they are, and he knows they're no different today than they were the day they hanged his daddy, or the day they sold you off, or the day they cut off his hand."

Momma sighed loudly, but didn't offer a response.

Johnny had been nodding his agreement all the while his father was speaking. He turned toward me and said, "I'm going with you brother."

I put my hand on his shoulder. The muscles felt like bundles of steel cables, and I knew he would be a tough and dependable partner to have in this venture. "Thanks, Johnny. I can't think of a better man to have with me on this, but you're not going."

Chapter Twenty-Two

She told me forgiving
Made us better and stronger
But three men need killin'
Can't wait any longer

Finding my mother and spending some time with her had filled a big hole in me. Getting to know my brother and stepfather was good too, and I liked them both very much. The temptation to stay on at their little farm was strong. I felt at home there, but after two days I knew I had to leave. I had another big hole to fill and it was time to get after it.

In a way I felt bad about not taking my momma's suggestion to leave the past behind. I knew she was serious and it meant a lot to her. After all these years without her I wanted to please her, and I would have done anything she asked. Anything but this. She was, however, the reason I'd turned down Johnny's offer to go with me. I couldn't put her other son at risk and cause her the worry that would go along with it.

The afternoon before I set off for Fort Smith, Joe offered to help me with Boone's feet. They'd grown long in the toe and the shoes were worn thin. Shoeing a horse was one of the few tasks I still struggled with because of the loss of my hand. I could start a nail with the steel sleeve on my left arm and then finish up with a hammer, but it wasn't easy and it took me three times as long as it should have. I was grateful for the help and Joe did a first class job of installing a new set of shoes that would easily last all the way to Fort Smith and on to Pine Bluff. Once I got there, Pete Kraemer could take care of any blacksmith work that needed doing.

I had intended to leave at first light, but Momma insisted on making breakfast for me. She had biscuits, eggs, bacon, potatoes and coffee and kept putting more on my plate until I had to take her hand and stop her.

"Momma, you can't feed me enough to last me all the way to Fort Smith. If I eat one more bite I won't be able to get on my horse." She did convince me to have one more cup of coffee, however. I guess I wasn't a whole lot more anxious to leave than she was to see me go, but I did manage to get in the saddle and on the trail by an hour after sunrise.

Boone loped off easy and willingly as we retraced our steps from a few days earlier. My life had changed in that short span of time and I fought back tears as I thought about it. When we reached the field where I had found Johnny, I stopped, looked back down the trail, and thought about taking my momma's advice. I thought about turning around and forgetting about the task ahead of me.

Then I thought of my grandpa, my hand, my daddy and the day my momma was sold off. And I thought of the Coolidge boys and Howard. I nudged Boone with my right spur and put him back in to that ground eating lope of his.

The return trip to Fort Smith took only six days. Momma had packed my saddle bags full of food and I had to spend little time looking for game. I shot two prairie chickens, but other than that, I lived on what was in my bags.

It was late in the afternoon when I arrived at his ranch, and found Bill Mason working a two year old gelding on a long line in one of the round corrals. He kept working the colt while I dismounted and put Boone and my gear away. Leaning against the top rail, I smiled and said, "Looks like you remembered some of what I taught you about trainin' horses."

"I did Sammy, but I reckon it's time to set the horse business aside for a while and get on with that other business we got in front of us."

"You're still on board, then?"

"More than ever, Mr. Tucker, I'm on board more than ever. Been thinkin' a lot while you've been gone, and this is something we've got to do for you and me and all of us."

When he'd cooled the colt down and turned him out, Bill asked if I'd like to sit on the porch and have a glass of brandy with him. "What do you think?" I laughed, "I've been on the trail for damn near a week straight and I'm drier'n a popcorn fart."

I told Bill all about finding my mother, her husband, Joe, and my brother, Johnny. There was no doubt he was happy for me. He put his hand on my shoulder. "That's great Sammy, that's just great. When are you figuring on heading out for Pine Bluff."

"I was thinkin' maybe day after tomorrow."

"Good, I got something to show you, but it can wait until morning." We spent the rest of the evening drinking brandy and talking about my family and my time at their farm.

I slept well that night. Finding my mother and knowing I was finally going to get on with the task I'd had on my mind since I was ten years old felt good. Knowing Bill was in it with both feet helped too. After having breakfast and getting Bill's two wranglers started with some young stock, he invited me to go with him to the carriage house.

A big grey gelding that was nearly a perfect match for

Boone was in a paddock next to the building. "That's part of what I want to show you," he said, "the rest is inside."

The rest was an ordinary looking wagon set up to be drawn by a team of horses. Bill opened a large wooden box that had been built into the bed of it. The inside was padded and the side facing the front was ventilated. The vent holes were hidden by the wagon's wide cushioned seat.

"I'm thinkin' we hitch Boone and this here grey to this outfit. When we get to Pine Bluff you get in the box and nobody will see anything but a white man driving his rig into town. I'll be coming to buy mules to sell to the army. We can lay our saddles in the bed and cover them with a tarp. What do you think?"

"It sounds good, if we can get those two ponies to get along and pull together."

We spent most of the day working the horses. Two good horses don't necessarily make a good team. Initially I harnessed them individually and drove them around the round corral without hitching them to the wagon. Next I hitched them double and did the same thing, just ground driving them. They squabbled some at first, but after a few nips and cow-kicks they settled down. By noon we had them pulling the wagon like they'd been doing it together for years.

We drove the wagon into Fort Smith that afternoon, and, when we got to the edge of town, I climbed into the box just to see how that would work out. It was quite comfortable in there, and while several folks greeted Bill as he drove by, nobody had any idea I was also on board. I felt good about this clever little wrinkle Bill had come up with. I liked the idea of having a partner who was capable of some creative thinking.

As for the horses, at first the commotion of the town

had the other gelding on edge, but old Boone had seen about everything there was in his day, and his quiet attitude settled his young team mate down quickly.

On the drive back to Bill's ranch I pushed my hat back and turned in his direction. "We got this worked out pretty good. We can stick to the main roads all the way to Pine Bluff and nobody will know I've come back. I'll just jump in that box when we see someone on the road or when we enter a populated area."

Just then a troubling thought struck me. "What about you, Bill, you lived in the Pine Bluff area until you were, what, twenty or so? Won't people down there recognize you?"

"I've thought about that, but I doubt if anyone will, at least not any white folks. That was more than twenty years ago and I was a skinny slave kid who almost never left the plantation. Could be, I suppose, some colored folks might know me, but I don't think it's likely. I'm going to take the chance and even use my own name and tell folks what I do in Fort Smith. I've got an idea about how we can make that work for us."

"Gettin' back to that box you built in this wagon, how 'bout we keep a bottle of brandy in there as an incentive for me to hop in when I have to?" Bill laughed for a moment, but then got serious.

"It all starts tomorrow, Sam. All these years of you waiting for your chance, and all these years of me denying who I am. All these years of swallowing the anger I've felt over what the Coolidges and Masons did to my grandmother, my mother, and me…and it all starts tomorrow."

"You know something else Sammy? I've been ashamed of passin' for white all this time…ashamed of turning my back on our people, and, when we finish this, I ain't gonna be ashamed any more, and I ain't gonna be passin' and I ain't gonna be denyin' who I am."

"I'm glad you came along Mr. Bad Wing Crow. I'm glad because you're a good friend and I'm glad because you gave me the chance to be part of this. I want you to understand something right now…this is my fight as much as it is yours."

What Mason said struck a chord with me. I guess it made me understand this whole thing on a deeper level, and I tried to let him know I understood.

"You used different words, Bill, but you said the same thing Pete Kraemer did when he insisted on getting into this deal. You talked about passin' and he talked about shufflin' and sayin' yes suh and yes mastah, but you both said the same thing, and you both know this is for all of us."

Chapter Twenty-Three

Pine Bluff, Arkansas
October 30, 1885

They maimed him for sport
Don't remember his name
Fire smolders inside him
Coals burst into flame

The saloon was dark inside with the only light provided by the front windows and a couple of kerosene lamps behind the bar. The overhead chandelier wouldn't be lighted until sunset. The faded red letters on the weathered wooden sign outside read; "Buster's Bluff".

Bill Mason entered the place and stood just inside the door for a minute, let his eyes adjust to the subdued light, and then walked over and leaned against the long cherry wood bar.

He took a spot a few feet from the only other customer in the place, a husky, middle aged man with dark hair and several days growth of stubble on his broad, square face. He was sipping a glass of whiskey and talking to the bartender.

The man didn't so much as turn his head when Bill came in and stood next to him. There was a noticeable bulge under the right side of his dark, soiled and wrinkled jacket. Unless he had an extra quart of whiskey in his pocket, Bill assumed he had a revolver holstered on his hip.

"What can I get for you, sir?" The bartender was a

smallish man with thinning red hair and a bushy mustache. Wearing a white shirt with billowing sleeves and a green vest, he looked like a dapper, slightly oversized leprechaun. He was friendly and even seemed a little timid; not at all like most of the brassy, indifferent types who poured the drinks in these places.

Bill waved his hand in the direction of the brass spigot a few feet to his right and said, "if the beer in that keg is cold, I'll have a tall one."

"Yes, sir. Got the coldest beer in town. I'll get you one right now, yes sir."

"You new in town?" The bartender asked as he set the mug on the bar.

"Yeah, the name's Bill Mason from up Fort Smith way."

"Welcome to Pine Bluff, Mr. Mason. What brings you to our town?"

"Well, I've been supplying the army with horses for a number of years, and now they've asked me to find them some good mules. Thought there might be some good broke ones available in this area."

The bartender nodded. "Could be you'll find some good ones around here. I'll ask the fellas that come in here for ya." He held out his right hand and introduced himself. "I'm Pat Collins, and the gentleman next to you is Mr. Buster Coolidge, the owner of this establishment."

"Pleased to meet you, Pat, and you too Mr. Coolidge."

Coolidge looked his way and nodded, but didn't offer to shake hands. The smell of the whiskey on his breath was almost overpowering when he finally spoke. "Mason, huh? Well, welcome to Buster's Bluff. Best damned beer and whiskey in town. As for buyin' mules, you might find some nigger share croppers willing to part with a mule or two if you ask around."

"Thank you. When I'm out west looking for horses I just put the word out and pretty soon I have plenty of ranchers who are willing to part with their ponies. I'm thinkin' the same thing ought to work here with mules." Coolidge nodded and grunted.

"Another thing perhaps you gentlemen could help me with. I expect to be here for a few weeks and I was wondering if there might be a poker game in town… one that would be willing to let me in." Collins looked at his boss expectantly and didn't have to wait long for his response.

"There's a game right here every Wednesday night at seven. Just show up with your cash and we'll see if there's room at the table."

The thought of taking some of Mason's money at the poker table must have loosened Buster's tongue up some and he went on. "Another idea about mules; there's an old nigger who works for my brother who might know where to look…name's Tucker. You can find him at the Robert Coolidge place four miles south of town most any day."

"Thank you very much. You've both been very helpful." He finished his beer, wiped his mouth with the back of his hand and spoke again. "Excellent beer, Pat… cold and refreshing, and I'll see you Wednesday evening Mr. Coolidge. Actually I'm staying in the hotel just across the way, so I may be seeing both of you sooner than that. I have a fondness for cold beer as well as poker."

The livery was at the opposite end of Main Street from the saloon; a distance of a half mile or so. The dirt street was dry and packed smooth, so Bill chose to walk there instead of on the crowded boardwalk.

The two greys were in a small corral outside the building

standing face to face and grooming each other. Clearly they had become the best of buddies in the relatively short time they'd been together. After checking on their water and hay, Bill entered the barn. Joe, the proprietor of the livery, was also the blacksmith. He was fitting shoes to one of James Howard's sorrel mares while Pete Kraemer looked on.

"Excuse me, Mr. Mason," Pete spoke almost apologetically, "uhh…Joe here told me your name, Suh. I know a thing or two about hosses, and them two grey's you got outside are about as fine as I ever seen."

"Well, thank you…uhh…"

"Name's Pete, Suh, Pete Kraemer."

"Nice to meet you, Pete. I was just going to go out and rub those two down a bit."

"If you don't mind, Suh, I'll come with and give y'all a hand. I sure do admire good hosses like that."

When the two men were in the corral they each began brushing one of the geldings. Bill spoke first. "I got invited to the poker game Wednesday night. I can sit in if there's room. If not I can hang around and drink beer and begin getting to know these three."

"There'll be room," Pete assured him, "they love gettin' new blood and outside money in the game. Just don't expect 'em to play fair."

"You do horse shoein', don't you Pete?"

"Yes Suh, I do."

"Does Howard know that?"

"No Suh, I don't believe he does."

"Good. Could you make one or both of his team of sorrels appear to be lame?"

"I could do that real easy, Boss."

"Don't do anything now, but I've got an idea that will involve you doing that. I'll tell Sam and you and Harold about it when we get the chance to talk. Make sure Howard doesn't know you do shoein', alright?" Pete nodded.

"And Pete?"

"Yes suh."

"Quit callin' me sir and boss…my name's Bill."

"Don't worry about it, Bill, I was just practicin'. Got one more thing for you. Sammy's thinkin' we should be doin' Howard first, and Buster last."

"Yeah, he was talkin' that way when we were drivin' down here from Fort Smith."

"When do you think we can all get together…uh…Bill?"

"I'm thinking Thursday. I can drive over to Harold's place late in the afternoon. Buster even suggested I talk with him about buyin' mules. I'll know more about these assholes after Wednesday night. Maybe I'll even have some of their money."

Pete smiled, "good luck with that."

At 6:55 Wednesday evening Pete Kraemer drove Howard's buggy down Main St. and stopped in front of the saloon right behind Mason's wagon. When Bill stepped out on to the boardwalk, Joe, from the livery, clucked to the team and turned back down the street.

Howard joined him on the walk way. "Mr. Mason?"

"Yes, sir, that's me."

"I'm James Howard, and I understand you'll be joinin' us for cards this evening."

"I sure will be if you've room for me at the table. I'm looking forward to it." He extended his hand and said, "call me Bill."

"That's a fine looking team of greys you have, Bill… mighty fine looking."

"Thank you, and they're every bit as good as they look. Never had a better pair than those two."

"I'd enjoy drivin' a team like that every chance I got if I owned 'em, but I thought you were staying right across the street at the hotel. I expected you'd just walk from there."

Bill smiled. "I didn't hitch 'em up just to come across the street. I took a little drive around the countryside this afternoon…wanted to get the lay of the land and give the team some exercise. It was getting close to seven when I passed the livery, so I asked Joe if he'd hop in the wagon and drop me off here."

"I see. Like I said, if I had such a fine team as that I expect I'd surely be using them as well. I'm in the freight hauling business and I appreciate good horseflesh."

"Well, you do have an eye for it," Bill smiled again as he spoke, "and those two ride well also. The one hitched to the right, the one with the diamond shaped snip, he's as good as any horse I ever rode. Although I'd have to say that pair of sorrel mares pullin' your rig wouldn't have to take a back seat to any team I've ever seen."

"Thank you, Bill, and perhaps we can work out a wager that might include some horses."

"I don't think so, Mr. Howard, I'm counting on those greys to get me back to Fort Smith when my business here is finished, but I'm not afraid of betting some cash money."

The Coolidge brothers and an older, gray haired gentleman were already seated at the table when Mason and Howard walked in. The oil burning chandelier was lit and gave a yellowish cast to everything beneath it, including the smoke from the thick, nearly black cigars protruding from the lips of the three men at the table.

Pat, the diminutive bartender, made the introductions. Robert Coolidge offered his hand, but didn't stand. He simply said, "Mason". The other man, whose name was Will Parker, stood and greeted Bill cordially. Buster managed a "good to see you again, Bill," barely looking up from his glass of whiskey.

James Howard broke the ice a bit. "When you mentioned you were from Fort Smith, Bill, it brought back some memories. Is Bill Tibbits still the Sheriff up that way?"

"He is, and has been for as long as anybody can remember. Do you know Bill?"

Robert Coolidge let loose a kind of half laugh, half snort. "We know him, but I doubt if he'd admit to knowing us. During the last part of the war we got him in a poker game and drunk enough to bet his real silver money against our Confederate dollars. We're still not welcome in Fort Smith after all these years."

Bill's eyes opened wide. "Need I take that as a warning?"

"No, those were the old days, and we didn't like the Sheriff much. This is just a friendly card game."

As soon as Pat had set everyone up with a drink, the game got started. Bill had played a good bit of poker over the years, and, after the first few hands, he got the impression he would not find himself overmatched in this group. From time to time, however, he noticed subtle eye contact between each of the Coolidge's and Howard. Whatever was going on, Parker didn't seem to be part of it.

Unless he had outstanding cards, Bill folded whenever he saw evidence of that kind of communication. Otherwise, he played his cards as he normally would have, and the strategy stood him in good stead. When the night was over, he had a hundred dollars more in his pocket than when he'd started.

The two Coolidge boys drank straight whiskey almost continuously and were feeling no pain by the end of the night. Howard drank only slightly more moderately as was the case with Parker.

Bill made a point of buying more than his share of rounds, but limited his intake, claiming he'd had an ulcer and couldn't indulge much anymore. For the first two hours he didn't ask any questions and talked only when he was spoken to or when it was a necessary part of the game. Only when it was clear that the other four players were thoroughly oiled up did he initiate conversation.

"Mr. Parker, am I right in assuming you're the owner of Parker's General Store?"

"You are indeed Mr. Mason. My father actually started the business in the early forties."

"So you are a lifelong resident of this city?"

"Yes I am."

"How about the rest of you gentlemen, am I the only outsider in the group?"

Robert Coolidge responded to the inquiry with a smile. "Since we've invited you to our table, we don't consider you an outsider, but it is true that the three of us were all born and raised in this area. We grew up and went to school together right here in the county."

"We did indeed," Howard added, "and we had some wild times. We probably did more to keep the niggers in line, both before and after the war, than anybody."

Buster's quiet, surly, attitude had evidently been softened some by the whiskey he'd ingested and he joined the conversation. "We kept some of them slave girls in line, too. Some of them prettier, lighter skinned ones."

"Y'all ain't supposed to admit that stuff, Buster boy."

Robert laughed as he cautioned his brother.

"The information shared at this table, I can assure you gentlemen, will stay at this table, but it sounds like y'all have had some experiences I've unfortunately missed. Would I be out of line if I asked what it was like dallying with those nigra girls?" Bill held up his hands and asked the question in a tentative, almost apologetic, tone.

"Well," Howard said, "since you asked, I wouldn't mind reliving some of those rather joyful times. You have to understand, though, we weren't the first to ever go to the cabins…the slave quarters…for educational and recreational purposes." Everybody at the table laughed at his characterization of the practice.

"No, we weren't the first," Robert added, "but we might have set a record for the most visits." Mason joined in the laughter that followed.

It was then that Bill noticed Howard looking intently at him and he began to wonder if he'd brought up the wrong subject, but, for the time being, Howard went on talking about the girls.

"That sort of thing had been going on for two hundred years and sometimes that moist black soil proved to be fertile." Laughter erupted once more. "Some owners actually intended to make babies with those girls. They figured you got a smarter nigger that way…a slave who could figure a few things out for himself when he was workin'. Anyway, Mr. Mason…"

"Please, call me Bill."

"Very well, Bill, by the time we got…uh…involved in this business, some of them girls were pretty light skinned and not hard to look at. I reckon they might have had more white blood in 'em than nigger blood. They never let on, but I think some of 'em liked it when us white boys came to visit…liked it almost as much as we did."

Howard's brow furrowed some and he looked again at Bill. "As I think about it now, some weren't much darker in color than you are, Bill. If you don't mind me askin', where did that come from?"

Immediately all eyes were on Bill's face. He felt some discomfort, but covered it with a broad smile.

"No, I've been asked that before and I don't mind a bit. I do have a shade darker skin than the rest of you, but, if that's what you're wondering, it doesn't come from Africa. My mother was born in Italy and my father in Spain. Both had dark, olive complexions, black hair and brown eyes. I had no chance of coming out as a blue eyed blonde, although the Mason name comes from the small amount of English ancestry on my father's side."

Bill deflected the conversation away from his appearance. "I've been around my share of women with that type of skin and hair and I know how beautiful they can be. I don't fault you gentlemen at all for succumbing to the temptation. In fact, right at this moment I'm feeling a bit cheated for not having had that pleasure myself."

"I suppose," Bill went on, "the opportunity to mingle with girls like that was unfortunately lost with the end of the war and…uh…emancipation."

"Well, it's…uh…a little different these days, Bill." James Howard's thick tongue forced him to speak slowly now in an effort to minimize the slurring of his words. "When the sharecroppers fall behind on what they owe, that don't mean we don't get paid, you see, we still collect payment. Uhh…interest you might say. Except we collect it from some of their wives and daughters. It really ain't all that different from the slave days. We can still whip a nigger, we can hang one if he's got it comin', and we can do what we please with them girls."

Bill forced a smile, but couldn't come up with any words. The thought of his mother and grandmother being used by men like this made his guts twist up in a knot. The way they joked about it made it worse. It was a game to them and they cared nothing for the pain, shame, and suffering they caused the women.

Buster was dealing the last hand and Bill was eager to be on his way. He thought he'd heard all of the horrible, revolting stories these three had to tell and doubted he could stomach hearing any more, but Buster, in his drunken state, had one more thing to share. His speech was so slurred it was barely understandable as he instructed the bartender to fetch it.

"Hey Pat, show Mr. Mason those two pickle jars you got sittin' behind the bar. Down there on the bottom shelf." Pat Collins got a disdainful grimace on his face that he tried to hide, but dutifully got down on his knees and fumbled around until he produced the items requested.

"Put 'em on the table in front of Bill."

It took a while for Bill's eyes to penetrate the murky liquid in the jars. There was a dark colored form half floating and half resting on the bottom of one of the jars. The other was nearly full of small, egg shaped objects.

When Mason realized what he was looking at, he gasped for breath and his stomach convulsed to the extent that he almost threw up on the table. Never in his life had he seen anything so vile, so inhuman, and so disgusting. Pat, fortunately, was the only one sober enough to notice Mason's reaction. He quickly picked up the jars and returned them to their place behind the bar, but not before Buster drove his point home.

"Ya see, Bill, there wasn't nothin' we wouldn't do to make

them niggers behave. Nothin' we wouldn't do."

When Bill had regained some of his composure, he made a vow to himself. "These sons of bitches are going to pay. Whatever I have to do, I'm going to make them pay."

*****

After they'd settled up, all five men got up from the table and walked out to the street. Pete Kraemer was waiting with Howard's buggy and Grandpa Harold Tucker was right behind him with Robert Coolidge's team. Coolidge made an introduction of sorts.

"Bill, my driver here is Tucker. He may be able to help you find the mules you're looking for. You can find him at my place most any day or he can direct you to his."

Harold smiled. "Yes Suh, Mistah Bill, I shore can hep you with mules. You jest stop by anytime and I'll hep you all I can. I got a pair of big Belgian crosses right now myself."

The introduction to my grandfather in front of the group, and the quest for mules, gave Mason perfect cover to visit his place the next morning. Harold and Pete always started work at noon on Thursdays after being on duty until past midnight on poker night. They were able to join Mason and me for the meeting and we worked out a detailed plan for taking care of Howard.

Near the end of the meeting, I sighed, hesitated and then spoke with some urgency. "Gentlemen, we have to get on with this thing just as soon as possible. I've been holed up here in this house for too long already. I hardly even go outside in the daytime…I don't have my horse…this kind of life ain't something I can handle much longer."

The other three all smiled. They knew I'd been at my Grandfather's house for only a few days. Mason was the one who responded to my rather desperate plea. "We need one more Wednesday night poker game, Sammy, and I think we can make it happen soon after that."

I sighed again. "I can't do it for that long. I can't stay cooped up here. Let me put some stuff together and get in that box on your wagon and you can take me down by the river…maybe ten miles southeast of here and I'll camp out. There's hardly anybody livin' down that way and there sure aren't any white folks."

Mason grunted in agreement, but it was Pete Kraemer who spoke. "I like that idea, Sammy, and if we changed the plan just a little bit, we could bring you a visitor."

I had one more thing to say as the meeting was breaking up. "Bill, since things are going to start happening so soon after your arrival in Pine Bluff, we need to protect you from suspicion."

"Makes sense," he agreed, "how do you suggest we do that?"

The look on his face was impossible to describe when he heard my answer. "I think we're going to have to shoot you and make your body disappear."

Bill recovered quickly and smiled. "Sounds reasonable to me."

It took me only minutes to gather up my bedroll, a canvas tarp, fish hooks and line, some food and the meager kitchen equipment I usually carried with me on the trail. By two that afternoon I had my camp set up in a small clearing in a thick, wide, strip of woods that separated the Arkansas River from the road.

Camp was no more than fifty feet from the river's edge, but the trees screened it from any boats that might pass by. The main body of the woods made it impossible for anyone to spot me from the road.

The solitude was welcome and the days went by quickly. I

busied myself with fishing, snaring rabbits, and improving the camp. This life suited me far better than being confined to my Grandfather's small farm house. It underscored what an undomesticated creature I had become after ten years of living the life of a nomad.

The imminent prospect of settling the score with the Coolidges and Howard kept my mind busy. During the day I was able to avoid thinking about Kate most of the time. Nights were harder, but I got pretty adept at shifting my thoughts from her to making plans for the demise of Howard and the Coolidge brothers. Thinking about exactly how Buster might spend his last moments on earth was particularly satisfying.

Chapter Twenty-Four

Such a fine team of horses
He's plannin' on buyin'
There's a surprise in the wagon
And he might end up dyin'

The autumn sky had been dark for more than an hour when Bill walked across the street from the hotel to the saloon that second Wednesday evening. Harold Tucker drove the team of blacks up to the front door and Robert Coolidge stepped down. "Be back here by 11:30 and no later, Tucker."

"Yes, suh, Mistah Robert, you can count on old Harold."

Before Mason and Robert had entered the saloon, Pete Kraemer drove Howard and his rig up to the front door. The buggy was pulled by a pair of bay geldings.

"You've got the old team tonight, James," Robert remarked, "where are those fancy red mares of yours?"

Howard grumbled as he stepped onto the boardwalk. "Damned things both come up lame in the front end. Must have got into somethin' that made 'em founder. That's the only thing I can think of would make 'em both sore at the same time. Hoof walls feel warm on both of 'em too. That pasture they were in is pretty lush. My nigra, Pete here, got 'em out of there and into a corral where we can feed 'em just a little bit of hay."

Bill shook his head. "That's a shame. I lost a good team that way. They foundered on green grass and I never could keep 'em sound after that. Sure hope that doesn't happen to those fine mares of yours."

Buster Coolidge and Parker were waiting at the table when the three men entered the building. Pat, the bartender, was nervously hovering over the table making sure everyone had drinks, cigars and anything they might want. He was so subservient it was like he was apologizing for being alive.

The game started immediately and went much as it had the week before. Mason was content this time to break even and he played his cards to make that happen. He didn't want to create any bad blood by taking the money every time.

After a couple of hours and five or six glasses of whiskey, Howard again brought up the subject of Bill's team of grey geldings. "You know a hundred dollars buys a mighty good horse these days, but I believe I'd go as high as three hundred each for that team of yours, Mason."

"Thanks, James, that's a generous offer, a very generous offer, but I couldn't part with 'em for that. I expect to be leading at least ten mules back to Fort Smith in a week or so and I need to know I'll have a good steady team I can count on in case some of those mules act up."

"Well," Howard said, "my bay geldings are as steady as they come. They just ain't quite as fancy. How 'bout if I take your team for a test drive tomorrow, and if I still like 'em after that, I'll throw the bays in on the deal and still give you three hundred apiece for your greys."

Mason smiled. This deal was coming together easier than he had expected. "I'll tell you what, James. Meet me at the livery tomorrow at noon. I'll use your team of bays to go look at some mules I've got lined up, and you take my team out for a good long drive. We'll talk about making a deal when the day's over, but I'm not making any promises. We can meet for a drink right here at six in the evening. How's that sound to you?"

Howard's beaming face betrayed how pleased he was with the arrangement. "That sounds good, Bill, that way we'll both know what we're getting. When you're through with my team tomorrow just take 'em to the livery and have Joe put 'em up. I'll do the same with yours." The two men shook hands to seal the agreement.

It was close to 12:30 when Pete Kraemer drove his boss to the livery the next day. The two bays were hitched to the buggy and the gimpy sorrel mares followed behind. Mason was waiting for them with his team hitched to his wagon.

Howard looked every bit the part of a man who was recovering from a night of hard drinking. His hat brim was pulled down over the bloodshot slits his eyes had become and his mouth hung half open.

Pete spoke softly in deference to his boss's condition. "Will you be wantin' me to go with you, Mistah James? I was thinkin' I might hep Joe work with the mares. We can pack their feet in cool mud and then maybe loosen 'em up some by movin' 'em around in the corral."

"Why don't you do that," Howard responded, "I can manage by myself and I want to do the drivin' anyway."

"Fine, boss, with both me and Joe workin' on it maybe we can get them mares fixed up. I'd sho nuf like to get them mares fixed up for you, boss."

"How about if we drive your team down the street and we'll have a quick drink before we set out. It might clear our heads some after last night." Mason laughed as he made the suggestion to Howard.

"That sounds good to me. A hair of the dog as they say."

Pete led the sorrel mares into the livery as the other two men drove off toward Buster's Bluff Saloon.

A hair of the dog turned out to be three glasses of whiskey for Howard and one beer for Mason. When they exited the building they found Joe, the livery man, waiting in the street with Bill's team and wagon.

"Pete was busy with them mares, so I thought I'd bring this rig up here to the saloon for you, Gentlemens. I kinda wanted a chance to handle these big greys anyhow. They are a fine, fine pair. I hope you don't mind." Joe smiled a broad friendly smile as he said the last part.

"That's fine, Joe, thank you," Bill answered, "We'll both just drive off from here. Meet me back here at six, then James?"

"Six it is, and Joe, I want you and Pete to be here at that time also so you can take the teams back to the livery. Six o'clock sharp, you understand?"

"Yes, suh, Mr. Howard, we'll be here."

The whiskey had Howard feeling a little bolder than usual. He drove the team down Main Street at a fast trot and urged them into a lope when he reached the town limits.

The road was rough in spots and every bump jarred Pete Kraemer who was lying hidden in the box behind the seat. He wanted to be at least two miles out of town before showing himself. At the pace they seemed to be traveling, that should take no more than fifteen minutes. If he put his pocket watch next to one of the air holes there was enough light to read it. It was one forty-five.

At two o'clock Pete lifted the hinged lid of the box. The

fast moving wagon was lurching from side to side and he steadied himself with both hands as he slowly got to his feet, and stepped out of the box. The sound of the fast moving horses and the creaking of the wooden wagon easily drowned out any sound he made. Pete vaulted over the seat and sat down beside Howard, who, until then, was unaware of his presence.

Startled, the white man's jaw dropped open and he was speechless for the first several seconds. "What…what are you doing here? How'd you get here? You were supposed to stay at the livery, you dumb nigger."

"I changed my mind about that, James, and I changed my mind about bein' your dumb nigger, too. Ain't it funny how people's minds just up and change sometimes?"

Pete drew a short barreled revolver from his coat pocket and shoved the muzzle under Howard's right ear. He pushed hard enough that Howard cried out in pain. "Did that hurt James?" He jabbed him hard again and said, "turn right at the next road."

"You'll hang for this you black son of a bitch…I'll…"

Pete's hands were the big, meaty, calloused ones of a blacksmith, and his fist was like a club. Before he had finished his threat, Howard felt the right one connect with his nose. There was a crunching sound followed by the warm wetness of blood running over his lip and into his mouth.

"I might hang someday, Mr. James, but you ain't gonna be around to see it. You done hung your last nigger."

Dazed, and with a bleeding, broken nose, split lips, and blackened, watering eyes, Howard was barely able to continue driving the team. His last remarks hadn't gone over well with the short, powerfully built black man, and he wisely chose not to say anything more.

They drove in a southerly direction for the next two miles in silence. Pete Kraemer felt like a heavy yoke had been lifted from his shoulders…a burden he'd been bearing for as long as he could remember. The broad smile on his face and the glimmer in his eyes stood out in stark contrast to Howard's beaten, and confused expression.

"How you like bein' old Peter's driver, Mister James? Ain't it sumthin' how things turn around sometimes?"

"You God damned… oh… oh… God!" Having momentarily forgotten himself, Howard again paid the price for his poor choice of words. He cried out in pain and buckled over as he felt Pete jam the gun barrel into his ribs.

"You workin' for me now, Mister James, and you gotta show me some respect. You'll catch on. I didn't learn how to do all this shit the very first day neither. You'll catch on. You'll be fine. Old Pete will hep you."

After driving another mile they drew alongside a large stand of trees on the left side of the road. It was late in the fall, and there were but a few yellow and red leaves remaining on the branches. Nonetheless, the woods were thick enough to provide a visual barrier for anyone traveling on the road.

"Turn down this lane to the left…into the trees, Mister James."

"That's the nig…uh…that's the old slave cemetery! What are we going in there for?"

"That's right," Pete poked him in the ribs, but not so hard this time, as he repeated the order. "Turn down the lane! You'll find out real soon why we're goin' in there."

With the team and wagon next to the graveyard and hidden by the trees, Pete pulled a jug of brandy from the box in the back of the wagon and took a long pull on it. "This may be the sweetest tastin' drink I ever had, Mister

James. We gonna sit right here in the shade and wait a spell, and I'm gonna have me a few more sips of this fine liquor."

The afternoon was sunny and unusually warm for so late in the fall. There was barely enough breeze to flutter the occasional leaf that fell from the branches overhead. Howard sat silent and bent over at the waist for a good half hour. The only sounds to be heard came from Pete. He carried on, talking almost continuously and occasionally sipping from his jug.

"This is the day, Mister James. This is the day when all that nigger talk, when all that treatin' us folks like animals, an usin' our women, an makin' us kiss your ass…this is the day when it all comes back to ya. This is the day you gonna' pay. You gonna pay up today. You gonna pay up for all that and for the lynchin's you done. You remember them lynchin's? We gonna refresh your memory on that real soon. Yeah, it's gonna all come back to ya real soon."

Things did happen soon, for those last words were barely out of Pete's mouth when the sound of wagon wheels and the clop, clop of horse's hooves could be heard coming down the lane that led to the graveyard.

"Help me, help me!" Howard virtually screamed the plea.

Pete thought about jabbing him in the ribs again with the revolver, but held back. "That ain't hep comin' fer you, Mister James. That's real bad news comin' down that lane. Real bad news fer you."

The team of bays and the rig came into sight and Howard shouted again, but quieted down when he saw that a black man held the lines. "Harold, Harold Tucker! Come and help me. This nigger's got a gun on me!"

Pete jammed the pistol into his ribs harder than ever before, and Howard doubled over and fell off the seat. "You are a mighty slow learner, Mister James. You need to stop usin' that word altogether."

Grandpa was driving and I had been hunkered down in the buggy out of sight. When we drew up alongside the other rig, I stood up, climbed over the seat and sat next to him. Pete grabbed Howard's hair and pulled his head up so he could see me.

"Mr. Howard," I said calmly, "I'm Samuel Tucker." I held out my left arm.

"When I was ten years old my hand was chopped off with an axe. It was chopped off for advising a white girl that she'd dropped her purse, and it was chopped off for my family standing up to you and the Coolidge's for abusing my mother. Do you remember Lizzie Tucker?"

"I… I didn't do that…I didn't do the hand…the Coolidge's did it. I swear I didn't do it!"

My lips formed a tight, grim smile. "I know you didn't do it, James. You were there, but you didn't hold me down and you didn't swing the axe." I held up my arm again. "This is a debt you don't have to pay, but you have others… you have others and we're going to square up on those right now."

I gestured toward Grandpa. "I think you know my grandfather, Harold Tucker. In a bit you're going to take a little walk with Grandpa and me." Grandpa and I got out and walked over to the other rig. I gestured to him, and Pete pulled some wrist and leg irons out of the box…the very kind of hardware they'd shackled my daddy with when they hanged him.

Howard shouted when we snapped them around his wrists and ankles. "You can't do this! You can't do a white man this way! Help me…somebody please help me."

Grandpa didn't wait for Howard to recover his composure. He took hold of his right elbow and I grabbed the left.

The graveyard was enclosed by a three foot wall made without mortar by carefully stacking field stones. There was one narrow opening in the moss covered wall and we escorted Howard through it. I must say, watching him walk with a shuffling, awkward gait, as a result of the irons, gave me no small amount of satisfaction.

The grass was tall and it hid most of the two hundred odd markers; markers made mostly made of wood and badly deteriorated. Grandpa had saved to get a granite headstone for my father. He steered us directly to that one. It read; James Tucker, 1839-1864.

Looking at the marker, knowing my father's body was lying at my feet, and knowing one of the men who'd put him there was standing next to me was overwhelming. Sadness and anger welled up in me to the point of overflowing.

I drew my left arm across my body in a position to backhand Howard. The steel sleeve would have smashed his already bloodied face, but Grandpa grabbed my arm and stopped me. He held his other hand up to settle me and he began to speak to Howard.

"We're standin' at the grave of my son, Jimmy. He was only 25 years old when you hung him. Only 25 when you took everything he had from him and everything he was ever goin' to have. Yeah, his name was James…same name you got, and he was my only son. You took him from me and you took him from Sammy, here, his only son. And you done it because he tried to stop you from abusin' his young wife, Lizzie. You were collectin' on a gamblin' debt and Lizzie was supposed to be your payment. Do you remember that, Mister Howard?

Howard spoke in a soft, trembling voice. "Those were the

old days…the slave days. Things were different then."

Grandpa's big right arm moved with amazing speed and the back of his hand caught Howard flush. It didn't break bones like the steel cap on my arm would have, but Howard went down as hard as I've ever seen a man fall. He lay there in the tall grass, making no effort to get up while Grandpa stood over him.

"Things were different, huh?" The old man's words were soft, measured, and cold. "Well things are different now, too. You could have said you were sorry, but of course you ain't. You're only sorry we got you here and sorry you're gonna be payin' up."

I'd never before seen this side of my grandfather. He was a strong man, I'd never doubted that, but he was always gentle, kind, and controlled. The pent up anger and sadness that had been simmering inside me all these years had now come to a boil and it had obviously done the same in Grandpa…maybe even stronger.

All my life I had harbored questions about why he couldn't have found some way to stop them from hanging Daddy, cutting off my hand, and selling my momma off. I understood it all now.

Grandpa picked Howard up off the ground and pushed him out of the grave yard and toward the wagon.

"Pete, back that rig up under the tree." He pointed. "That big Oak right there." The old man had clearly taken charge of this situation, and none of us was inclined to question his actions.

When the wagon was in position, he threw a half inch hemp rope over a low hanging branch, stood Howard up on the back end of the wagon, and slipped the hangman's knot over his head.

"Take the slack out of the rope, Pete, an' tie it to the base of the tree. Pete Kraemer did as he was instructed while I watched.

The old man took Howard's hat and threw it to me. Pete was now in front of the wagon holding the horses still. With a red bandana, Grandpa gagged Howard and let him stand for a while making unintelligible sounds of protest, before ordering Pete to get away from the team. Then, with surprising agility, he vaulted onto the wagon and settled into the driver's seat.

I hadn't been present when my father was hanged, but I'd asked Grandpa about it. They'd stood him on the back of a wagon with a noose around his neck just like we were doing with Howard. According to Grandpa, he'd shown no fear and made no plea for mercy. Like Grandpa, my daddy was a powerfully built man with heavy shoulders and a thick, muscular neck. When they drove the wagon out from under him his neck didn't snap and he slowly strangled. Even though I wasn't there, I'd seen that horrible image in my dreams many times.

James Howard wasn't nearly as brave and stoic as my father had been. His whole body shook as he stood perched on the back of the wagon and he never stopped trying to speak through the gag. His face was red and beaded with sweat and his shirt was becoming soaked.

A chill came over me and I couldn't help but recognize what a pitiful sight this man was. For a moment my mother's words about sinking to the level of my adversaries came back to me.

The time for such reflection was short lived for my grandfather. He picked up the lines and turned his head back toward the grave of my father. "The day has come, Jimmy."

He clucked to the team of greys and lightly tapped their

powerful hind quarters with the buggy whip. "Get up boys…walk on boys."

Chapter Twenty-Five

Will the Arkansas River
Carry his bones to the sea
Will the fish pick them clean
It don't matter to me

The sun had set and Bill Mason was nursing a cold beer at the same table where the poker game took place each Wednesday night. He looked at his time piece and turned to speak to the bartender. "Its six thirty-five, Pat, and James was supposed to be here at six. I hope he didn't have any trouble. I'm worried about him. When he left this afternoon I was afraid he'd had too much whiskey to be drivin' off by himself."

"Oh, Mr. Howard's often a few minutes late, Mr. Mason, I wouldn't worry about him none."

Just then they heard the sound of horses and a wagon coming up the street followed by the frantic voice of Pete Kraemer. "Mr. Mason! Mr. Mason! I think somethin' awful has happened!"

Mason and Pat hurried out the front door onto the boardwalk to see Kraemer trying to hold the lathered up team of grey geldings steady.

"Mr. Mason." There was deep concern in Pete's tone. "Your team…your team, here, came back to the livery by their lonesome and all sweated up like this. Mr. Howard wasn't with 'em. The wagon's got mud splashed up underneath like maybe it was in the river. You know, from the muddy bank. I'm thinkin' somethin' awful done happened to Mr. Howard. I shoulda gone with him today, I know I shoulda."

"Well, let's not assume the worst, Pete," Mason said, "maybe he got out of the wagon and something spooked the horses. He might be walkin' back to town right now. We'll get some lanterns and go out lookin' for him. Pat, why don't you tell the Sheriff what's happened and see if you can get him to come along. I'll take this team to the livery and have Joe and Pete cool 'em down and put 'em up for the night. They're too hot and used up to do any more today. We'll take Howard's rig and his team."

Sheriff Rueben Granquist was a fat, red-faced, balding man nearing seventy years of age. He had just finished his evening meal and was enjoying a glass of whiskey, and he was none too happy when Pat rapped on the front door of his home and began shouting.

"Sheriff Rueb, Sheriff Rueb, we got a problem, we got a big problem…"

"Tell me about it in the morning, Pat, whatever it is, there ain't nothin' I'm gonna do about it tonight."

"But Sheriff," the little bartender went on, "it's Mr. Howard. His team came back without him and Bill Mason is fixin' to go lookin' right now. The wagon looks like it's been in the river, and he wants you to go with him."

"James Howard is missing?"

"That's right, sir, James Howard."

"Very well," the Sheriff sighed, "tell Mason to bring his rig by the house as soon as he's ready and I'll go along."

Bill had kerosene lamps hanging from each of the four corners of Howard's buggy when he drove up to the house. The Sheriff handed him a bottle of whiskey and two glasses. "Hold on to these while I get my ass up into this damned thing." With great effort, and a lot of groaning, the old lawman managed to hoist his three hundred pounds into the seat.

"Thanks for coming, Sheriff," Bill said as he handed the bottle and glasses back, "I thought we'd drive straight to the river and see what we find there."

Granquist poured a glass of whiskey, handed it to Mason without asking, and poured another for himself. "Let's go. Howard likely got drunk, fell out, and is either sleeping along the road or walkin' back right now, but I guess we have to look."

The drive to the river took thirty minutes and three glasses of whiskey. The moon was full and they didn't need the lanterns to see the tracks of a wagon that had entered the water.

"Damn, Sheriff, the water's too high to be fordin' this thing here. How in hell did he think he was going to make it across?" After asking the question, Mason took a walk downstream a distance of maybe eighty to a hundred yards.

"Well, it looks like he didn't make it. Here's tracks comin' out right here and they look the same as the ones goin' in. He must have got in trouble in the current and the horses managed to get turned around and back to shore. I'm afraid James…"

The Sheriff cut him off. "I'll send some men back in the morning to look. I expect it'll be a body they'll be lookin' for, but maybe they'll find him sleepin' in the weeds." Once more, without asking, he handed Bill a full glass of whiskey.

Two deputies and a handful of volunteers, including

Bill Mason and Pete Kraemer, searched the river and its banks for two days. Near sunset on the second day they found Howard's hat stuck in a mass of logs lodged against a sandbar. There was now little doubt the man had drowned.

Pete Kraemer could barely control his grief. Mason was amazed by the depth and sincerity of it. He had to work hard to suppress a smile let alone outright laughter. Even the deputies expressed admiration for the man's deep loyalty to his employer.

The search was called off and the speculation was that Howard's body would eventually be found floating far downstream, or be snagged and pulled off the bottom by a fisherman.

Chapter Twenty-Six

Salina, Kansas

He knew the secret now
How he wished it wasn't true
On the long ride ahead
He'd decide what to do

His long strides made the wooden plank floor squeak as he walked across it.

The room served as Jack Botsford's law office, Justice of the Peace office, and Mayor's office. The large, beautifully finished maple desk sitting on an Oriental rug looked like an island of opulence in the otherwise Spartan, barnlike room. A few wooden chairs, a file cabinet and a bookshelf were the only other furnishings.

The sparse light was limited to what filtered through the two large windows looking out onto the main street of Salina. On a cloudy late afternoon like this one, it took a while for a visitor's eyes to adjust. "Is that big lump behind the desk you, Jack?"

Mayor Jack Botsford looked up from his desk and smiled. "Yeah it's me, Bob. We're going to miss you around here, you know. You've made this shit hole of a town a whole lot safer and more civilized than it was before you came."

His mood was somber as he addressed his town's chief lawman. "I knew, when they made you a U.S. Marshal, they'd be askin' you to move somewhere… somewhere that ain't as tame as Salina's become, but I didn't think it would be quite this soon."

Bob Poole nodded and fibbed a little. "I know, Jack, it was a bit of a surprise…comin' as soon as it did and all. I'll be headin' out in the morning, you know. Reckon I'll stop at the Willis place and see how Kate and the Davis's are doin' and then head south."

The mayor sighed. He and Poole had an enormous amount of respect and affection for each other. "Take good care of yourself, son. You know I hate to see you go."

"I have some regrets myself, Jack, this town's treated me well. You've treated me well, and I appreciate it."

Botsford's sullen expression was quickly replaced by a wide grin. "Well, I ain't done treatin' you well quite yet." As he said the words, he drew a bottle of rye whiskey and a couple of glasses from one of the desk drawers. "Let's have one last snort."

Poole smiled also, but feigned alarm at the suggestion. "It's a little early in the day to start drinkin'… and right here in the mayor's office?"

Old Jack laughed out loud. "Maybe, but you're a U.S. Marshal and I'm the fuckin' mayor and justice of the peace. Who do you think's going to do anything to us? The complaint would go to you and I'd be the one to hear the case."

That first glass of rye tasted like a second one, and after the third the marshal covered his glass with his hand. "If I don't stop now, I won't be able to ride in the morning." Botsford reluctantly put what was left of the bottle back in the drawer. The two men shook hands. Marshal Bob Poole got to his feet and walked out the door.

The next morning, just after sunrise, he was on his way

out of town; mounted on the roan gelding with a little sorrel pack horse trailing behind. When he reached the edge of Salina he stopped, looked back, and thought about how this was just another in a long string of places where he'd arrived alone and left alone.

As he sat there, he thought about his old friend, the one called Bad Wing Crow, and muttered to himself. "You and I ain't a hell of a lot different, Sammy. Neither of us ever stays in the same place or with the same people very damned long."

He hadn't said anything about it to the mayor, but he'd actually requested the transfer to Pine Bluff, Arkansas. The feeling that Sammy might have gotten himself in a bad spot had been weighing on his mind for some time, and he felt a need to find him.

After all these years he still thought about how Tucker had kept him from taking a bullet from those two horse thieves down in Texas. "You weren't more than a kid, Sammy," he thought, "but without your fancy shootin', my bones would have been picked clean by buzzards and been bleachin' in the sun for seven or eight years by now."

Poole had seen Jim and Nettie Davis from time to time when they came to town for supplies, but Kate hadn't accompanied them on the last several trips. He wanted to check on her so he could give a report to Sam when he found him. It was his intention to find him and he had no doubt he would. A one-handed black cowboy with a big reputation as a gun man could go unnoticed for only so long.

The roan gelding willingly entered the little creek that ran along the edge of the Willis farmstead, but the pack horse balked and stood on the bank. Bob reined his mount in and had him stand with all four feet in the water while he let the sorrel look at the situation for a bit.

One of the things Sammy had taught him about horses was to give them some space and use just enough persuasion to get them to do what you want without making a big fuss.

As he waited for the little horse to make up his mind, he happened to look up stream just as Kate came to the opposite bank carrying a wooden bucket. She was no more than fifty feet away. She spotted him at about the same time, and she turned and ran for the house, holding her bulging belly with one hand and the empty bucket with the other.

Poole sighed, closed his eyes and shook his head. "Damn, I wish I hadn't seen that. Damn!" He gave a short tug on the lead rope and the pack horse crossed the stream behind him like he'd been planning on doing it all along.

Nettie Davis came out to meet him when he rode into the farm yard. She had a forced smile on her face and she was fidgeting with the odd looking bump beneath her apron. "Mornin', Sheriff. Jim's out huntin' deer and Kate's in the house. Hasn't been feelin' well. Don't know if you ought to go in, ya might catch what's been ailin' her. I sure could bring out a cup of coffee for you, though, and I got some biscuits I just baked. I could sure fetch them for you, too."

Poole dismounted, turned toward the woman and shook his head. "I got a good look at her, Nettie, and I ain't about to catch what's ailin' her. Let's go inside and talk this over."

When the marshal was seated at the kitchen table, Nettie went to get Kate. It was a few minutes before she returned, holding the girl by her left arm. Her cheeks were reddened and streaked with tears, she held her head down and made no eye contact with Poole. The sight of her touched him and nearly brought tears to his eyes. She looked like a lost and broken little girl.

Nettie explained the plan to keep Kate out of sight and claim the baby was hers. Poole sighed. "That may work, Nettie. For now, though, you can take the pillow out of your dress and sit on it."

He stood up and walked to where Kate was sitting. Putting his hand gently under her chin, he lifted it. "Look at me, Kate. I'm your friend and Sammy's about the best friend I ever had. I'm sorry you got this trouble, Darlin'. I'll help you if I can."

She wiped her eyes, and, for the first time, looked squarely into his. "Promise me you won't tell Sammy if you should see him again. Please, Sheriff, promise me."

"Well, if you folks ever came into town, you'd know I'm not the Sheriff of Salina anymore. I'm a federal marshal now, and it's likely I will be running into Sammy. I'm heading down Arkansas way and I'm pretty sure that's where he is." He hesitated for a moment and then went on. "As for not tellin' him, I can't promise that, Kate. I'll think about it, but I can't promise."

When Poole had finished his second cup of coffee and the last of the biscuits, he went out, snugged the girth on the roan, and mounted. Nettie and Kate stood on the porch waiting for any last words he might have to say. He sat in the saddle for a bit before offering the sparse amount of advice that came to mind.

"The next person who comes ridin' in to this place ain't gonna be me, Kate. Be more careful. And Nettie, work on that pillow deal. I don't know what you can do, but the way you had it you weren't going to fool anybody." He touched the brim of his hat, squeezed his long legs, and the roan trotted off to the southeast.

The young marshal was undaunted by the prospect of riding solo across several hundred miles of sparsely populated country. He'd done it many times before and figured he could handle about anything that came his way.

Kate's request…her pleading request…that he not say anything to Sammy about her pregnancy was another matter. It weighed heavily on his mind. How could he not tell his friend of the predicament the woman he loved was in? How could he not tell him he was about to become a father?

Mentally as well as physically, there was nothing timid about Bob Poole. A decisive, principled man, he was barely off the Willis farm when he made up his mind. "I have to tell Sam. He'd never keep anything that important from me."

Chapter Twenty-Seven

Still in Salina country
A few weeks later

The Marshal had told her
He'd given her warning
But there was nowhere to hide
When they rode in that morning

The Van Heel brothers, Paul and Bertram, were the two toughest, most unruly men in Salina. Somewhere in their late thirties, they were big boys, weighing well over two hundred pounds each. With round faces and sandy blonde hair, they looked enough alike to be twins. For all anyone knew, they might have been twins. Nobody ever cared or dared to ask.

Known mostly for their drinking and vicious brawling, the Van Heels were also petty thieves, but they were far from big time outlaws. They rolled drunks and rustled a calf here and there; usually claiming they'd just rounded up a stray on open range. Not even close to being clever, it was through luck that they had managed to avoid serious jail time or the noose.

On the second day after Poole had taken over as Sheriff of Salina, the brothers had started a ruckus in the Red Fish Saloon. The patrons looked on as Paul held a young cowboy's arms while Bertram beat him.

The kid was a bloody mess and about to drop to the floor when Poole walked in. Without hesitating or saying a word, he buffaloed Bertram behind the right ear with his long barreled Colt.

Seeing his brother crumble to the floor, Paul loosened his grip on the beaten young man who dropped as well. As soon as he had a clear view of Paul's face, the Sheriff planted his big right fist in the middle of it. Within thirty seconds of Poole entering the room, both Van Heel brothers were lying unconscious on the dirty, rough sawn, spittle stained, floor planks of the Red Fish.

Bob pointed to four men who had been watching the melee, apparently without the courage to intervene on the cowboy's behalf. "You four…drag these assholes to the jail. I'll meet you there in a few minutes."

After tossing down a shot of whiskey, he turned toward the rest of the crowd. "This shit ain't gonna happen on my watch, boys. Get used to the idea."

For the remainder of Poole's time as Sheriff, the Van Heel boys kept themselves in check. They were flat out scared of the big lawman.

Now that he'd been gone for a few weeks, their courage had come back and they were returning to their old ways. Early one November morning they rode east out of town hoping to find a calf or two that needed a new home.

*****

There hadn't been much in the way of livestock on the Willis farm when Jim and Nettie Davis took the place over…just a few chickens, a milk cow, and a heifer. The rest had been run off when the three killers had come and wiped out Kate's family.

The stolen mule had been recovered, and he now teamed up with Jim's old grey mule for the plowing and such. Of course Kate still had the chestnut mare she'd gotten as a result of the run in with those same outlaws.

Since they weren't producing meat on the farm, they depended heavily on the wild game Jim brought back from the vast Kansas prairie. There was plenty out there; deer, antelope, prairie chicken and more, and Jim was a skilled hunter.

However, he had to travel several miles from the farm to find the best hunting, and depending on how he fared, he'd normally be gone over one night or sometimes two.

This particular morning found him field dressing a whitetail doe. When he was finished, he hefted the carcass onto the wagon alongside the buck he'd shot the evening before. He covered them both with canvas. With eight Prairie Chickens stowed under the seat in a burlap bag, it had been a successful hunt. There was no need to stay another night.

The canvas protected it some, but he didn't want to risk having the meat sour in the warm afternoon sun. It was mid-morning when he clucked to the mules and turned them toward home. He guessed the six mile ride would take three, maybe four hours. The prairie was rough and rolling and cut with an endless number of deep draws. Taking a straight course was impossible and travel was slow.

Like most black men of his day, Jim Davis had been through a great deal of hardship. He'd survived slavery, share cropping, and all that went with it, and he'd emerged as a strong, confident, self-reliant man. He didn't spend a whole lot of time worrying about what he might find around the next corner, or what somebody might try to do to him. He'd stood up to every surprise he'd encountered and every man who had tried to best him.

On this morning, however, he felt a little on edge. Didn't know why he felt that way; maybe it was because the wind was picking up and it looked like some foul weather was brewing. Whatever the cause of it, the feeling made him push the mules just a little faster than usual.

*****

There'd been a hard frost the previous night, and Kate and Nettie were busy harvesting the last of the squash and carrots from the garden, when the Van Heels splashed across the creek on their big spotted horses. The garden, being close to the tree lined creek, was the worst place on the farm to be if you didn't want to be seen by unexpected visitors. Kate turned to run toward the house as soon as she saw them, but it wasn't soon enough.

Paul spurred his horse and cut her off like he was heading a calf. "Whoa, there missy. Ain't no reason for you runnin' inside on a nice mornin' like this." Kate's eyes moved from Paul to Bertram who moved his horse to block Nettie's path to the house. The faces of the two brothers were cold and portrayed nothing but evil. She felt like she'd gone back to the day when her family had been attacked and killed just a few months earlier. She couldn't believe this was happening again on the farm that, for all of her memory, had been such a peaceful and happy place.

Bertram looked her up and down slowly. "Somethin' don't look right here, darlin'. Looks like you are fixin' to have yourself a little one. Now how'd you get with child when you got nothin' but niggers around here? You gonna have yourself a little black baby, darlin'?"

Paul laughed at his brother's remarks. "Maybe we can help her out some, Bert. Maybe it ain't too late for one of us to just kinda slip in and see if we can't make that baby white. While I'm doin' that, you could have some fun with the nigger girl. Then you could have a try at whitenin' up the little monkey this one's got inside her."

Nettie stepped in front of Kate. "You men just go on and leave us be. She's married and that's a white child she's carryin'. And…uh… her husband and my Jim will be back here right soon and you best be outa' here when they come."

"Yeah, honey, I'm sure your buck and her white husband are gonna' be here any minute now." Paul laughed and nudged his horse a few steps closer to the women. Bertram moved his horse up closer as well.

Kate stepped out from behind Nettie. She had a metal trowel in her right hand that she held behind her back. Her face remained blank as she spoke. "So you aren't going to leave, and you're planning to have your way with both of us? I don't think you should do that. I think you should leave right now."

The two brothers looked at each other and laughed loudly. Bertram looked down from his horse and spoke. "That's right, sweetheart, and we're gonna get started right now. After all, we only got a few minutes 'til your men folk get here, and they might not feel like sharin'.'

He drew his pistol and laughed as he went back and forth, pointing it first at Kate and then at Nettie.

The second time he swung the gun in Nettie's direction, Kate lunged and jabbed the sharp point of the trowel into his right hand. Bert swore as the pistol fell from his hand. Kate reacted quickly and trapped it against her breast before it hit the ground. She fumbled with it for a few seconds before getting a grip with both hands and pulling the hammer back.

When Paul saw she had the weapon, he spurred his horse and reined it toward her. Kate fired, but the slug went wild as the horse's shoulder caught her full on and sent her sprawling. The back of her head connected solidly with the hard ground, but, somehow, she managed to maintain her grip on the pistol.

She tried to will herself to raise it up and fire again, but she was dazed and couldn't lift her arm. Paul leapt off his horse and stomped on her wrist. She cried out in pain as she felt a bone snap and her grip on the weapon loosened.

After picking up the Colt and stuffing it in his belt, Paul looked down on the pregnant girl and smiled. His boot was still pressing hard on her broken wrist. "Looks like yer try at bein' a hero didn't work out so good, now did it honey? An' it looks like all the fight's gone outa you now. I 'spect this next part's gonna be real easy."

Bert had also dismounted and was standing behind Nettie with his big right forearm clamped tightly around her neck. His hand was bloody, but not seriously injured. Nettie could barely breathe, but didn't struggle. "Please," she gasped, "please don't choke me…don't hurt me. I'll do what you want. I'll do whatever you want."

Kate was regaining her senses and was surprised by the words she'd heard her friend speak. She looked up at the resigned, defeated look on her face and realized Nettie had been down this road before. She'd been abused by white men and had learned the hard way that no good would come from trying to fight.

"Take the nigger into the house, Bert. I'm going to the barn with this one and see if I can't find some nice soft hay."

"Leave somethin' for me, Paul, I need to square up with that white bitch for stabbin' my hand."

Paul picked Kate up by her hair until she was on her feet and dragged her toward the barn. The same barn from which she'd watched as her family was murdered. Though she had promised herself she'd never again stand helplessly by and let something like this happen, like Nettie, she didn't fight back.

She had two reasons. Her swollen and discolored right

arm throbbed and hung at her side. It was useless. More importantly, she had to protect the child inside her.

*****

At first it looked like a dark cloud low on the horizon. When Jim was within two miles of the farm, he got a knot in his belly. It was smoke; thick, black, smoke, and it was right where it shouldn't have been. He cracked the whip.

The young sorrel mule willingly went into a gallop at the man's urging. The old grey tried his best, but at twenty-four years of age, he had neither the legs nor the lungs for such a run. As they moved ahead, the traces on the sorrel's side remained taut while the grey's were mostly slack. Much of the time he was actually holding the rig back.

Jim didn't like their chances of getting to the farm in time to do anything about the fire, even though he knew the grey was giving all he had. Nonetheless he kept laying the whip across the beast's rump. It was cruel, but there seemed to be nothing else he could do.

The old mule's breath seemed to get more labored and raspy with each stride. In spite of feeling the repeated sting of the buggy whip, he was able to maintain the gait for less than three quarters of a mile before sinking to his knees and skidding to a stop. Jim knew there was no point in trying to get him back on his feet. The animal had given everything he had and then some.

Leaving the grey lying on the ground and still hitched to the wagon, Jim unbuckled the sorrel's harness from the tongue, freed the traces from the evener, and vaulted onto his back. Once again the strong, faithful beast moved out at top speed.

Though his powerful stride never shortened until the man reined him in at the edge of the farmyard, more than a mile from where the dash had begun, it wasn't soon enough.

The flames from both the house and the barn leapt at least thirty feet above the roof tops. The buildings were totally engulfed and looked ready to collapse. Any possibility of entering either of them was gone, and if anyone was inside, they were surely dead.

Tears were flowing freely down Jim Davis' cheeks as he ran around and around the farmstead frantically shouting his wife's name. The smoke, the heat, the emotion and the exhaustion finally caused him to collapse face down in the dirt…just like his old mule had done.

Chapter Twenty-Eight

Pine Bluff, Arkansas

Has the day finally come
Has it come at long last
Don't want to be hasty
And get it done too fast

It was the first Wednesday after James Howard's disappearance and the Coolidge brothers, along with Will Parker and Bill Mason, were seated at their usual table in the saloon. The Coolidge's were still mourning the loss of their cousin, but not enough to interrupt the tradition of the weekly poker game.

The evening went as usual. The Coolidge boys played pretty well until they got drunk, Parker drank less, but he wasn't real sharp at poker when he was sober. Mason made a point of not winning too many hands, and Pat Collins hovered about making sure everyone had drinks, cigars or whatever they wanted. He was especially subservient and attentive to Robert and Buster. He would have gone out back and urinated for them if he could have.

Will Parker was the first to leave the table when the game was over. Mason remained seated. He waited for the other two men to finish their drinks before he spoke. "There's something I'd like to speak to you gentlemen about. Let's step outside and talk for a few minutes…just the three of us."

Together they walked out to the boardwalk in front of the saloon. Mason herded them a short distance away from where Harold Tucker was waiting with Robert's buggy. Buster was scowling and growing impatient. "What's this all about, Mason? It's damned near midnight and I'm tired."

Mason spoke softly. "It's about your cousin, James Howard, Buster. I was down south of town yesterday talkin' to a white share cropper about some mules, and he told me something interesting. He said he saw James' driver, Pete, in my wagon with James on the day he disappeared. They were near the old slave cemetery when he spotted them."

Robert Coolidge looked puzzled. "Didn't Pete claim he was at the livery all day workin' with Howard's team of sorrels?"

"He did, and he said he didn't know anything about where James went that day or what happened until my team and wagon came back without him. He's also the one who noticed the wagon had mud on it from the river."

Buster seemed to sober up a bit and joined the discussion. "Damned nigger must have been lyin' about everything then. Did you say anything to the Sheriff?"

Mason shook his head. "No, I haven't mentioned it to anyone except you two. Since James was your cousin, I thought you might want to handle it on your own. You know, without getting the law involved."

"We will handle this ourselves," Buster agreed, "like in the old days, we can damn well do whatever we want with a nigger and there won't be a lot of questions asked. Where's this Pete livin' now that James is gone?"

"I know where to find him." Mason answered, "He found himself a woman. She's the widow of a share cropper, and he's livin' with her southwest of town."

Buster was getting more and more agitated as the

conversation went on. "Let's go get the son of a bitch right now!"

Robert joined in to calm his brother down. "Take it easy, Buster, it's late and we been drinkin'. Tomorrow will be soon enough."

Bill agreed. "That makes a lot of sense. How about if I round up Pete in the morning? I'll tell him I need his help with some mules I'm picking up. You boys meet me at that old slave cemetery at about noon."

"Are you sure you can find him and get him there?" Buster asked.

"Damn right I can, and let's not mention anything about this to anyone…not even your wives…agreed?"

The Coolidge's both nodded and Robert spoke. "We'll see you at noon, Bill, and thanks for your help with this. We won't forget it."

Bill Mason walked back to his hotel with a satisfied smile on his face. "No, boys, tomorrow will be a day you won't forget…not for as long as you live."

Before eleven o'clock the next morning Grandpa had the team of blacks all groomed and hitched to the buggy. Robert Coolidge climbed aboard the rig and turned to his driver. "You work around here today, Tucker. I'll be back later this afternoon."

Tucker feigned disappointment. "You ain't wantin' old Harold to go along an' drive for you, Mr. Robert? I'd sure be happy to do the drivin' for you today."

"Stay here like I told you, damn it. See if you can get your lazy ass to get some work done."

"Yes suh, Boss, I'll get busy right now."

Coolidge's fancy looking black geldings were feeling fresh this morning and he wasn't able to get them settled down like Harold could. After the first half mile he gave up and let them have their way. They moved out at a gallop with Robert barely managing to keep them on the road and the buggy right side up. When they reached Buster's place in Pine Bluff, the horses were lathered up, but tired and more manageable. The trip had taken less than half the usual amount of time.

Buster came out to the buggy looking, as you would expect, like he'd had a hard night. Without saying a word to his brother, he put a fifty foot length of half inch hemp rope under the seat and climbed aboard the buggy. His eyes were bloodshot and he smelled of whiskey. As usual, he had his Colt revolver on his right hip. A leather thong held the holster securely against his thigh.

The morning was cold and cloudy and both men hunched their shoulders and pulled their collars up against the weather. The conversation was sparse as they drove toward the old cemetery. It was eleven forty-five when they turned onto the narrow grassy lane that led to the graveyard.

"Looks like we're the first ones here," Buster commented, as Robert parked the rig under the huge Cottonwood tree next to the rock wall that defined the boundary of the burial ground.

Reaching into his coat, Buster pulled a flask from the inside pocket. "Might as well have a little snort while we're waitin' for the fun to start."

"For Crisesake, Buster," Robert growled, "you haven't sobered up from last night yet."

"I'll drink any God damned time I want to, and it's none of your God damned business." Buster was red faced and angry enough to make Robert hold his tongue. Liquor could make his brother crazy with rage and Robert knew better than to cross him when he was that way.

Right at noon, Mason guided the team of greys into the same little clearing where Coolidge's rig was parked. Buster's flask of whiskey was now empty. Pete Kraemer looked frightened and confused when he saw who was waiting for them, and he tried to jump out of the wagon. Bill grabbed hold of his arm and kept him in place while Buster staggered out of Robert's buggy with the rope in his hand. Pete stopped struggling when Robert pointed a sawed off double barreled shotgun in his direction and ordered him to sit still.

"I can blow your brains out with this twelve-gauge, nigger, or you can settle down and answer some questions. If you get the answers right, maybe we won't need the rope Buster's holdin'."

From hiding, I watched Pete's eyes shift back and forth from Robert to Buster and then around the perimeter of the clearing. So far, he didn't like the way things were going.

I'm sure he was thinking this confrontation had gone on plenty long enough when I stepped out of the bushes next to Robert's wagon. One of my Colts was pointed at his head. At the same moment, Grandpa came out of the brush on the other side of the clearing. The shotgun he held was trained on Buster, whose pistol was still holstered. I was hoping he would reach for it, but he didn't.

"Drop the shotgun, Coolidge, or it'll be your brains splattered on the dirt." Somewhat to my surprise, he immediately set the gun on the floor of the buggy. "Open your coat," I ordered, "and show me you don't have any hand guns." Again, Robert complied.

Turning toward the other rig, I pointed the pistol at Mason and told him to let go of Pete and stand next to Coolidge's buggy. I moved to holster my sidearm and turned toward Buster, but out of the corner of my eye I saw Mason's hand slide inside his coat. I raised the revolver and fired. Bill grunted, staggered back, and clasped both hands over his chest. Blood was oozing from between his fingers as he fell to the ground.

Walking a few steps, I stopped when I was maybe twenty feet from Buster and squarely in front of him. I put the pistol away and glanced at my grandfather. "You can put the shotgun down, Grandpa, and drag Mr. Mason into the bushes. We'll throw him in the river along with these two… right after the hangin'. Get the pistol from inside his coat."

A week earlier, Grandpa had taken charge of settling up with Howard, and none of us argued with him. Today I was running the show and neither Pete nor my grandfather was of a mind to challenge me on that. I guess there's something about us Tuckers. When our minds are made up…they're made up…and it shows.

I kept my eyes trained on Buster, but from where I stood I could see the relief on Pete's face and his mouth break out in that broad smile of his. "You don't suppose you could have waited a little longer, do you, Sammy? I know you're mister bad-ass Bad Wing Crow, but these guys could have blown my head off while you was makin' up your mind when to get this here situation under control."

I laughed. "Well, maybe I did cut 'er a little close, Peter, but so far things are workin' out pretty well. You could have pulled that snub-nosed Smith and Wesson out of your pocket if you didn't feel like waitin' for me."

Pete's face twisted up into a scowl. "Yeah, that would have been a fine idea. I ain't no quick draw guy like you, and I can't hit nobody with that thing unless they're sittin' on my damned lap."

Pete was an amusing guy, and I couldn't help but laugh at

his effort to chastise me. "Well, Peter Kraemer, you're still kickin', and now it's time for Buster and I to have our little dance."

By this time Grandpa had returned from dragging Mason's body into the brush. "He didn't have no pistol on him, Sammy."

I shook my head. "Well, it sure looked like he was goin' for one. Please get up in the wagon and sit next to our friend Robert. Break his neck if he tries anything." Neither Grandpa nor Robert was armed, but, I knew and Coolidge knew, the old man could over power him without working up a sweat.

My attention was now focused on Buster. I was surprised by how calm, steady, and unafraid he appeared to be. It didn't make a nickel's worth of difference to me, but I was a bit surprised. Clearly he had more sand in his belly than his brother.

"So you're Bad Wing Crow, huh? I've heard about you. And I bet you're the little nigger kid who tragically lost his hand in an accident fifteen or twenty years ago. You were choppin' the head off a chicken, weren't you?" Buster sneered as he sarcastically recounted the event.

I kept my eyes locked on his, smiled, and spoke in barely more than a whisper. "That's correct, boss, and I'm the little kid whose daddy you hanged and whose momma you used and treated like an animal. And I'm also the little kid who's going to hang you and your brother from that big Cottonwood. I might shoot you first, but I'm going to hang you either way."

Buster didn't appear to be the least bit fazed by my remarks, and, again, I didn't really give a shit. I wanted him to understand what this was all about, but it wasn't going to be a war of words.

"You know somethin', nigger," he said, "I got a pistol at my side just like you do, and I'm mighty good with it."

When the talking is still going on, a man doesn't expect you to pull your iron. It was a handy bit of information I'd learned a long time ago. I smiled at Buster and kept smiling while I talked. "I've heard that, boss. Now are you talkin' about that pistol right there?"

On the word 'pistol' I drew, and on 'there' the first of two rounds smacked into the holster. They were followed by two more that smashed the handle of the Colt it cradled. Buster's eyes got big and the smile and the cocky look on his face faded just like I knew it would.

The piece I'd just fired was now empty so I put it back in its holster. I opened my coat to let Buster see the one I kept in the cross draw rig. He looked down at the damaged gun at his side and then back at me.

"You think that thing will still fire?" I asked. "I sure wouldn't bring a busted up piece like that to a gunfight. You want to try it? Do you want to call me nigger again? Or do you want to unbuckle that gun belt and drop it on the ground?"

Without offering any further conversation, he did as I suggested. I walked up close to him, jabbed the steel piece on the end of my left arm into his belly and ushered him to the back of the wagon. Pete brought out some wrist and leg irons, and we shackled the two brothers. Then we stood them on the back edge of Mason's wagon.

We put Buster's own rope around his neck, and Pete couldn't keep himself from commenting. "Mighty decent of you, Mr. Buster…bringin' the rope to your own hangin'… mighty decent."

We had another rope for Robert, and when both men had nooses around their necks and the ropes were slung over a branch of the Cottonwood, Grandpa drove the wagon out from under them.

Chapter Twenty-Nine

The marshal came to town
Be awhile before he'd get it
Didn't know what had happened
Knew damn well who did it

The first thing Bob Poole did when he arrived in town was to squeeze his big frame through the swinging doors of the Busted Bluff Saloon and order himself a beer.

When Pat Collins asked who he was, he pushed his coat to one side to reveal his shiny, newly acquired U.S. Marshal's badge. After taking a big gulp of beer, he smiled and offered his hand to Pat. "The name's Bob Poole and I'll be working here in Pine Bluff. When I finish this beer, or maybe another one, I want to talk with Sheriff Granquist. Do you know where I might find him?"

"His office is right down the street, Marshal, and I think you can find him there now." The little man was more nervous than usual as he spoke. "Usually he, uh, works out of his home, but we got some serious problems here and, lately, him and his deputies have been spendin' more time at the office."

The marshal took another gulp of beer and wiped the foam from his lips with the back of his hand. "What kind of problems are you talkin' about, Pat? You said your name was Pat, right?"

"Yes sir, Pat Collins. Well, about a week or so ago Mr. James Howard went missing and it looked like…to the Sheriff and everybody…it looked like he fell out of the wagon he was drivin' and drowned in the river. Then, day before yesterday, his two cousins, Robert and Buster Coolidge, disappeared. Buster is the owner of this saloon."

"Now the Sheriff don't know what to think. Every Wednesday night those three played poker at that table right over there, and one of the gentlemen who'd been playin' with them lately…Bill Mason…he's missin' too. Mr. Mason ain't from here in town. Came this way from… uhh…Fort Smith I think it was. Came to buy mules for the army."

"Well, thanks for the information, Pat. Give me another beer, please."

When he'd finished his second beer, Poole left the saloon, untied his horse, and led him down the rutted dirt street toward the Sheriff's Office. "Sammy Tucker," he thought, "you're in this right up to your ass, aren't you? You told me the story of the Coolidge's and Howard, but I never heard of this Mason guy."

Granquist's office wasn't far, but the marshal walked slowly to give himself time to mull over what Pat had told him. He had a lot of other stuff going through his mind as well.

His assignment was to take over law enforcement in Pine Bluff, but he was to give Reub Granquist up to a year to retire. So, for a while anyway, they would overlap, and getting along with the Sheriff would be important.

Even though he'd grown up in Texas, he knew the folks here would be wary of any agent of the federal, or Yankee, government. The wounds from the war were still raw and open.

Granquist was sitting behind his desk when Poole walked into the office. He pretended not to notice when the portly old lawman slipped his glass of whiskey into a drawer. Noticing the badge, the older man spoke. "Well, you must be Mr. Robert Poole, United States of America Marshal. Been expectin' you to show up one of these days to show me how to do my job the way the Yankees do it."

Poole smiled. "You got the name right, Sheriff, but I got no plans to interfere with how you run the county. I'm just an old south Texas boy got into Sheriffin' just like you did, and they just now went and made me a marshal. I ain't no different than you…just a different badge and I can't help it if it was Yankees that gave it to me. And, please, call me Bob."

Granquist seemed to soften some at Poole's ingratiating remarks. "Well, Bob, why don't you call me Reub and let's see if we can't get along here for awhile."

"That's what I've got in mind…uh…Reub. I've heard a lot of good things about you and I'm lookin' forward to workin' with you until you decide to retire. You've been in office a long time, and I just hope I can learn something from all your years of experience."

What the marshal had really heard was the Sheriff was just what he was now looking at…a fat lazy drunk. Beyond that, Granquist was known to take bribes and to allow any local white man to do whatever he chose to a black person. For now, though, kissing the man's fat backside seemed like the prudent thing to do.

It could be that his survival, as well as mine, just might depend on it. He knew without a doubt I was in this deal with the Coolidge's and Howard. Like he had said, in it right up to my ass and maybe deeper.

Poole took a chair in front of the desk. "The fella down

at the saloon, Pat I believe, said you've got some of your leading citizens missing. What do you figure has happened to 'em?"

The Sheriff sighed and pulled his glass of whisky out of the drawer along with the bottle and an empty glass. "It's close enough to quittin' time, Bob, would you care to join me?"

Poole laughed. "I was hopin' you'd get that back out of your desk and offer me one."

The two men were quiet for a bit while they enjoyed a couple sips of whisky. Eventually the Sheriff responded to Poole's question about the missing men.

"When Howard disappeared, we was sure he'd drowned in the river. We found where his team and wagon went in the water and got swept downstream to where the horses found solid footing and managed to get out. Howard had been drinkin' and it looked like he fell or got washed out of the wagon by the current. We found his hat way down river."

"Now, with the Coolidge's and Mason missing too, we don't know what to think. Mason had been in town for only a few weeks, but he'd been playin' poker every Wednesday night with the Coolidge's, Howard, and a fella named Parker. Now four of those five have vanished in a little over a week, and I don't know what the hell happened to any of 'em. I know Parker well enough to know he ain't involved."

Bob Poole grunted and took another swallow of whisky.

"Well, Reub, this is your show. I was plannin' on just getting to know the area and some of the folks here in the next week or two. While I'm doin' that, I'll see if I can learn anything about this here…uh…situation, but I won't interfere in your investigation. If I stumble on to anything good, I'll sure let you know, but otherwise I'll stay out of your way. That sound agreeable to you?"

Granquist smiled. "I like the way you think, Bob. You seem to be a reasonable man and not the Yankee intruder we was expectin'. We're gonna get along fine."

"I think we are, Reub. I think we are."

*****

The sun had been up for less than two hours when my grandfather answered the knock on his front door. The old man's face betrayed his alarm when he spotted the badge, but he said nothing.

"Mr. Tucker, I'm U.S. Marshal Bob Poole and I'm a friend of Sammy, your grandson. Is he here by any chance?"

Grandpa hesitated for a few seconds before awkwardly putting together an answer. "No sir, Marshal, he…uhh… he ain't here. I ain't seen Sammy in six or seven years. Don't know where he is…could be anywhere."

"That's too bad, I was hopin' to talk with him. Tell you what, if you should happen, just by some chance, to see him, tell him to meet me right here at this time tomorrow morning."

The old man's eyes widened, and, again, he was at a loss for words. "Well…uh…well, like I said I ain't seen him in…"

"I know, Mr. Tucker, six or seven years, but tell him anyway."

Chapter Thirty

Were the horses really stole
Were the hanged really hung
Did the boys pay enough
For the trouble they brung

The next morning was colder than normal even considering winter was at hand. The frost was heavy and a thin layer of ice covered the puddles remaining from the previous evening's rain.

Bob wore a sheepskin coat and hat…the kind with the ear flaps that tie under the chin. He looked more like a sheepherder than a U.S. Marshal, and I smiled at his appearance when I met him at the front door of Grandpa's house. "Good to see you, Bob, how about some coffee?"

"Coffee sounds good, Sammy, and it's mighty good to see you, too."

Grandpa joined us as we sat down at the small wooden table and he immediately started to apologize to Bob for having claimed he didn't know of my whereabouts. "Uhh… Marshal, yesterday when you asked me if Sammy was here, I… uhhh."

Bob interrupted him. "Don't worry about it Mr. Tucker, we're all happy you had the good fortune to run into him after all those years, and were able to ask him to meet me here this morning."

Bob and I laughed. Grandpa got the joke, too. "Yes, sir, that was mighty strange…me runnin' in to him right after you left and all, and after all them years."

After Grandpa poured the coffee, he took a pan of sour dough biscuits from his wood fired oven and set them on the table along with a jar of honey. Bob inhaled the smell of the freshly baked morsels. "We got a lot to talk about, Sammy. More than you know, but I believe I'll warm up with a few swallows of coffee and one of these fine biscuits before we get started."

"Sounds good to me, Marshal."

I was enjoying calling Bob by his new title. "You know, Marshal, this is the same little table I sat at when I was ten years old, and these biscuits are the same, Marshal, as the ones Grandpa made back then."

Poole scowled. "You can cut the 'Marshal' shit, Sam. We gotta' make sure you and your grandfather are still eatin' biscuits for many years to come. I sure hope you ain't done nothin' to keep that from happening. We'll get to that directly."

After a few more biscuits, Bob leaned back in his chair, wiped his lips, and got on with it. "I had a talk with Sheriff Granquist when I got to town the other day, gentlemen. He told me the two Coolidge brothers and their cousin have suddenly gone missing…along with a fella named Mason. Now I don't know how Mason fits in, but we all know about your history with the other three."

The longer Bob talked, the more anxious and agitated he sounded. "Whatever you did with 'em, Sammy, I hope like hell you didn't do anything so bad, or so sloppy, that we can't get you and your grandfather out of here alive."

"Would you please pour Bob some more coffee, Grandpa,

maybe that will help get him settled down some."

Grandpa filled the Marshal's cup, while I continued. "There's an abandoned plantation eight miles east of town and then two and a half miles south. It's called the Cordill place. It hasn't been worked since shortly after the war. I think you ought to ride out there and look around."

I flashed a big smile in my friend's direction. "A smart law man like you just might be able to figure this case out just by doin' that. If you get stuck, I'll be right here and ready to help you out. I did some deputyin' up in Salina a while back and I…"

"Yeah, I know all about your experience as a deputy, Sammy…you shot an apple as I recall. But this ain't that God damned funny." Poole glared at me as though he really meant it. "I'll ride out there, though, and I guess I'll just see what I see."

Bob pushed his chair back, rose to his full six foot five inch height, and turned toward Grandpa. "Thank you for the coffee and biscuits, sir. Best I ever ate."

As he turned to leave, I spoke up. "When we first sat down you said we had more to talk about; more than I knew. What did you have in mind, Bob."

"We do have more to talk about, Sammy…we do. But I think we'd do better by lettin' that part sit for now. We'll just let it sit."

Grandpa had an unusual, kind of wistful look on his face as we watched Bob walk to his horse. "You know somethin', Sammy, I believe that's the first time a white man ever called me sir…the very first time."

"Bob Poole ain't like most white men, but I've known some others…some other good ones. The man who made this steel cap for my arm is another, and I knew…uh…I knew a woman too, Grandpa, a very special woman."

Next morning, Poole loped the big roan almost steadily on the ten and a half mile ride to the old Cordill place. The clouds of the night before were gone and the morning sun warmed the day quickly.

At the four mile mark he stopped and tied the sheepskin coat and hat behind the saddle. He figured he'd be more comfortable in the white beaver felt Stetson and the deer skin vest he pulled from his saddle bags. He chuckled, and talked to himself as he put them on. "I look more like a federal marshal this way."

My directions were clear and Poole had no trouble finding the place. It was close to eleven thirty when he rode up the tree-lined lane, past the main house, and made his way among the barns and the old slave quarters. The place was overgrown with weeds and debris, and there was an eerie feeling to it.

The buildings were weathered and in disrepair with shutters and doors hanging askew. Nonetheless it was easy to imagine what it must have been like only two decades earlier, with all the activity, the people, and the despair that would have been there.

The last building was a stone brig. He assumed it had been used to punish slaves who had run or otherwise misbehaved. Just outside the brig were two wooden timbers standing upright and sunk into the ground four feet apart. Each timber had a heavy iron ring bolted to it at about the six foot level. A chain and wrist iron hung from each ring. Poole had never had much direct contact with slavery, but he knew what these things had been used for. It made a chill run up and down his spine.

As he approached the fields behind the buildings, he could make out three figures standing in the middle of a small patch of plowed ground. He nudged the roan into a lope, and quickly closed the distance between himself and the men. They all appeared to be white and were holding shovels. When he was close enough so they could see him clearly, they began running in his direction and shouting for help.

The piece of uneven turned over earth was small, maybe half an acre in size, but each of the three fell flat on his face before reaching the edge. The Marshal laughed. "Hold up, boys. Just stay where you are and I'll ride over there."

When he reached them, he remained mounted as he introduced himself. "I'm U.S. Marshal Bob Poole, and I'll bet you're the Coolidge brothers and either Mr. Mason or Mr. Howard, right?"

Robert Coolidge's speech was slurred as he answered. "That's right, Marshal, he's Howard, Mason's dead, and there's a nigger, horseback, in that clump of trees right over…uh…right over that way, and he's got a shotgun, a pistol and a bull whip. Him and two other niggers hung us, stole my team and carriage, and shot Mason dead. Then they brought us here and they make us dig in this field in the daytime and lock us in the slave jail at night."

The men were having trouble standing and they reeked of liquor. Poole noticed a large earthenware jug lying in the dirt behind them.

"How about if you fellas stay here while I ride over to that stand of trees and see if I can't flush out your…uh…your overseer."

James Howard, who was the drunkest of the lot, responded. "We'll stay right here, but you'd better be ready with yer gun. That sumbitch'n nigger'll kill you if you ain't."

The Marshal held his revolver across his lap, and out of view, as he rode toward the clump of Burr Oaks at the edge of the field. He was not, however, surprised to find no horse and no rider.

On the very far side of the grove he came upon Robert's team of black geldings, harnessed to the carriage, and tethered to a stout oak. Dismounting, he tied the big roan to the back of the rig. He couldn't keep from smiling as he settled in to the driver's seat and spoke aloud, "Sammy, what in the hell have you done here?"

He drove the rig to where the three men were standing. "You boys can get up in here and I'll drive you to Pine Bluff, but before you do, would you mind telling me how you all got so drunk when it ain't even noon yet?"

Buster spoke up. "That nigger, Pete Kraemer, he done it. Every morning he fills that jug with water for us and he don't give us nothin' else til night. Today he filled it with corn liquor, and that's all we had, so…uhh…that's what we drunk."

Poole nodded. "So this Pete Kraemer; he's the one that hangs out in the trees with the shotgun, the pistol, and the bull whip?"

"That's right, Marshal." James Howard was doing the talking now. "He's the one that locked us in that damned jail every night and made us dig in this damned dirt all day. Just drive over to that cell and look in there for yourself. We had nothin' but straw to sleep on and a pot in the corner. Treated us like we was the niggers."

Poole took the man's suggestion and turned the team back toward the buildings. When they were abreast of the old brig, he tied the lines off and set the brake on the carriage. "You gentlemen just sit where you are and I'll take a look."

The first thing the marshal noticed was there was no visible means of locking the heavy oak and steel door, although there were screw holes where a hasp and staple might have been.

It squeaked loudly as he pulled it open. The cell was

about eight feet square and filled nearly to the ceiling with old furniture and miscellaneous other junk. "Are you sure this is where he kept you locked up?"

"Damned right we're sure," Buster snapped. "They done this to make it look like we wasn't in there, but this is the place."

There were a couple empty earthenware jugs on the ground in front of the small building and Poole picked one of them up and sniffed the opening. "Smells like more corn liquor, boys. Your imprisonment, if that's what it was, couldn't have been all bad."

Buster turned beet red, clambered out of the rig, and got right in Poole's face. "You sumbitch, are you sayin' we're lyin'? Those God damned niggers done this to make it look like we just been hangin' around here drinkin'."

Poole shoved his big right hand into Buster's throat, squeezed, and slammed him back against the side of the carriage. "You would do well, Mr. Coolidge, to call me Marshal. If you call me anything other than Marshal again…anything doesn't please me, I'm going to put a rope around your neck and lead you back to Pine Bluff like the jackass you seem to be."

The strength of Poole's grip and the fact he stood at least half a head taller than Buster seemed to make an impression. Of course Buster was a good deal braver when he had his revolver at his side. Whatever the motivation, he settled down and got back in the carriage without any further discussion.

The drive back to Pine Bluff was quiet and uneventful for the most part. On a few occasions Buster and Howard hung their heads over the side of the rig to vomit. Otherwise, they slept. Robert slept throughout the trip.

It was late afternoon when they pulled up in front of the

Sheriff's Office. The marshal escorted the three men inside. Sheriff Granquist was so surprised to see them he didn't even try to hide the bottle and the glass of whiskey sitting on his desk.

"Here they are, Reub. Do with 'em what you want, but I believe I'd let 'em sleep here tonight. They've got a hell of a story to tell you, but I think they'll do a better job of it in the morning when they've sobered up some."

At nine the next morning Poole returned to the Sheriff's Office. Granquist was in his usual position behind the big oak desk, and the Coolidge brothers and Howard were seated in wooden chairs on the other three sides of it. Poole suppressed his laughter when his eyes adjusted to the low light and he noticed each of them had a glass of whiskey in his hand.

Granquist spoke first. "Mornin' Bob."

"Mornin' Sheriff, gentlemen."

"I been talkin' to these boys and we got things pretty well figured out. The three niggers that done this to 'em is Pete Kraemer, who was James' driver, Harold Tucker, and his one-handed grandson, Sammy Tucker. The only thing I don't understand is how you happened to stumble onto the Cordill place and find 'em."

"Good work, Reub," Poole spoke through clenched teeth, "and that's a question I would expect from a veteran lawman like yourself."

"When I went out ridin' yesterday, I was just tryin' to get the lay of the land. You know, maybe talk to some folks and get some information that might help you with your investigation. I had no idea about findin' these three, but a sharecropper I ran into said his boy had seen something strange out at that plantation. Said he saw three white men diggin' in a field like they were lookin' for worms to go fishin' or something, but they'd dug up an awful patch of ground to be doin' that."

The Coolidge brothers and Howard groaned at Poole's description of their field work, but they all, including the Sheriff, seemed to accept his explanation of why he'd gone to the Cordill place.

Poole went on. "It's good that we know who we're lookin' for, but, the question now is, when we get 'em caught, what are we going to charge 'em with that we can make stick with the federal circuit judge?"

The four men looked at the Marshal with incredulous expressions on their faces. Robert Coolidge spoke. "What in the hell are you talking about, Poole? Reub here is the justice of the peace, he'll hear the case, we'll hang the damned niggers, and we'll be done with it!"

The marshal gestured with his hands as he was inclined to do when he wanted to make a point. "Easy boys, that's the way we would have done it in Texas a few years back, too, but times have changed. Now that they're puttin' us marshals all around, we've got to go through the right channels."

"You're lucky you got me instead of some Yankee from up north. We'll get those boys hung, but we've got to do it right. I wired the judge this morning and I expect him to be here in Pine Bluff in a week or ten days. We've got that much time to catch these niggers and put our case together."

"Put our case together?" James Howard asked. "Those three hung us, stole my team and rig, locked us up and made us work like niggers in the field, and they killed Mason."

Poole smiled. "Boys we're in good shape with the word of three white men against three niggers. But we've got to make it look at least reasonable to the judge. Now, how is it they hung you and you ain't dead?"

"Well, uhh…"Buster stammered, "they threw the rope over a limb of a tree, stood us on the back of the wagon, and drove off, but they didn't tie the rope to nothin', so we just fell on the ground."

Poole nodded. "See, that's what I'm sayin', they hung you but you ain't hung. They stole your team and rig, but it was right there with you when I found you. They forced you to work and locked you up at night, but you were unguarded and drunk in the field when I found you and your cell was so full of stuff you couldn't have fit in it."

"You…uhh…" it was Buster again, "you ain't gonna tell the judge that are you?"

"No, I'm not," Poole answered, "I could change the story some for the judge if we needed to, but we don't even have to talk about it. We don't need all those charges to get those boys found guilty and hung. The most serious thing they did, in the eyes of the law, was kill Mason. Did all three of you see him get shot?"

Robert answered. "Buster and me saw it. James was already at the Cordill place locked up. It was the one handed nigger that shot him. They were all three there and armed, but it was the one-handed one that shot him, and the old man drug him off and threw him in the river."

"And you know what else?" Howard sounded excited as he threw his piece in. "They've still got Mason's team of Grey's and his wagon, so that's somethin' we can hang 'em for too."

Poole held up both palms in the direction of the other four as a sign that everything was under control. "That, gentlemen, is all we need. Under federal law, they're all accomplices, they're all guilty of first degree murder, and we can hang 'em all. We don't have to stretch the truth one bit, and, like Mr. Howard says, they're guilty of horse stealin' to boot. We only got to hang 'em once boys…only once. It's Reub's case and it's all gonna be legal and proper. All we gotta do is get 'em caught."

He offered his hand to the Sheriff. "Congratulations, Reub."

Sheriff Granquist, who had mostly stayed out of the discussion until now, shook Bob's hand and looked real satisfied. "I like it Bob. I like it a lot, and I like the way you think. Let's have another snort." The Sheriff only had the four glasses, so Poole took his straight from the bottle as they drank a toast to their plan.

Chapter Thirty-One

We sure could'a hung 'em
But we gave 'em a break
Now they ain't real grateful
Could be a mistake

The Coolidge brothers and Howard wanted to join in the search for Peter, Grandpa, and me, but Bob convinced them it wouldn't look good for the victims of a crime to apprehend the suspects.

He suggested the Sheriff's two deputies look for Pete at the widow's cabin where he had been rumored to be. Poole would go straight to my grandfather's house. He reasoned that Grandpa would recognize the deputies but not him, and that might allow him to catch the old man off guard.

Sheriff Granquist was to stay in his office to await the arrival of the prisoners…an assignment that suited his talents perfectly.

As Marshal Poole rode toward the Tucker residence, he frequently looked behind him to be sure the deputies hadn't decided to follow. He urged the big gelding into his fast lope, knowing, if someone was following, they'd have a hell of a time keeping up.

Grandpa and I were in the barn out back of the house when he arrived. We watched Bob ride up and tie the roan to the hitching rail. We had my grey gelding, Boone, along with a sturdy bay mare I'd acquired for Grandpa, saddled and ready to go in case we had to make a quick exit from the Pine Bluff area.

"No need to knock, Bob." I said, as I walked around the corner of the little house to meet him. "Let's go inside."

Bob led the way. We each took a chair at the kitchen table. "Got no biscuits for you this time, Marshal, but I can make some coffee quick like," Grandpa offered.

"How 'bout we just sit down and talk and see if we can figure out a way to keep you boys from hangin'."

Poole's face was all screwed up in a scowl as he turned to me. "If you've got an explanation for what happened to this Mason fella, maybe we can do that…keep you from hangin', I mean. The Coolidge brothers say they saw you shoot him dead, Sammy, and they saw you, Mr. Tucker, drag him off to the river."

"Well," I said, "I've got a story about that, but before I tell it, how about you tellin' me about that other news you mentioned yesterday. I've got a feelin' that might be important."

Poole nodded. "I can do that, I reckon. Does your grandfather know about…uhh…the Willis family and Kate?"

"He knows all about Kate and me."

Bob was tense and he spit it all out in a flood of words. "Well, I stopped at the farm, before I came down here, to see how she and the Davis' were doin', and I came upon Kate when she wasn't expectin' me. She's with child Sam… your child. She's been hidin' it and I don't think anybody knows about it up that way. Nettie's been tryin' to look pregnant when she's seen in public so she and Jim can claim the baby's theirs when it's born. Kate asked me not to tell you, but I said I couldn't promise such a thing, and now I told you."

Grandpa looked at me with eyes and mouth wide open but didn't say anything. I was speechless for a good bit as well. This was the last thing I had expected. Not knowing what to say was the least of my problems. I knew I had to do something and this struck me as a problem with no good solution.

I knew I couldn't and wouldn't let Kate deal with this by herself, but how could I go to her without making things worse. It just seemed like there was no workable answer. I guess the shock of it had my mind froze up.

Bob tried to snap me out of the dilemma by getting back to the subject of Mason's shooting, but before we'd really gotten into it, we heard his horse nicker. We all went to the window, moved the curtain aside, and saw Granquist's two deputies riding up to the front of the house.

Grandpa's eyes narrowed and he turned toward me. "Sammy, get down in the cellar right now. Marshal, put handcuffs on me and take me to jail."

I started to object, but he shut me up. "Sammy, there was nothin' I could do to save your daddy, without gettin' myself killed and leavin' you alone. This time it's different. You got somebody needs takin' care of and you got to go to her. Anyway, the marshal here can look out for me. Now get in the cellar."

Reluctantly, I did as I was told, but, as I opened the cellar door, I told Bob to send me a telegram…to send it to Fort Smith in the name of Bill Mason…and let me know what was happening with Grandpa.

I knew if Bob had Grandpa in irons, the deputies wouldn't be likely to search the place, and that was my only chance to get out of there without a shoot out.

A shoot out with the deputies didn't scare me in the least, but it would complicate the situation for all of us. I also knew I had to get to Kate and take care of her. I'd just have to trust Bob to look after Grandpa and try to get him through this.

Bob opened the front door, with Grandpa in tow, just as the deputies walked through the gate. They were the Livingston brothers; a scruffy, scrawny looking pair.

"I don't know what you boys are doin' here, but I got one of 'em." Bob proclaimed. "Doesn't look like you two went lookin' for Kraemer."

"Well…uhh…" Jeff, the younger but slightly brighter of the two, stammered. "Uhh…Reub thought you might run into two or maybe all three of 'em down here, so he sent us to help you."

"Sure," Poole grunted, "and if y'all had trusted me and gone where you were supposed to go, we might have all of them in custody right now. I'm takin' the old man to jail. You two assholes are going to come with me." Bob could be intimidating as hell when he wanted to be. The deputies walked toward their mounts without an argument.

The other deputy, the one who went by the name Curly, stopped and turned back. "We gonna make this nigger walk to town? Ain't he got a mule or somethin' we can sit him on?"

"No, I looked in the barn and out back earlier," Bob answered. "There ain't any livestock on the place that can be rode. You two boys are the smallest of all of us. You can ride double on that big sorrel and we'll put the old man on the bay."

"What…? I heard somethin' back by the barn when we rode up. Heard it when your horse was talkin'."

Curly's objection was cut short when Bob pushed him

and snapped, "There's a couple of goats behind the barn, now get on the God damned sorrel, both of you!"

When they arrived at his office, Poole didn't wait for the Sheriff to get out of his chair or hide his whiskey. He grabbed the keys and escorted my grandfather to a cell. Then he stood in front of Granquist's desk for a moment while he decided what approach to take with the old lawman.

He decided to keep it low keyed. "I appreciate you sendin' your two boys to help me out Reub, although, as things turned out, I had the situation covered by the time they showed up. What do you want to do about finding Kraemer and the one handed nigger?"

Granquist smiled, "nice work on getting the old man, Bob. Did you get anything out of him about where the kid might be?"

Poole nodded. "I did get an idea…something he let slip, and I'll get on that next. What about Kraemer?"

"Well, Bob, the Coolidge boys put up quite a fuss, and I decided to let them have a go at findin' him. What can it hurt after all?"

Poole took a deep breath to calm himself. "Which way did they go?"

"East," the Sheriff grunted, "they went east."

"Good," the marshal answered, "that's the direction I think the one handed one went. He may be with Kraemer. I'll take these two," he glanced in the direction of the deputies, "and see if we can catch up with em."

Poole handed Granquist a piece of paper. "I picked up this telegram this morning. Judge Cass will be here maybe as soon as day after tomorrow. We don't want that old man lookin like he's been beat up. We got everything we need to hang him legal, and we don't want to do nothing some Yankee judge can get his teeth into. Right, Reub?"

"Sure, Bob. Makes sense to me."

Poole nudged the roan into a lope on the only road that led east out of Pine Bluff. The two deputies, mounted on a pair of geldings that looked as undernourished and scruffy as the Livingston brothers themselves, did their best to keep up.

Bob didn't relish the idea of having these boys along, but he figured Grandpa would be safer if nobody but the fat, drunken Sheriff was there to keep watch on him. After two miles of the roan's steady long-strided lope, Curly hollered. "Marshal, can we slow down to a walk or a trot for a bit? You're killin these horses and us too."

Poole had the deputies intimidated, and he liked it that way. He knew they would be less likely to get out of line if he kept the heat on them.

Turning around in the saddle, just for a stride or two, he snarled. "Quit yer God damned complainin' and keep up or I'll drag your asses behind me. We're doin' the job you were supposed to do this morning." The two kept quiet after the warning, but their exhausted mounts couldn't keep pace and began to fall behind.

After another mile, with the deputies trailing by a good quarter mile, Poole spotted a wagon coming toward them. Within minutes he was able to see it was drawn by Robert Coolidge's team of blacks. He stopped and waited in the road.

The deputies caught up as the wagon drew near enough that its occupants were identifiable. The Coolidge brothers were seated side by side with Robert holding the lines. Buster had a white rag tied around his right hand, swollen, cut lips, and dried blood under his nose. Both of Robert's eyes were blackened.

Poole suppressed a smile. "Looks like you boys ran into some trouble."

Buster turned toward the bed of the wagon. "Not as much trouble as this nigger ran into. He resisted arrest."

The marshal rode up closer and saw the man lying unconscious on the hard, rough sawn planks that were the floor of the vehicle. His face was swollen to the point of being misshapen and half dried blood was caked to his ears and nose.

"I assume this is Kraemer. Is he alive?"

Buster shrugged. "He was when we threw him in there. We're just hopin he'll be alive long enough to hang."

As he took a closer look at the beaten man, Poole was able to do a pretty good job of piecing together what had happened. His scalp was split in at least four places. "Looks like you whipped him pretty good with the barrel of a gun and maybe stomped on his face after he was down."

"He got nothing he didn't have comin'. Look what he did to us." Robert pointed to his eyes as he spoke.

Bob dismounted, took a blanket from behind his saddle and a jacket from his saddle bag and vaulted onto the back of the wagon. Placing the jacket under Pete's head and the blanket over his body, he turned to the Coolidge brothers. "He looks to be in bad shape. Let's try to keep him alive for the judge. He'll be here in no more than a day or two."

After tying his horse to the wagon, Poole climbed into the front seat, gestured for Robert to move over, and took the lines. He did his best to avoid ruts and holes on the drive back to Pine Bluff in the hope of not aggravating the injuries Pete Kraemer had sustained.

When the wagon pulled up in front of the Sheriff's

office, he stepped over the seat back and kneeled beside the injured man. His eyes were closed. Poole wet his finger and held it close to Pete's nose and mouth. He was barely breathing.

Though he had never met Pete Kraemer, Poole could feel the rage building up inside for what had been done to the poor man.

He jumped out of the wagon and the Coolidge brothers crowded up on either side of him. "Is the nigger dead?" Buster's inquiry was met with a backhand blow from the marshal's right that sent him sprawling in the street. His left hand did the same to Robert.

Standing over the fallen men, Poole could barely restrain himself from stomping them into the dirt of Pine Bluff's main street. He knew better than to take his eyes off the brothers and he wasn't surprised by what happened next.

Buster, still smarting from how Poole had intimidated him when he'd picked them out of the field at the Cordill place, wasn't of a mind to absorb this further humiliation without a fight.

Rolling over in the street, he got up on one knee and reached for his side arm. The marshal's right boot caught him flush in the face just as Buster's hand closed around the handle of his revolver. In an almost simultaneous movement the barrel of Poole's gun crashed down on his head, leaving him unconscious and, once again, prostrate in the street. The lawman picked up Buster's weapon and turned to Robert who surrendered his gun without being asked.

Robert wiped his bloodied lip and sat up. "Whose side are you on, Marshal? Ours or them niggers?"

"Your brother tried to pull iron on me. As far as me smacking you two in the first place, I did that because you're apparently trying your best to screw up our case."

After nearly a minute of silence, he spoke again. "We have a federal judge on his way to hold a legal trial. I wanted to have all three prisoners alive, well, and in custody. When you nearly kill one of them, and for all I know he will die, it undermines our chance for a conviction and a hanging. I don't know anything about this Judge Cass. Who knows how he'll react to you boys beating this man so bad…while you're arresting him when you ain't even officers of the law…while you're the victims of the crime he's supposed to be tried for."

"Well," Robert offered, "how's he gonna know we did it…even if Kraemer dies?"

Poole swallowed hard. "Maybe he won't find out. If he dies maybe we can tell him we just couldn't find Kraemer, but we have to make damned sure nothing happens to old man Tucker. We need to have at least one defendant who doesn't look like he's been the victim of vigilante justice. Do you understand that I'm a U.S. Marshal and there's only so much I can do to smooth things over for you?"

"The war's long over, and there are some things you used to be able to get away with that you can't now." He hesitated for a few seconds and added; "maybe not a lot of things, but there are some. When your brother wakes up, tell him this is the last time he'll fight with me and live to tell about it."

This thing stuck in Bob's craw like a dried horse turd, but it seemed like the only way to handle the situation for the present. He was the only white man in Pine Bluff who cared one whit if my grandfather lived to see the judge, and there were any number who would gladly join a lynch mob.

I had told Bob I thought Grandpa would be alright if he got a fair trial in front of a federal judge, but we ran out of time before I could tell him why. For now he had to have faith that I knew what I was talking about.

Even though Bob had been a lawman most of his adult life, he would have had no qualms about killing the Coolidge brothers…perhaps even beating them to death as they'd likely done to poor Pete, and he'd given it some serious thought just moments earlier. Now just wasn't the right time.

Chapter Thirty-Two

Old Tucker was on trial
Home boys held a grudge
Lookin' forward to a hangin'
But what about the judge

Poole saw to it that the local doctor gave Pete his best effort even though he was treated and housed in one of the jail cells. Pete began to have periods of consciousness on Friday, and Judge J. E. Cass arrived in town on Monday. Bob had spent his time guarding the jail. He even slept in the cell between the one Grandpa occupied and the one they'd put Pete in.

When Sheriff Granquist asked why he wasn't out scouring the countryside to find me, he replied, "the more I've gotten to know your deputies, Jeff and Curly, the more impressed I am with them as lawmen, Reub. They know this area far better than I do, so I think its best we leave the manhunt to them, while you and I stay here and guard the prisoners we have."

If the Sheriff knew Bob was really protecting my grandfather and Pete from him and any other locals who might want to administer their own justice, he didn't let on.

"I'm lookin for Marshal Robert Poole," the words were out of Judge Cass's mouth no more than a second after he burst through the front door of the Sheriff's office. He had wired Poole that he'd be there at 1:30 on Monday afternoon, and that's exactly when he showed up.

He was a sturdily built man of medium height, with hair thick and dark and just a sprinkling of gray. Poole judged him to be in his mid-sixties, maybe pushing seventy, even though he gave the impression of being robust and far from elderly. He spoke with a heavy New England accent.

The marshal walked across the room with hand extended. "I'm Bob Poole, your honor, pleased to meet you." The judge took his hand and simply said, "Marshal". "And," Poole went on, "this is Sheriff Reuben Granquist."

Granquist remained behind his desk as he acknowledged the visitor. "Welcome to Pine Bluff, Judge. As justice of the peace I usually handle these matters myself, but I reckon times are changing."

"Well, times are indeed changing, Sheriff, but justice doesn't change, and you can be assured justice will be served in any matter that comes before my court."

The jail cells were adjacent to the office area and the judge walked toward them to have a look. "Your wire said you expected to be charging three suspects with homicide, Marshal, and I see only two prisoners."

The Sheriff jumped in before Poole had a chance to respond. "Well, Judge, there were three niggers that done the killin', but we only got two of em. That one that's all busted up went over a cliff on his horse while tryin to escape capture, and the third is still on the loose."

"We'd like to get on with the trial and hangin' of these two we got in custody. No sense keepin 'em here and feedin 'em any longer than we have to. We've got two witnesses, reliable, long-time residents of Pine Bluff, that seen the whole thing. Here's the charges we've filed against the… uh…the suspects, Harold Tucker and Peter Kraemer."

Instead of getting up and handing it to the judge, Granquist remained seated and slid the file to the front portion of his desk top. Cass got an indignant look on his face, but walked over and picked up the paperwork without comment. He nodded as he perused the charges.

"So the victim, this Bill Mason, was shot while unarmed, and all three suspects were present and carrying weapons... huh? Then, I see, he was dragged off and thrown in a river. Was his body ever recovered?"

Poole was irritated with the old Sheriff trying to control the conversation. He spoke up loudly just as Reub was trying to put an answer together. "No, your honor, the body was never found."

Cass smiled. "I appreciate the courtesy, Marshal, but you needn't address me that way unless court is in session. Judge, or Ed, will do just fine. When will the prosecution and defense attorneys be ready to proceed?"

Granquist's fat face twisted in disbelief. "What do you mean defense attorney? These niggers ain't hired no attorney and they don't need one."

The judge's eyes opened wide, but before he could speak Poole turned toward the Sheriff. "I got Warren Stevens to agree to represent them, Reub. He'll wait to be paid when Tucker's assets are sold after the hangin."

"Well, alright then, I guess that's the way we do it now, but I'll need to be reimbursed for feedin 'em both, too." Granquist grumbled.

The judge turned toward the two lawmen and scowled as he spoke. "That all sounds fine, gentlemen, but I must remind you that the defendants haven't been tried, and you are a bit premature to be planning a hanging and the disposal of property."

"I understand that, sir," Poole came back, "and to answer

your original question, I've been told both attorneys will be ready to proceed tomorrow."

"Very well, court will convene at ten tomorrow morning. Where do you suggest we hold the hearing?"

The judge looked toward the Sheriff for an answer. "Well," Reub started, "we could have it at the saloon, I'm sure Buster…"

"Why don't we just have it right here in the office?" Poole interrupted. "We don't have to transport the prisoners that way and there should be plenty of room here for any folks who want to witness the hearing. Is that agreeable with you, Judge?"

"Right here at ten tomorrow will be just fine." Before he left the office Cass gave the marshal just the slightest hint of a smile.

By 9:30 Tuesday morning there were more than thirty men and a few women who had crowded into the Sheriff's office. The Coolidge brothers and James Howard sat right up front within three feet of the Sheriff's desk. Most of the crowd stood behind the two rows of chairs that had been provided.

At ten sharp, Judge Cass struck his gavel three times on the desk and addressed Bob, "court is in session. Please bring the first defendant forward."

"I will your honor, but I'm afraid the second defendant, Mr. Kraemer, hasn't recovered sufficiently from his injuries to appear before the court this morning. "Very well, let's have Mr. Tucker." Poole escorted Grandpa to the front of the desk.

"Are you Harold James Tucker?"

"Yes, sir, I am." Grandpa answered in a firm voice. He seemed relaxed and at ease and showed no sign of emotion.

"Well, Mr. Tucker," the judge went on, "you have been charged with the crime of murder in the first degree in the death of one William Mason. How do you plead to this charge? Guilty or not guilty?"

Before Grandpa could answer, his attorney spoke up. "Your honor, I'm Warren Stevens, council for Mr. Tucker, and before my client enters a plea, I'd like to bring something to the court's attention."

Cass scowled. "I'll allow this interruption, Mr. Stevens, but I certainly hope this information…this information you can't possibly wait to introduce… is relevant."

Stevens smiled. "It could hardly be any more relevant your honor. I'd like to introduce the victim of this alleged homicide, Mr. Bill Mason." Stevens, a fairly recent transplant from Des Moines, Iowa, could barely contain his delight as he gestured toward the front door.

Bill entered the room smiling and looking fit and healthy. Jaws dropped and there was a buzz in the room. The Coolidges and Howard jumped to their feet and Buster walked toward Mason. "What kind of bullshit is going on here, Mason…are you in with these damned niggers?"

The judge shouted, "Marshal Poole, this man is in contempt of court. Take him into custody and place him in a cell." Bob had his big right hand wrapped around Buster's neck before the judge had gotten to the word contempt.

When he had Buster secured in the cell Grandpa had just vacated, Bob walked slowly to Bill's side. He made a point of looking into the eyes of every man in the room as he did. He was the only man in the courtroom who was armed and he was bigger than any of the others present. He was making it clear that it would be unwise to challenge him.

So Buster's little insurrection was quelled just that fast. The judge gave Poole that knowing smile once more before summoning the two attorneys for a conference.

"Gentlemen, the defendant is on trial for the murder of William Mason. If this man," he looked in Bill's direction, "is indeed Mr. Mason, we're finished here and the charge will be dismissed."

"God damn it, say something John." Sheriff Granquist shouted.

"You're out of order, Sheriff. Keep quiet or you'll be in the other cell." The crowd buzzed loudly in response to the judge's warning.

John Jansen, the balding, portly, prosecutor, spoke up. He evidently felt compelled to obey the Sheriff or at least do something to earn his fee.

"Now, your honor, we have two of our citizens, both white men, who witnessed this crime, and…"

Cass held up both hands and shook his head. "For God's sake, Mr. Jansen, these men are charged with murder. If the alleged victim of the crime is alive and well, and he's in this courtroom, it doesn't make a hell of a lot of difference who the witnesses are or what they say, now does it?"

"Uh…no sir, it doesn't."

The judge asked Bill Mason to stand before him and swore him in. "Will you state your name, sir?"

"William Mason, your honor. I have some papers here… bills of sale from livestock purchases and so forth, as well as my U.S. military identification card. It's required for supplying mules and horses to the Army." The judge took the documents and looked them over thoroughly.

"As further assurance to the court, is there anyone present who can attest to this man's identity?" Rather surprisingly, three men, including the diminutive bartender, Pat Collins, affirmed the man was Bill Mason.

"Well," the judge said, "it's quite obvious you haven't been murdered by Mr. Tucker, Mr. Kraemer, or anyone else. Did either defendant attempt to kill you or harm you in any way?"

"No, your honor. The only times I've seen Mr. Tucker or Mr. Kraemer is when they drove Robert Coolidge and James Howard to and from our Wednesday night poker games. Nobody has tried to harm me in any way since I came to Pine Bluff. Folks here have been real good to me. For the last week or so I've been south of here buyin' mules and now I'm ready to head back to Fort Smith."

"We also have a charge of horse theft against these same two defendants…uh… alleging they stole a team of horses from you. Did either of them steal, or attempt to steal, any horses from you, Mr. Mason?"

"No, your honor, they did not. My team of grey geldings is tied up right outside the Sheriff's office. I assume they are the horses in question... they are the only ones I brought to Pine Bluff." The judge rose from his chair and looked out the window. "The charge of horse theft is dismissed, then, along with the charge of murder."

"Mr. Tucker, all charges against you and Mr. Kraemer have been dismissed and you are free to go. I apologize for the inconvenience you have suffered as a result of this very unusual and irregular situation. Marshal Poole will escort you and Mr. Kraemer…uh safely…to the location of your choice. Do you have any questions for the court?"

"Well, yes sir, I do. I have this here paper signed by me and Mr. Robert Coolidge. It says he will buy my land and house for eight hundred dollars when I'm ready to move off it." He took a slow, deliberate look around the room, boldly making eye contact with each of the white men present. "I think it's time I move out of the Pine Bluff area."

Cass nodded. "Very well, Mr. Tucker, unless Mr. Coolidge wants the court to look into the question of him and his cohorts filing false charges against you, I will suggest that he pay you the money immediately plus another hundred for your inconvenience." Robert Coolidge was dumbstruck, but made no effort to speak or move. "I said immediately, Mr. Coolidge, and make it in cash."

The crowd filed out, but court remained in session until Coolidge returned with the money. By two that afternoon, Grandpa had picked up his belongings and was seated beside Bill Mason, in his wagon, heading for Fort Smith. Mounted on the big roan gelding, Bob Poole trailed behind. His little pack horse followed untethered.

Poole and my grandfather placed Pete in the back of the wagon on a mattress. He was no longer experiencing short periods of consciousness. They knew he shouldn't be transported, but if he had any chance of surviving he had to get out of Pine Bluff. Grandpa looked at Bob and shook his head. The old man had seen a lot of death and suffering in his nearly eight decades. He knew, and the look on his face convinced the marshal as well.

They were two miles north of town when a single rider appeared from behind a stand of Scrub Oaks. Dressed in black, he was mounted on a flashy looking black Morgan gelding that was acting fresh and wound up tight.

Grandpa was surprised to see neither Poole nor Mason show any sign of concern about the visitor. He was surprised again as the man drew closer and he recognized him as Judge J. E. Cass.

"How are you getting along with that horse, Ed?" Mason asked.

"I'm happy with him, Bill. He's a little feisty for the first hour or so, but you can't wear him out. He'll go all day and he travels right smooth."

"So you won't be askin' for your money back, then?"

"No, I won't, but I think my old ass would be more comfortable sittin' on that wagon seat with you and Mr. Tucker, if you don't object."

Mason grinned, "you probably don't want to eat the dust and farts of them mules I've got trailin' behind either."

He stopped the team and waited while the judge tied the Morgan to the back of the wagon and climbed aboard.

Bob Poole rode up alongside the rig and greeted the judge. "Nice to have you join us, Ed. You did a hell of a job in court today." Grandpa looked from one man to the next. He was totally baffled. The other three smiled at his confusion.

"How about if I explain a few things to Mr. Tucker," Cass suggested. Not waiting for permission, he went on. "I was once a lawyer in Boston, and a poker player in my spare time. A number of years ago certain circumstances, events that don't need to be described here, caused me to give up the practice of law and get out of New England rather quickly."

Cass' explanation of his hasty exit from the northeast caused Poole to laugh loudly. The Judge gave him what was supposed to be an angry glance and went on.

"It was after I left the east that I met Mr. Poole and Mr. Mason. I got to know Bill, who is a fair poker player in his own right, as a result of my giving up law in favor of gambling. You see, in recent times I've made my living playing cards in Texas and Louisiana…mostly on river boats. That's how I got to know Bill. Because of my legal background, and my customary black attire, folks on the boats started calling me Judge."

"Bob did me a big favor back in Texas a couple years ago. We ran into each other again, just recently, when he was on his way to Pine Bluff. I was playing cards on a boat just up the Arkansas a bit. He told me he was coming down this way to help out a friend and asked me to watch for telegrams. I got one telling me to be here by Monday."

"At the time, I had no idea Bill was in the picture. This horse, oddly enough, is one I won from Bill in a card game last April. I might add he did a hell of a job getting me here on time. Bob and I got together yesterday morning. He filled me in on what he knew about the case and told me I was now a federal judge. You gentlemen saw the performance. What did you think?"

My grandfather couldn't stop smiling and shaking his head. "Land sakes, I never heard tell of such a thing. I sure am happy 'bout how it all came out, though. I'm sure enough happy 'bout that." He turned to look at the motionless, blanketed form in the bed of the wagon. "'Cept for poor Pete."

Poole joined the conversation. "When I took him to jail, Mr. Tucker told me how Bill's killing had been faked." He turned toward Grandpa. "I then had no problem agreeing with the Sheriff and charging you and the others with his murder. It worked out well. I figured you all would have to be charged with something or we'd have a lynch mob on our hands. Damn, I would have loved to have seen it when you made them think they were being hanged."

Bill Mason smiled at the picture the statement conjured up, but then spoke in a somber voice. "Yeah, we screwed around with them and they got beat up some, but we let them live when they deserved to die. They really deserved to die. And now they've gotten away with beating poor Pete nearly to death. I don't think this is going to sit too well with Sammy. It sure don't sit well with me."

Grandpa looked at Mason with tears in his eyes. "I believe the boy is gone already, Mr. Bill. If you look under them blankets I believe you'll see we haulin' old Pete to his grave. We haulin' a dead man right now." He was right.

*****

Later that afternoon, the Coolidge brothers and Howard got together at the saloon. Buster had been released from jail as soon as Deputy Curly Livingston could confirm that Cass and Poole had checked out of their hotel rooms. When Pat Collins brought a bottle and three glasses to the table, Buster turned on him. "You little Irish bastard, I ought to fire you for stickin' yer nose into our business in court."

"I'm sorry, sir, I didn't think I was doin' no harm by identifyin' Mason. I thought we'd all be happy to see him alive."

"Well, after this keep yer damned mouth shut unless I tell you to say something."

Robert raised his hand in an effort to settle his brother down. "I don't think Pat meant us any harm, Buster. He was as surprised as any of us to see Mason walk in that door."

Robert went on. "It's pretty plain to see Mason was in on this whole thing with them three niggers, and I suspect the federal marshal was too."

"Yeah," Buster added, "and don't forget the fuckin' judge. I wouldn't be surprised if he was part of it too. We got three niggers and three nigger lovers to settle up with as far as I'm concerned."

At this point, James Howard entered the conversation. "Gentlemen, it's one thing to kill niggers, but white men are another story…especially when one of them is a judge and another a marshal. As for me, I'm done with all of this.

If you two go after the niggers let it go at that. Leave the three white men out of it."

Robert nodded. "You may be right, James, you may be right."

Buster wasn't so easily convinced and he wasn't happy with Howard's decision to bow out. He'd already polished off two glasses of whiskey and it fueled his anger until it bubbled out of him. "We always stuck together in the past, James, and now yer turnin' chicken shit on us? If I get a clear shot at Mason or those other two, I just might take it, but I sure as hell figure on killin' them niggers. I figure they headed toward Fort Smith and that's where we're goin' tomorrow."

Howard got up and walked toward the door. He turned back and sighed. "I'll go with you, God damn it, but let's wait another day and plan this out so we don't get made out to be fools again."

Chapter Thirty-Three

We got out of Pine Bluff
Things were tied up real neat
Would have ended right here
If they hadn't killed Pete

My time in the saddle is when I do my best thinking and I used the ride from Pine Bluff to Fort Smith well. I had to help Kate and find a way to be with her. Getting her to Oklahoma Territory was the obvious answer. I don't know why I didn't think of that the day I found my mother and her family. The question now was how to get her there. Traveling across country with a pregnant white girl would be asking for trouble and I didn't want to expose Kate and our child to that.

It occurred to me to have Bob take her there. She'd be as safe with him as she'd be with anybody in the world. He could even pose as her husband if anyone had questions.

The very real prospect of seeing Kate and starting a life with her in Oklahoma was something I'd barely dared to dream about. Being with the woman I loved, having a home and our own child…this was the kind of thing that wasn't supposed to happen in the life of Samuel Tucker. It brought a level of peace to my mind I had never known before.

*****

I arrived in Fort Smith at about noon on Tuesday and went immediately to the telegraph office. Behind the barred window stood a barrel-chested, middle aged man with black hair and a few days growth of stubble on his broad face. He looked more like a blacksmith than a telegraph operator. When I approached the window, he raised his eyes to look in my direction, but said nothing.

I forced a smile. "Excuse me sir, has a telegram arrived for Mr. Bill Mason? He's expecting one from Pine Bluff. I work for him and he asked me to pick it up. He's away on business, but should be back in a day or two."

The man sneered, walked from behind the counter and stood with his face no more than a foot from mine. I turned my head to escape his foul breath when he spoke. "I didn't know Bill had any niggers workin' for him. What's your name, boy?"

The prudent thing would have been to act the part of the subservient colored man, but I just wasn't real good at that anymore. As I said before, I had left both my inclination to put survival first and my inclination to avoid trouble back in Salina, and I wasn't about to take any shit from this loudmouth. War had been declared, as far as I was concerned, and I was in the thick of it.

I withdrew my left arm from my coat pocket and held the metal sleeve out where he could see it. In the next motion I pulled back the right side of my coat to expose the gun on my hip. I took it out of the holster, spun the cylinder, and set it on the counter where he could reach it. Next I opened the left side of my coat and held my hand a few inches from my cross draw piece. I gestured with my head toward the Colt on the counter. "If you're done shootin' off your mouth, why don't you try to shoot that."

He backed up a couple of steps and raised both hands above his waist. All of a sudden he seemed to be at a loss for words.

I figured it was time to answer his question about my name. "They call me Crow…ain't really my name, but they call me Crow."

It was my turn to sneer now as I stared into his eyes, and spoke slowly, "what's your name, boy?" His eyes got big and the tough drained out of his face at the same time. Maybe he'd heard of me, maybe not, but evidently I'd made an impression.

"Uhh…I'm Jerry…uh…Jerry Laposa," he stammered as he stepped further back from me. "I didn't mean no harm by what I said Mr. Crow. Uh…a telegram came for Mr. Mason just yesterday. I'll get it for you right away."

He hurried behind the counter and slid the message through the opening under the bars. "Thanks, Jerry," I picked up the telegram and the pistol and turned toward the door, but stopped just before I opened it.

"Mr. Mason will appreciate your cooperation, Jerry." I was enjoying being on a first name basis with him. "And Jerry…take a deep breath…feels good to be breathin'…don't it? Remember how good that feels, Jerry."

I waited until I was mounted and on my way to Mason's ranch before reading the telegram: "Mr. Mason, Mr. Tucker and I are in good health and expect to arrive at your ranch early next week. Everything worked out fine in Pine Bluff. Two other gentlemen are with us."

I was enormously relieved to hear that my grandfather was alright, and I assumed the other two gentlemen were Pete Kraemer and Bill.

Playing the Bad Wing Crow card in front of the telegrapher was a mistake and I knew it. But, like I said, I was at war. I had a belly full of that good old southern boy bullshit and was in no mood to swallow any more.

I got a good feeling as I rode through the front gate of Mason's ranch. It was almost like coming home. The same two cowboys, Nate and Burt, were still working there and they welcomed me.

That very afternoon I worked a couple of particularly rank broncs that had been giving them a hard time, and the boys were grateful. That night I took my old bunk and settled in to await the arrival of Bob, Grandpa, Bill and Pete.

I also felt reasonably contented with what had happened in Pine Bluff. At least I felt finished with it. We'd punished and humiliated the Coolidges and Howard substantially.

It didn't square things for what they'd done to me and my family in the past, but nothing could have undone any of that. And I'd complied, for the most part, with my mother's wishes of not stooping to their level.

Initially, I had planned on hanging Robert and James and shooting Buster, but my mother's words, and the look on her face when she said them, wouldn't let go of me. It wasn't until the day before we got Howard that I decided to change the plan. Of course, if Buster had forced my hand I would have gladly shot him. But, as things turned out, I had a choice and chose not to.

With respect to the change of plan, Grandpa was easy to convince. He understood what Momma meant, but Pete was slow to come around. He went along with it, but never stopped trying to persuade me to hang or shoot all three.

Mason, usually such a reasonable man, wanted them all killed and fought my decision to the end. He argued that his own family history of abuse at the hands of the Coolidge family would have justified the original plan and said what they'd done to us Tuckers was even worse.

It was late in the afternoon of the following Wednesday

when I saw Bill's wagon approach the front gate. Two riders led the procession and six or eight mules followed. I jumped off the colt I was working and hurried toward them.

Poole and the big roan were easy to recognize as were Bill and Grandpa who were seated in the wagon. The other rider's face was hidden by the brim of his hat, but he sure didn't look like Pete Kraemer. As the distance between us closed, I knew it wasn't him.

Without greeting any of them, I looked up at Poole and asked, "where's Pete, Bob? Where's Pete?"

"He's dead, Sammy." He gestured with his head to the back of the wagon. "The Coolidges got to him before I could and they killed him… beat him to death."

I felt like I'd been kicked in the stomach. If I'd listened to Pete and Bill and not let those three bastards off the hook, he'd still be alive. It was like I'd killed him myself.

I walked back to the corral to be alone. I went through the motions of continuing to work the colt. It took me half an hour to finish the ring work, unsaddle him, and put him up.

Grandpa, Poole, and Mason knew Pete had become a good friend to me during the short time I'd known him, and they left me alone with my thoughts and grief.

The sun was going down as I walked to the house and found all four sitting on the porch. Each held a glass of brandy. Poole stood up. "I'm sorry, Sam. I thought I had it covered, but the fat fuckin' Sheriff let the Coolidge boys go lookin' for you and Pete."

I held out my hand and he took it. "You got Grandpa and me out of there, Bob. Thank you. I'm the one who could have kept Pete from getting killed, and I'm the one who's going to settle up with the Coolidges. You got any more brandy, Bill?"

Bill brought me a glass, filled to the top, and then introduced me to Ed Cass. In spite of my foul mood, I found him to be a likable guy, and I thanked him for his help. We spent some time reliving the events that had unfolded in Pine Bluff.

Bill talked about his faked murder and how badly my home made wax bullet had stung when I'd shot him, and how he'd managed to splash tomato sauce on his wound. We talked about that kind of thing for more than an hour before I brought up the next order of business.

"Bob, I need to have you go to Kansas right away. Take Kate and Grandpa to Oklahoma Territory. Take them to the Joe Black Fox farm and you'll all be welcomed. That's where my mother is. She's married to Joe. I don't know why I didn't think of that right away. It didn't occur to me until I was on the ride from Pine Bluff.

Nobody in Oklahoma Territory cares what color you are. Most of them have a little bit of everything in them. It's a perfect place for Kate and me and our child, and I'll get there as soon as I can. But first I'm going back to Pine Bluff and do what I should have done in the first place, and I'm leaving in the morning."

Bill and Bob tried to persuade me to either not go at all or to take them with me. I turned them down on both counts. Poole looked me squarely in the eyes. "I'm not leaving for Kansas until this is finished. If you can't leave it like it is, I don't need to travel right with you, but I'm stickin' around close where I can back you up." There was no point in arguing with him.

I thought back on how Pete had talked about how good it felt to stop kissing white men's asses and to be riding with the famous Bad Wing Crow…how excited he was at the opportunity to turn the tables on those who had oppressed us for so long.

"Pete, if your watchin', keep watchin', because I'm going to square this up for you. I'm going to finish it for you."

Chapter Thirty-Four

Didn't know when I lit out
They'd be comin' this way
Could the old man and me
Finally have our day

The Coolidge brothers and Howard left Pine Bluff a day and a half after Poole's outfit had set out for Fort Smith. As was the case with many plantation owners at the time, they rode gaited horses. These animals were bred to cover a lot of ground smoothly and rapidly. They weren't as fast, flat out, as a stock horse like Boone, but they could get a man from here to there in a hurry without jarring the hell out of him. Mason's wagon, with the mules trailing behind, had to travel a good bit more slowly.

As I rode down the Main Street of Fort Smith that morning, I stopped at the livery to have the smithy snug up the shoe on Boone's left front.

Something about the flea-bit roan gelding in one of the corrals caught my attention. I'd seen him before, but couldn't quite place him. Figured I'd probably just passed him on the trail somewhere. I didn't spend a lot of time worrying about it and was back on the road as soon as the smithy was finished. I pointed Boone toward Pine Bluff and struck a lope.

A heavy rain had washed the road of all but the most

recent tracks. As was my habit, I took notice of those that remained. Three sets of deep fresh prints stood sharp and clear among the rest, and the pattern and spacing was indicative of a running walk. At the moment I didn't connect the hoof prints with the roan at the livery, but something made them stick in my mind.

I was more than four miles down the road toward Pine Bluff when it hit me. "That's Howard's horse," I nearly shouted the words.

Sitting down in the saddle and applying my right heel, Boone slid to a stop, rolled back over his hocks, and began loping back toward Fort Smith without missing a beat.

My first stop was the livery. It was mid-morning when I rode into the barn. The smithy, a colored man called Bull, looked up at me with a welcoming grin. "You got another loose shoe already, Mistah Tuckah?"

I shook my head. "The roan, the one in that pen over there when I was here this morning, did he belong to a man named Howard?"

"Didn't get the names, but three white men, all with them single-footin' plantation horses, they boarded here last night. Wasn't none too friendly. Didn't say hardly nothin' 'cept ask how to get to Mason's place. They left more'n a hour ago…maybe close to two hours, and headed north. You run into 'em, be damned careful."

I held out my left arm. "I know all about 'em, Bull. Known 'em since I was a kid."

I loped Boone down Main Street toward the road to Mason's ranch. There were so many horse and wagon tracks in town I couldn't pick out one set from any of the others, but I didn't have to. I knew these three were headed to Mason's. They weren't any more ready to let this thing go than I was and that was fine with me. My only regret was I hadn't finished it earlier and saved Pete…and I regretted I hadn't stayed at Mason's to greet them when they arrived.

I knew the trio from Pine Bluff had gotten to the ranch long before me and I had to be ready for about anything. I had no intention of prancing down the lane and through the front gate.

When I was within a half mile of the place I rode cross country to the back side until I intersected the creek bed. It would provide cover to get me and Boone to within a hundred yards of the buildings. I planned to hunker down there until I figured out what to do next.

The little creek wasn't much more than a trickle and it hadn't cut a very deep crease in the landscape. On top of that, the brush growing along it was sparse and little of it was more than four or five feet tall. I dismounted and led Boone. We stayed toward the bottom of the little draw. In some cases the best path was right through the water. I moved slowly and never broke cover. When I was opposite the ranch buildings, I tied Boone behind a heavy patch of brush and hunkered down to wait and watch.

When the three men had ridden in to Bill's ranch earlier that morning, they went straight to the two year old pen and tethered their mounts to the top rail. The wranglers, Nate and Burt, were in the pen roping a couple of colts to work in the round corral.

The visitors didn't waste any time with explanations. They entered the corral and jammed the barrels of their pistols into the small of the unarmed young cowboys' backs. Howard and Buster ushered them toward the house. Robert, with his revolver in hand, followed.

Mason and Poole, having been alerted by Bill's old coon hound, spotted them and walked out to the porch with guns at the ready. Grandpa stood behind them.

Nobody said anything until less than fifty feet separated the two groups. Buster, in a show of bravado, took a pull from his ever present flask of whiskey and then spoke just loud enough to be heard. "Throw them pistols in the dirt and tell us where the one-handed nigger is."

When nobody responded, he shoved the muzzle of his gun into Nate's thigh and pulled the trigger. The bullet, shattering the bone, dropped him instantly. The fallen cowboy screamed and writhed in pain as his blood spurted onto the ground.

Buster stepped over him, pushed Howard aside, and jammed his Colt into Burt's spine. "Throw down your guns and tell me where Crow is or this one's gonna get it right through his back."

Poole grimly nodded at Bill and dropped his pistol in the dirt in front of the porch. Mason did the same.

As Buster roughly pushed Burt forward with the muzzle and cocked the hammer, Grandpa shouted. "He run off somewhere an' we don't know where. Sammy figured this business was over when we left Pine Bluff. Don't shoot no more."

Buster evidently believed Grandpa and spared Burt. He told Bob to pick Nate up and drag him to the porch.

When Poole bent over to help the wounded man, Buster cracked him over the head with the barrel of his revolver. "That squares things up some, Marshal, but I ain't through with you yet."

Poole was dazed but remained conscious. He took a few seconds to clear his head, clenched his teeth, and dragged Nate to the porch. The cowboy screamed in pain and passed out. Mason bound his wound tightly to slow the bleeding and covered him with a blanket.

Bill, Bob, and my grandfather were seated on the edge

of the porch floor with their wrists lashed to the railing. Their captors sat behind them in rocking chairs and drank Mason's brandy.

That's the picture I saw when I settled down in the creek bottom. It seemed a little ironic that I was watching them through a Confederate Army spy glass.

It was early afternoon, a bright clear day, and the position I'd chosen was southwest of the ranch house. At this time of year the sun would be low in the sky and right behind me in another three to four hours. I liked the set up, but I wished I didn't have quite so much ground to cover before I'd be within effective pistol range.

As proficient as I was with hand guns, I wasn't worth a damn with a rifle. The plan I had in mind wouldn't work with a rifle anyway. If clouds moved in it wouldn't be good either. I was counting on the sun to help me out.

After standing watch for two hours, I got a break. Buster got up, and threw an empty bottle to the ground. I could hear him swear as he started toward the horses. Robert said something I couldn't make out, but it wasn't hard to figure out what was going on.

Having run out of his favorite brand of whiskey, Buster was heading to town for more, and his brother's feeble efforts to stop him had no effect. I reasoned this would make things easier for me at the ranch.

The part I didn't like was that Buster was drunk. I wanted him to be sober enough to fully experience the little dance I expected to have with him before the day was over.

A half hour after watching Buster ride through the front gate and turn toward town, I crept to where Boone was tied. Using my lariat to extend the bridle reins, I walked directly behind him, driving him across the creek and into the open expanse of pasture on the other side. His body blocked me from view and the sun obscured the saddle and all other details. He looked like nothing more than a loose horse grazing his way across the pasture.

There was a single, bushy Juniper about halfway across the open ground and a three foot buck rail fence at the far edge of it. We moved slowly across the open until the tree screened us from view. Once there, I swung into the saddle and hooked the big grey with both spurs. Though Boone was digging with everything he had, it felt like the world had slowed down.

With the reins in my teeth and a pistol in my hand, we reached the fence at a full gallop and cleared it with two feet to spare. The exhilaration of this one man, one horse cavalry charge was beyond description. The sense that things were moving slowly persisted, but I was enjoying every second. I felt not a twinge of fear and a whole lot of fire in my belly. This was the way I should have done it in the first place.

By the time Robert and Howard knew what was happening, I was within pistol range. I knew this was a hostage situation and they would shoot the captives one at a time to get me to surrender.

I also knew if I rode in on them at thirty miles an hour with guns blazing and got right in their faces, they'd shit in their pants and their plan would fall apart. It worked better than I could have hoped. In their panic, they each got off only a couple of wild shots that had little chance of hitting anything.

As soon as we'd cleared the fence, I took a few shots that were directed at Coolidge's and Howard's feet. They were meant to keep them off balance and unable to take aim at me until I was on top of them, and I wanted to make sure I didn't hit Grandpa or my friends.

My first shot at close range caught Howard in the right shoulder. He dropped the gun, fell back against the house, and slowly slumped to the floor.

Poole knew the hide-behind-the-horse trick and was ready for me. We'd used that a couple of times while hunting antelope. He'd worked his hands free, and, when Robert stepped in front of him and fired, he grabbed his right wrist with both hands and snapped it like a twig.

Howard's wound was enough to knock him off his feet, but it wasn't going to kill him. It hadn't been my intention to just wound him, but that's the way it turned out.

He was diving for cover and I was riding at full speed when I shot at the middle of his chest. Even Bad Wing Crow doesn't get a hundred percent bullseyes. If I hadn't seen the gun fly out of his hand, I would have kept shooting at the center of his torso. Instead, I turned toward Robert just in time to see Poole take care of him.

Bob gathered up the fallen weapons and untied Mason and Grandpa while I kept watch on the wounded prisoners. He looked at me and smiled. "I knew what you were up to, Sammy, and I have to say that was about the sweetest damn thing I ever saw in my life. You looked like hell on horseback comin' out of the sun and over that fence. That big old pony of yours can flat out dig."

The three of us stood, looking at each other, catching our breath and laughing for a good bit before Grandpa offered his take on the action. "So that was this Bad Wing Crow I been hearin' about, huh? I believe this is the day we been waitin' for, Sammy. I believe this time it's really the day."

"Yeah it is Grandpa." I pulled the crumpled piece of paper from my coat pocket and handed it to him. "This is the day we've been waiting for ever since you gave me these three names."

I hadn't seen "Judge" Cass and I asked about him, hoping he hadn't been hurt. Mason told me he'd gone looking for a poker game and was either in Fort Smith or on the river somewhere. "Bill," I asked, "can you and grandpa load Nate into the wagon and get him to the Doc? Bob and Burt can stay here and keep an eye on these two. I'll go find Buster."

Poole sighed and shook his head. "I'm the federal marshal here, Sam, don't you think I should go with you?"

"No, I don't."

"Shouldn't we get these two," he said, glancing at Robert and Howard, "to the Doc also?"

"No, they'll be alright for now. I need to think on this. They may not require medical treatment. I'm still thinkin' about that."

I mounted Boone and was about to ride off when I noticed Bill Mason had a troubled look on his face. It wasn't like him to keep his thoughts to himself and I called him on it. "I'm thinkin' you got something to say, Bill. I want to hear it before I ride."

Bill looked my way with a tight smile. "I guess that's fair enough Sam. It's something I've been sittin' on for a while not knowin' if or when I should bring it up. It's something I was wantin' to handle myself, but I guess now is the time to tell you about it."

"One night when we were playing poker, and the Coolidge's and Howard were braggin' about how they used to keep the niggers in line, Buster had Pat Collins put two quart pickle jars on the table in front of me.

One of 'em was full of men's private parts…it had a label on it that said nigger nuts. The other had a small hand in it. It was a left hand and it was gray and shriveled, with the fingers all curled up. I know it was your hand, Sam. Apparently Buster shows these things off on special occasions…when he's drunk and wants to brag about his exploits…like they're trophies or something."

I shouldn't have been surprised to learn these guys would stoop so low, but the information caught me off guard. I felt like the wind had been knocked out of me. After taking some deep breaths, I turned to my grandfather.

"Grandpa, when they hung my daddy, did they cut him?" The old man's head sagged and he turned away. It took him awhile to begin to speak, and, when he did, he struggled with each word.

"They had…uh…they had your daddy's hands shackled and they was tryin'. They was tryin' to cut him, but he fought with his knees and butted them with his head. I moved forward to help and that's when he shouted at me. He said, 'Papa, get back. You got to take care of my boy.' So I backed off and didn't get into the fight.

He was so strong and he fought so hard all they could do was get the rope around his neck. They used a mule to pull him off the ground. It was after they hung him that they cut him. I had to do what he told me, Sammy, but I'm ashamed to this day for not helpin' him."

What I'd just heard from Bill and Grandpa cleared away any remaining doubts I might have had about how to handle the Coolidges…that's not to say I was struggling with a lot of doubts after hearing what they'd done to Pete. I turned Boone toward Fort Smith.

Chapter Thirty-Five

My momma's admonition
A haunting warning voice
Don't sink to their level
But there wasn't a choice

The last of the day's light was fading when Buster tied his horse to the rail in front of Roxie's Saloon. It was the third joint he'd visited since coming to town.

He leaned against the bar, set his pistol on it, and swore as he ordered whiskey. The owner of the establishment, Roxanna Phillips, poured his drink. His surly attitude and the cold look in his eye caught her attention. With her auburn hair tied in pigtails, she looked sweet and innocent, but she'd spent too much time in the saloons of Arkansas and Texas to miss seeing Buster for what he was…trouble… trouble that was about to happen.

With Buster looking the other way, she swayed over to a poker table on the far side of the room. It was the table Sheriff Bill Tibbits liked to call his own.

"Bill, that fella at the bar with the black vest…the one to the left of Steve King…we need to send him on his way. He's lookin' for trouble for sure."

Tibbits was holding a good hand and wasn't of a mind to be bothered, but he couldn't ignore Roxanna. He never had to pay for a drink in her place, and his table was always waiting for him. He set his cards face down and gave a warning look at each of the other players. It was a look that said "don't touch a damned thing 'til I get back".

"Shit," he swore as he glanced toward the bar and recognized Buster. He squeezed the back of the lady's hand. "We ain't gonna wait for no trouble. I'll run that son of a bitch out of here right now, Darlin'. I'll run him all the way out of the county."

When the Sheriff got to his feet and began walking his way, Buster saw him. He also noticed J. E. Cass get up from the same table. Cass had heard Roxanna's warning and decided to get clear of any kind of a fracas that might be in the works before it started. He was willing to concede the hand to Tibbits. He hurried, not quite quickly enough, toward the front door.

As the Sheriff approached to within a few feet of the bar, his revolver holstered, he started to speak. "Coolidge, you ain't welcome…" His words were cut off when Buster turned toward him with the muzzle of his Colt pointed at his belly.

"You're the one who ain't welcome in here Tibbits, and neither is that phony judge you were playin' cards with." He shot into the wall and missed Cass by no more than two inches.

The judge stopped and turned in the shooter's direction. "I…uh…I'm sorry. Did I do something to offend you, Mr. Coolidge?"

The humor was lost on Buster. Motioning with his gun, he squinted and spoke in that soft, condescending tone he so often used. "Both of you, out in the street."

When Tibbits and Cass had exited, he stood in the doorway and turned back toward the twenty or so patrons remaining in the saloon. "I'm lookin' for a one-handed nigger…the one they call Crow… Bad Wing Crow. Tell me where he is and you can have your Sheriff and your phony judge back."

"Samuel Tucker at your service, Mr. Coolidge. You, however, may call me Crow or whatever name you'd like. You can even call me nigger this one time…this one last time."

Slouched in the saddle, with a broad smile on my face, I looked down on him. I was no more than twenty-five feet from where he stood on the boardwalk. Tibbits and Cass were to my right and they began backing further into the street for safety.

Turning to the Sheriff, I saw that his side arm was still in its holster. "This business is between me and Mr. Coolidge, Sheriff. I trust that's alright with you?" Tibbits nodded and backed further away.

I held my left arm up and to the side. Though it was dusk, there was still enough light to see the metal sleeve where my hand should have been. My right hand was hidden inside my canvas duster.

My challenge to Coolidge was spoken softly and slowly. "What are you fixin' to do with this one-handed nigger now that you've got him, Boss?"

Buster wasn't frozen with fear like most men who are suddenly facing a gunfight. He moved with astonishing quickness. In the rapidly failing light of day, flame flashed from the muzzle of his revolver. The bad news for him was, mine flashed first. His shot went wild when my round caught him in the right shoulder. The gun flew from his hand. This time I wasn't aiming for the center of his chest.

The coolness I had shown a moment earlier was replaced by total rage. Rage fueled by the memory of what he'd done to my father and my mother, and for chopping off the hand of an innocent ten year old boy and keeping it as a souvenir. For a moment I considered shooting him in multiple locations…the knees, both shoulders, the belly… but I didn't.

I reached for my rope. Hanging him, like he'd done to my daddy, suddenly seemed more appropriate, but my change in plans almost cost me.

Buster jumped on what should have been my play. Making it appear he was wounded worse than he actually was, he staggered and acted like he was going down, but made a dive for the fallen pistol. He came up with the gun in his left hand and fired in my direction just as my lariat settled around his neck.

The bullet pierced my duster and just nicked the flesh of my upper right arm. In the whirl of emotions I was feeling, I hadn't been as careful as I should have been. I'd given Buster one too many chances, but I got away with it.

Before I had time to finish what I had in mind, I heard the throaty report of both barrels of a shotgun right behind me. The smoking scattergun was in the hands of a smiling Bill Mason.

The heavy loads of number four shot caught Buster in the midsection and nearly cut him in two. Bill's eyes met mine. "Sorry to steal your play, Sammy, but I've never wanted to do something as much as I wanted to do that."

I smiled back at him. "I appreciate the help, my friend."

Even though Buster was mortally wounded or perhaps already dead, I decided to go ahead with the hangin'. It was something I'd had in mind for a long time, and I saw no reason to stop now.

Dallying the rope around the saddle horn, I spun Boone and hooked him with both spurs. Dirt and mud flew as all four feet dug for traction in the rain-softened surface of the street.

The horse took off like his ass was on fire. He didn't falter when the slack in the rope was taken up. The popping sound of Buster's neck snapping was so loud it all but echoed off the buildings of Fort Smith's Main Street.

After he catapulted off the steps, Buster hit the street face first some thirty feet to the east. I rode another fifty yards or so at a gallop, turned Boone back, and dragged the body to where the Sheriff stood with his eyes wide and his jaw hanging slack.

"You saw what happened Sheriff, do you and I have any further business?"

"No sir, I believe we're finished here. The hangin' was a little out of sequence an' probably not necessary, since he was already shot, but I reckon you boys had every right to kill him any way you saw fit. I didn't like the son of a bitch anyhow."

I touched the brim of my hat and managed a tight smile. "Sheriff."

When I turned to ride out of town, I wasn't at all surprised to see Bob Poole in the front of the crowd sitting astride the big roan. He'd arrived in time to watch the whole thing. Instead of staying with the prisoners, he had Grandpa bring Nate to the Doc while he came looking for me. Obviously he'd wanted to be on hand if I needed backup.

"You aren't real good at following instructions, are you Bob?"

He twisted around in the saddle and gave me his best hard-ass lawman look. "And you aren't real good at remembering which one of us is the federal marshal."

I smiled. "Let's call that a draw, Marshal."

I felt an immediate and tremendous sense of relief after finishing my business with Buster…a feeling I'm at a loss to describe. I turned away from Bob and took a few minutes to think about it.

I was glad Bill had a chance to be a part of it…a big part of it. He later told me how it had galled him to pretend to be friends with the Coolidge's and Howard and to listen to the tales of their exploits. Looking the other way when the pickle jars and their grisly contents were brought out was the hardest part.

This evening, the rage Bill and I had carried inside for so long had subsided to a large extent. Maybe, I thought, we would finally be at peace after all the years, but we still had work to finish.

I looked back toward Poole. "We need to…uhh…deal with those two back at Bill's ranch."

"You got that all figured out, do yah?"

I took a deep breath and sighed loudly as I let it out. "Yes I do, Bob…at least where Robert is concerned. I reckon he and Buster figured it out for me. I might give some more thought to what to do with Howard.

Poole looked at me with cold, unflinching eyes. "I hear what you're saying, Sam, we got no choice. Look what happened when we let 'em off the hook last time. They beat Pete to death and then came looking for you and your grandfather. They deserve to die, my friend, and they'd kill all of us right now if they had the chance."

Mason stepped up close and nodded his agreement. I looked down at the saddle horn, thought for a few seconds, and then looked at Bob and Bill in turn.

"That's exactly what they'd do, boys. Those miserable,

low life bastards would shoot us down like dogs and they'd laugh about it. Maybe they'd keep parts of us in pickle jars to show off like something they'd won at the fair. I reckon we've done all the thinkin' we need to do."

Mounted on his fiery black Morgan, Ed Cass rode up behind us in time to overhear the last part of the conversation and offer his two cents. He'd obviously had a few glasses of whiskey at the poker table.

"On the other hand, Gentlemen, Bob is a U.S. Marshal, the local Sheriff hates those two, and I can be a federal judge when circumstances demand it. We pulled that off with a hostile Sheriff in Pine Bluff, why couldn't we do it here with the local law on our side?"

Bob smiled. "Maybe we could try that, Ed, but I don't think Tibbits is likely to play along with you being the judge. He's played poker with you for Crise sake."

"We could charge them with kidnapping and assaulting a federal marshal, and shooting Nate," Cass went on, "and we could turn the whole thing over to Tibbits to prosecute. He could get a real judge to hear that one. Bill, Nate and Burt could testify. They witnessed the whole deal."

I decided to put an end to the discussion. "This ain't that hard to figure out, gentlemen. Turnin' Robert over to the law wouldn't be respectin' Pete and my daddy. I just don't feel right about doin' Pete that way, and I don't feel right about doin' my daddy that way."

Chapter Thirty-Six

What is this I'm about to do
A fair and just solution
Or is it nothing more
Than a heartless execution

Coolidge and Howard stood on either side of the hay wagon which we had rolled into the round corral. Their backs were to the house and other ranch buildings. I stood on the opposite side of the corral leaning against the top rail. I'd placed the short barreled shotgun on the wagon within arm's reach of Coolidge and a Colt revolver on Howard's side of the vehicle. Both guns were loaded and the hammers were drawn back.

Robert, the tall, dapper, and usually composed plantation owner, was obviously not having one of his better days. He was red-faced, and sweating and fidgeting. His badly swollen injured right arm hung limp at his side.

Howard, on the other hand, seemed calm and at ease… like he was resigned to the fate that was about to befall him. His eyes were cast toward the ground and he didn't look up even when I spoke.

"Pick up the guns and shoot whenever you boys are ready. You can do it one at a time or both together. Doesn't matter to me."

Coolidge responded verbally to the challenge. "We can't beat you in a gun fight, Tucker. James doesn't know how to handle a gun and I ain't got but one good arm, and it's my left arm at that."

I laughed. "I ain't got but one good arm either, Robert. You want me to tell you how that came to be, or do you remember?"

"That was a long time ago, Tucker, and…" In mid-sentence he lunged for the shotgun. I guess he thought that would catch me off guard. I put two slugs in his chest before he could get the gun up to level and pointed in my direction. He fell back against the wagon, his arm sagged, and he fired both barrels into his left foot.

I'd kept one eye on Howard's side of the wagon as Coolidge made his play, but saw no movement. I looked directly at the shorter, stocky, rather harmless looking man and shook my head. "It's your turn, James. You probably should have made your move when Coolidge did, but it's your turn now and you'll have to go it alone."

"Some terrible things were done to you and your family, Tucker, and I went along with it when I knew I should have tried to stop it. But I didn't take an active part in cuttin' off your hand, hangin' your daddy, or beatin' Pete Kraemer. I'm sorry those things happened and I'm sorry for not tryin' to stop 'em from happenin'."

"Never once did I stand up to Buster and Robert and I followed 'em anywhere they led. If you think I deserve to die for that, you can shoot me and I wouldn't blame you for it, but I'm not reachin' for that gun."

I extended my arm, raised my pistol, and fixed my eyes on the center of Howard's forehead.

"Hold on Sammy." My grandfather took a few steps toward the corral, being careful to stay out of the line of fire. "What he said is true. He hung back both times. He didn't try to stop them other boys neither, but he hung back, an' he wasn't there when they killed Pete."

James Howard kept his eyes fixed on mine even after I eased the hammer of my Colt back from the cocked position and lowered my arm.

*****

It was close to noon when we helped Howard out of the wagon and handed him over to Sheriff Tibbits. He was quiet and contrite. He knew how close he'd come to being delivered to the Sheriff feet first.

My grandfather's words had tipped the scales in Howard's favor. In a way, sparing him was a small concession I made to my mother. Looking back, I'm glad it happened the way it did. I know I wouldn't have felt right about shooting him under those circumstances. I called it a small concession, but I expect it looked pretty big from Howard's perspective.

A soiled piece of canvas covered the body lying in the bed of the wagon. "I reckon that's Robert Coolidge?"

"Yeah, Sheriff, that's him."

Bob tried to sound like he was expressing regret as he described Robert's demise. "Old Tucker set his shotgun down to help the prisoner get up on the wagon and he grabbed it, Sheriff. He was trying to shoot his way to freedom, and he was, unfortunately, mortally wounded in the process. I would have had him in irons, but he sustained a broken arm in yesterday's melee an' we put this splint on it."

He lifted the canvas to show Robert's right arm. "I reckon I have to take a share of the blame for this happenin'." His lips were tight as he turned toward the body and slowly shook his head. "All this violence is a terrible thing, Bill, just a terrible thing."

Tibbets suppressed a smile. "Do you want to tell me which one of you did the shooting?"

"When he turned around and leveled the shotgun at us, Mason and I both fired…'bout three shots each." Poole answered. "I really can't say who hit him and who missed."

As I thought back on it, what happened between me and Robert seemed like what they call poetic justice…a gun fight between two men with one hand each. I didn't feel bad about it in spite of my mother's admonitions. I hadn't really struggled much with the decision about how to deal the Coolidge boys after I heard what they'd done to Pete.

Pete was a good friend, and I couldn't let either of his killers get away with it. I couldn't do it to him. He'd groveled and shuffled and kissed enough white asses in his day. Letting Robert off the hook would have been like Pete kissing ass again from the grave. Couldn't let it happen… figured I owed him that much.

What they'd done to my father, of course, was too horrible to imagine. The Coolidge's deserved to die for that. What Bill had told me about the pickle jars and the trophies they contained was the final nail in their coffins.

My only regret was for not doing it sooner. If I'd had a real hanging at the slave cemetery down in Pine Bluff, like Pete wanted, he'd still be alive. That bothered the hell out of me. Don't know as I'll ever get over that.

As for Howard, he just got lucky. He said the right thing at the right time and Grandpa came to his aid. Another ounce or two of pressure with my trigger finger and his head would have exploded like a bomb had gone off inside a watermelon.

Tibbits was proving to be the most reasonable lawman I'd ever known. He accepted Bob's explanation and asked no more questions.

"I'll get him to the undertaker and we'll ship him and his brother back to Pine Bluff in the same wagon. This is good timing…it's the best time of year to be haulin' bodies. In the Spring or Summer they get ripe in a hell of a hurry in this country. In the late Fall, like this, they stay nice and cool, but they don't freeze solid neither. It's a good deal all the way around."

Howard stood trial in Fort Smith and was convicted on the kidnapping charges. He was acquitted on the assault charge concerning the shooting of Nate. The jury heard testimony saying Buster had pulled the trigger, and most of them had seen him bounce down Main Street with my rope around his neck. I guess that seemed like enough to close the case.

Howard was sentenced to ten years at hard labor. He was initially sent to Little Rock, but, as Bob told me later, for the majority of his sentence the state leased him out as a field worker to private plantation owners.

It seemed ironic that he ended up working the fields like a slave. To me, that seemed like more poetic justice. I don't know if he served all of his time or if he died or was paroled. Our paths never crossed again and I didn't worry about it.

With Buster, it had been a fight, and a fight he was looking for. With Robert it was more of an execution. Normally that wouldn't have set well with me, but life is complicated and sometimes there just aren't any real good answers. We chose to compromise on this one.

That evening Grandpa opened a jug of his corn liquor and we drank a couple of toasts. Our eyes were already filled with tears when I turned to the old man, clicked my glass against his, and raised the stump of my left arm to the sky. "We had our day, Grandpa. After all this time we had our day."

"An here's to your daddy, Sammy." Grandpa turned to the southeast, raised his glass, and addressed my father directly.

"I'll go to my grave wishin' I coulda' done somethin' to stop 'em from hangin' ya, Jimmy, an' I shor wish I coulda' stopped 'em from takin' little Sammy's hand. But they had guns both times an' they'da killed me. Like you told me, I had to be alive to raise the boy, an' that's what I done. I know yer proud of him an' I hope yer proud of what we done to square things up."

Chapter Thirty-Seven

After all these long years
We thought we'd made it right
For all the bloody battles
There was yet one to fight

Three fancy gaited plantation horses, along with their saddles and tack, were left behind by the Coolidge brothers and Howard.

Initially, Tibbits tried to claim all three, but he eventually settled on Howard's roan gelding. He said he'd keep it, along with the prisoner's other personal belongings, to be returned to him upon his release…as though that was going to happen.

Marshal Poole took possession of the other two, saying he'd use them to help compensate the victims of the crimes the trio had committed. Of course, we were all victims in one way or another, so was I pretty sure a squabble was coming.

Grandpa was seriously taken with Buster's beautiful palomino mare and the fine Austrian saddle she carried. He'd never owned anything but mules, and owning such a horse was something he'd never even imagined. She was gentle as a lamb, big and stout enough to carry a man of his size, and she moved like water flowing down a stream.

Poole, Mason, Cass and I all agreed the old man should have the mare. She'd be a perfect mount to get him from here to Oklahoma territory.

The third horse, Robert's black stud, was coveted by all four of us. Cass suggested we play a single hand of poker with the high hand claiming the horse. I have no idea why we all agreed to that, but we did. "Judge" Cass won the hand of course. Nobody caught him at whatever he did, but we knew he did something. Mason was quick to point out that Cass, as a gambler with no permanent residence, had little use for a stallion. Bill bought him for $200 to use in his breeding program.

Bob and I ended up with nothing, but we didn't feel all that bad about it. We were already well mounted with Boone and the big roan.

Grandpa agreed to stay with Mason and help him out until Nate's leg healed up. Bill said he needed to travel to the Territory in a few months to pick up more Mustangs and Grandpa could ride along with him as far as the Joe Black Fox farm.

I was burning up to see Kate. Bob agreed to ride with me to Kansas and take her to what would be our new home in Indian Territory. There was no longer any reason to send Poole alone.

Surprisingly, after everything that had happened in the last few months, nobody seemed to be after me. Well, maybe those guys in Wichita, where Pete and I had the ruckus…they could be on the lookout for me, but I was sure they weren't hunting me down. It would be easy enough to skirt Wichita to the east on the way to Salina and to the west going to Oklahoma.

Bob's presence would be important on the second part of the journey. If anyone asked why the three of us were together, Bob could say Kate was his wife and I was the hired man.

On the second morning after we'd settled up with the Coolidge's and Howard, we set out for the Willis farm. As usual we traveled light, and with Bob on the long-legged roan and me on Boone, we were set up to make good time.

Our spirits were high and it was good to spend the time, one on one, with my old friend…my best friend. It hadn't been many days since Bob had made the same trip in the opposite direction, but he didn't mind. Life on the trail had always suited both of us.

Averaging near to 35 miles a day, with two layover days to rest the horses, we made the ride in just over two weeks. As the miles between me and Kate became fewer, my excitement grew and my spirits soared. That all changed as we drew to within a couple of miles of the Willis place.

At first, I didn't make much of the vultures circling up ahead. They were somewhere between us and the farmstead and I figured they'd found the remains of something a wolf or coyote had killed.

We picked up the pace anyway and loped straight toward the airborne scavengers. I felt a chill when I saw the grey mule, dead, still in harness, and still attached to Jim's wagon.

It was then I saw the wisps of smoke. It was rising from too many places to be chimney smoke. Fear gripped me stronger and more completely than it had since the tragedies of my childhood. Without saying a word to Bob, I hooked the grey and galloped the last mile. Bob and his mount were beside me, going stride for stride. My heart about stopped when we were near enough to see the farmstead clearly.

There was nothing left of the house or the barn but a few

charred timbers and a mound of ash. My breath came in short, shallow gasps. I felt like a bucket of mush as I slid from the saddle and sank to my knees.

Bob dismounted and walked toward me. "We don't know what happened here, Sammy. We don't know nothin' yet. Now get hold of yourself and let's find out. Kate and the Davis's may be just fine."

After a minute or so I managed a few deep breaths and got to my feet. We walked toward the house. We didn't see Jim Davis until we circled around to the back side of the pile of blackened rubble that had once been the barn.

He was digging in it with a pitch fork. Covered with dirt, soot, and sweat, his hair was singed and he had burns on his hands and arms. He was dazed and seemed unaware of our presence. Though he talked constantly, his words were mumbled and mostly inaudible. His wife's name was about the only thing I could make out and he said it over and over again.

Standing behind him, Poole put his hands gently on the man's shoulders. "Jim, it's me, Bob Poole, and Sammy's with me." Davis turned toward him with a blank, shocked expression on his face but didn't speak. He was a sorry picture…anything but the fearless, powerful Jim Davis I remembered.

Bob put a big hand on either side of his face and shook him just a little. "Jim, you have to talk to us. You have to tell us what happened here. We can figure this out if we keep our senses about us." He shot a glance in my direction to let me know that admonition applied to me as well.

My breath was coming back and I slowly began to pull myself together. It took every ounce of will and strength I had, but I knew I had to get back in control. Any chance we had of finding Kate, our unborn child, and Nettie, depended on it. Being smart and in control had kept me alive this long. Now there was a lot more at stake than just me.

We helped Jim to a wooden bench near the garden and he and I sat down. Poole asked again. "What happened here, Jim?"

The man's chin sank to his chest and he closed his eyes, but he did begin to talk. He spoke so softly I had to strain to make out his words. "I was on the prairie…out on the prairie huntin'…gone for two nights. Came home yesterday and the place was afire. It was all afire. Black smoke an' roarin' an' so hot I couldn't get close to the house or the barn. Every inch of both buildin's was blazin'."

"An' I… I smelt somethin'…smelt somethin' like flesh burnin'." Pausing, the shaken man took a couple of deep breaths before going on in that weak and trembling voice. "Couldn't tell if it was comin' from the house or the barn or both. The wind was whippin' somethin' awful. I ain't seen no sign of Nettie or Kate. Been lookin' all day an' all night, but ain't seen no sign."

I stood up and turned to Bob. "Why don't you sit here with Jim while I study the sign, or whatever's left of it. Might be there are tracks or something left that can help me figure out what happened here, and where…and where Kate and Nettie might be."

The hard, dry ground of early winter, the wind, the ash, and Jim tramping around the place for a full day didn't make the job an easy one. In fact, I knew it wouldn't be possible to piece together the whole story. I'd just have to put together whatever I could and hope it would be enough to lead us in the right direction.

The memory of the gruesome findings I'd made on this very farm just six months earlier chilled me to the bone, but

I had to go ahead with the task at hand. I had to look at the sign and read it for what it was…not what I wanted it to be. I took paper and pen from my saddle bag and carefully sketched out and documented everything. For more than an hour I worked, covering every inch of the farmstead, before reporting to Bob and Jim. I was still nervous as a cat, but feeling a lot better as I approached them.

"The women were working in the garden and two riders got up on them quick enough to block their path to the house. Maybe they didn't hear 'em coming because of the wind. One of the men took Kate and the other took Nettie and walked them away from the garden. They weren't struggling. The tracks in the main area of the place are not clear enough to tell where they took 'em or what happened from then until they left…except they lit the house and barn on fire and did it from the west…upwind…side of each building."

"They rode out to the south…three horses and Kate's mare was one of 'em. She was carryin' a load…carryin' a rider or maybe two. The mare was reachin' deep with her hind feet to take some of the load off her front quarters so she'd be better balanced. Kate and I worked on that with her. I don't believe she would have strided that way unless she was carryin' a rider and had a bit in her mouth."

My story brought Jim around to the extent it looked like he could function. Poole and I rode out, cut the dead mule loose, and hauled the wagon back to the farmyard.

Jim was setting up his camp next to the garden when we rode out again. Judging by the sun, I'd say it was right close to noon, probably later. With the short days of the season, we'd have no more than five hours of tracking light to work with.

This time we were heading south. Though the tracks were faint, they weren't muddled up with any others, and we followed them easily and at a good pace. In a low spot, where the ground was damp and soft and the tracks were sharp, I stopped and pointed out something to Bob… something I'd noticed back at the farm.

"The horses those boys are ridin'…look at the size of their feet. Look at how the hind feet plant closer together, inside the prints made by the front. Those ponies have some draft blood in 'em. I'd bet they're half plow horse. Who do you know in Salina rides horses like that?"

Poole took a few seconds. "The Van Heel brothers ride those big spotted geldings…those Tobianos. Don't know of anybody else." I nodded. "I was thinkin' the same thing. I sure don't like the thought of Kate and Nettie bein' with them. We need to pick up the pace."

We moved out at a brisk trot which was as fast as we could go and still see the tracks. After a couple of miles, their trail cut a two-track road angling south by southwest. The riders had turned on to it and Bob and I were able to pick up the pace to a fast lope. I knew we were gaining ground, but I wished we were gaining faster. They had started out the day before, and could be as much as twelve hours ahead of us.

Daylight was fading fast, and we had to make camp for the night. We had no choice. It was already too dark to make out the tracks. Worse yet, dark clouds were building up in the west. Rain or snow…either one…could wipe out the trail completely, and Kate would likely be lost to me forever. It was with that grim foreboding that I climbed into my bedroll.

The cold, moistness of the first snowflake was barely perceptible on my cheek. Then another fell and another until my face was wet and cold. My chances of ever finding her were being buried a flake at a time. I pulled the canvas shell of my bedroll over my head, closed my eyes, and thought of what Kate might be going through at this moment. I tasted my warm salty tears and cursed the falling snow and the hopeless feeling that came with it.

Chapter Thirty-Eight

It's a cold dirty war
No place for the faint
Prisoners are taken
And sometimes they ain't

I was out of my bedroll at first light, just stomping around and trying to stay warm. The sky had cleared sometime overnight, but not before it had dropped six inches of heavy, wet snow on the ground.

I uncovered the small pile of fuel we'd put together the night before. It was nothing more than buffalo chips and pieces of sage, but I reckoned it would burn long and hot enough to brew some coffee. Bob rolled out just as I got the fire going, and he boiled up the coffee.

Sleep had been fitful and hard to come by and I sure didn't feel rested or up to facing the daunting challenges of the day. The wagon road was visible as two ruts in the prairie grass and sage, but the hoof prints of the horses were buried. We could follow the road easy enough, but we would have no idea if or where the riders left it. My hopes of finding Kate were fading ever further.

Bob seemed to know what I was thinking. "It ain't over, Sammy. I don't like this snow any better than you do, but we're gonna get on that wagon track and stay on it 'til we find somethin'. I don't know what we're gonna' find, but we're damned well gonna find somethin'."

He handed me a cup of coffee that steamed visibly in the cold morning air. "Drink that and let's get started before the guys we're chasin' do. If it is the Van Heels, they weren't sittin' around the campfire singin' songs the last two nights…they were doin' some serious whiskey drinkin'. They won't be startin' out early this mornin' and they didn't yesterday either. We just might've gained on 'em more'n you think."

I nodded in his direction. "Let's get the horses ready and get after it."

The horses had spent a cold night and were feelin' fresh and eager to be on the trail. We'd hobbled them in a low spot, so they had a little protection from the wind if not from the snow and subfreezing air.

They both fidgeted some when we pulled their shoes and rasped their feet to keep snow and ice from building up on their soles. When we mounted they moved out with more than their usual spirit.

We were two hours down the road when I motioned for Bob to stop. I got out my glass and looked toward a barely visible speck on the southern horizon. "Uhh…three horses comin', Bob. Looks like one of 'em ain't carryin' nothin'. Oh God, three horses…two riders."

*****

Poole had been right. On the night of the snowfall, the Van Heel brothers, huddled in their sheepskin coats, were sitting around the fire drinking whiskey straight from the jug. Like the previous night, they were well on their way to being knee-walkin' drunk.

With no warm clothes, Kate and Nettie were lying in the men's bedrolls trying to stay warm. Their wrists were bound and secured to a rope around their waists. They pretended to be asleep.

"You don't think anybody's gonna' see this fire, do ya Paul? She's burnin' pretty high 'n bright."

"Naw, it's already dark an' snow's fallin'. Ain't nobody gonna' be out lookin' fer us now. If we left any kind of a trail to follow, by mornin', she'll be covered up. We got nothin' to worry about, brother."

Bert took a long swig, wiped his mouth, and swung his head toward the women. "What we gonna' do with these two? We been havin' our fun with 'em, but we can't keep 'em forever."

Paul nodded and his lips contorted into a crooked smile. "I been thinkin' about that myself. I heard once about a whorehouse in Wichita that bought girls…Chinese and niggers and such, but I don't think we could get away with sellin' the white one."

"What we gonna' do with her then?" Paul smiled that same cold smile again. "I believe we gonna' sober up and have some more fun with her in the mornin'." He laughed and went on. "An' sometime tomorrow or maybe the next day the coyotes will have their turn with her. Ain't nothin' gonna be wasted."

*****

The eastern sky was just beginning to brighten as Kate slowly and carefully turned to look into the face of Paul Van Heel; the man whose bedroll she'd been forced to share the past two nights, and the man who had raped her three times and then handed her off to his brother. He snored loudly, with his mouth open. His foul breath smelled of whiskey and it made her gag. Everything about the man stunk…his body, his breath, his clothes, his bedroll…they all wreaked.

She hated him more than she'd ever hated anyone…even more than the three who had killed her family. Perhaps the depth of her hatred was borne of the instinct to protect the child she carried inside her. She had many reasons…she'd been kidnapped, beaten, raped and treated like an animal. At the moment, sorting them all out didn't matter. If she could find a way, Paul Van Heel was about to feel the full force of her rage.

Wearing only the light dress she'd had on for the last two days, she eased herself out of her coverings into the frigid morning air. Her injured wrist throbbed, but the cold deadened the pain some. The snow stung her bare feet, but she paid it no mind.

Lying next to Bertram, on the opposite side of the fire circle, Nettie looked up at her with wide and fearful eyes. Kate held up both hands, as far as her bonds would allow, as a signal for her friend to be still. Nettie got the message and allowed only her eyes to follow Kate's movements.

The small campfire had long since gone cold and the rocks surrounding it were frozen to the ground. In his drunkenness of the night before, Bertram had left his heavy-bladed Bowie knife lying next to the fire. With her left hand, Kate picked it up, cut the rope around her waist and freed her wrists. Next, being careful to make no sound, she used the knife to pry a round stone, about the size of an apple, from the soil's icy grip. A bigger one would have been better, but she had only one good hand.

Holding it in her left palm, she tip-toed to the head of the bedroll where Nettie lay with her captor. She kneeled, motioned for Nettie to move her head away from Bert's, took a long deep breath, and lifted the stone high above her head.

Bert turned toward Nettie and he started to reach for her with his right arm. It was one of the last few movements he would ever make.

Kate's rage gave her extra strength as she brought the stone down on his right ear with all the force she could muster. He turned his face toward her and tried to raise his hands to protect himself, but Kate was too quick for him. She struck him several more times on his forehead and face until he moved no more. She stood up and turned toward the other man.

Paul was lying face up and beginning to stir. The dull sound of his brother's head being smashed had begun to awaken him.

Kate made her way to where he lay. He raised his head slightly and turned toward her. Still very groggy, he was trying to form words with his thick dry tongue when she smashed the same rock into the center of his face. She uttered no sound as she slammed the bloody weapon over and over again into his fat, round mug until it was no longer recognizable.

By now, Nettie had cut her bonds, pried loose another stone, and was pounding the lifeless Bert with it. Unlike Kate, she sobbed and screamed with rage as she pulverized her tormentor's head to a pulp.

The clothes, hands, arms and faces of both women were splattered with blood. They used the wet, slushy snow to wash the worst of it off, but didn't waste much time on it. Nettie tore some strips from Bert's shirt and wrapped them around Kate's right forearm to create a makeshift splint. The nearly one inch thick wrap supported the limb and made it less painful when Kate moved it.

Donning the oversized, heavy coats and boots of the Van Heel brothers, they saddled the horses and rode north.

Epilogue

July 1, 1888
Oklahoma Territory

A place where trails converge
Among family and friends
A peaceful quiet home
Is this the way it ends

We lay on a blanket near the lazy little creek that bisected our quarter section. Kate rested her head on my chest. I took in her scent with every breath and stroked her pretty blond hair. I'd known more contentment in the last two and a half years than in all the years before. Things had turned out well…better than I ever expected.

The afternoon sun was plenty hot, but the trees provided shade for comfort, and there was a breeze just strong enough to make the leaves flutter. Kate had one end of a string tied around her wrist. The other end was secured around the waist of Mr. James Peter Tucker who had celebrated his second birthday just two months earlier.

The boy never stopped moving and the string was to make sure he didn't wander off too far or fall in the creek. Each time it got tight, Kate sat up and reeled him in. Sometimes he came back on his own and dropped weeds or dandelions on Kate's chest. He thought he was bringing her flowers, tried his best to say the word, but it came out something like "fawa".

The reunion with Kate on that snow-covered Kansas

prairie had been everything I could have ever imagined. It was the best day of my life.

We never really talked about what had happened to her and Nettie while they were with the Van Heels. She tried to a few times, but I wouldn't let her. I just looked straight into her eyes and said, "don't ever blame yourself for anything done to you by those men. You're a hero, Kate, you're the reason you, Nettie, and little James are here right now."

We had all talked at some length that day about what to do with the bodies of the Van Heel brothers. In the end, we went with Bob's suggestion to leave them where they lay.

"We could haul their remains to Salina and tell the story or we could let the Sheriff try to figure it out for himself. My guess is nobody in Salina gives a shit about what happened to those two, and I doubt if they'll even look for 'em." I couldn't argue with that.

I did some work with the Van Heel's big pintos and had them driving as a team in less than two days. After picking up supplies in Salina, we lit out for Oklahoma. Jim, Nettie and Kate rode in the wagon with the chestnut mare and the mule tied behind.

The Doc did a nice job of splinting Kate's arm and made a sling. The bone was cracked but not displaced, and it eventually healed up fine.

Bob and I rode alongside the wagon. When we passed the spot where the Van Heels had camped, I saw vultures circling, but we didn't stop to look.

We arrived in the Territory less than a month after we'd finished up our business in Fort Smith and Salina. It was five days before Christmas, and Momma kept thanking Jesus for our safe arrival. She was so overcome with joy, I had to continually settle her down and reassure her that we were really going to stay.

Joe and Johnny were less effusive, but welcoming as well. I guess it had to do with the Cherokee culture. Kate and I couldn't have felt more a part of the family if we'd been born there.

On the morning of December 27th, while Joe and Johnny were tending to the livestock, Momma asked about the Coolidge's and Howard. She and I were sitting at the table having coffee.

"Sammy, darlin', I been wonderin' what you did with those three men that brought such pain to our family. I know you done somethin', and as a Christian woman, I'm worried some about it."

I'd known the question was coming, just didn't know when, and I was ready…didn't have every word figured out, but I had the core of it set to go.

"Well, Momma, we reminded 'em of all the things they'd done to you, me, and Daddy…and we made 'em squirm some. Made 'em think they were going to be hanged and made 'em work in the fields like slaves, but in the end we turned 'em over to the Sheriff in Fort Smith."

She patted my arm softly and said, "I'm proud of you, Sammy."

On balance, I think I was proud of the way we'd handled it also, and I didn't feel bad about leaving some of the details out of my explanation to Momma.

The loss of Pete stuck in my craw and I guess it always will. In a perfect world I would have saved him…saved him from death at the hands of those thugs. But in a perfect or even a decent world this whole story never would have taken place. It was only the incredible inhumanity of the time that allowed it to happen.

I suppose, to some extent, I let the Coolidge's drag me down to a lower level. In the process, however, I did avenge the loss of Pete and my father, and I honored them by naming my son after them. It was the best I could do. As I said, the world isn't perfect.

The end of March was at hand when Bill Mason delivered Grandpa to the Black Fox farm. The weather was good and the ride from Arkansas on that fancy gaited horse was as comfortable as such a journey can be. Grandpa's and Momma's reunion was emotional beyond description... something neither of them had dreamed possible.

Soon after Grandpa had arrived, we bought out a Cherokee family's homestead adjacent to Joe and Momma's place. Ironically, we used the money Grandpa had gotten from Robert Coolidge.

By Spring I had the house fixed up and the modifications included a nursery and crib. Grandpa and I planned to raise hay and small grain crops, and I would acquire and train horses for Bill Mason to pick up and sell to the Army. I even made arrangements with my old friends, Henry and Luke, to provide me with stock from Texas.

Jim and Nettie Davis homesteaded a place a mile to the west of mine. Poole stayed around for a week or so before riding back toward Kansas. Once or twice a year he makes it back for a visit.

A Cherokee holy man married Kate and me with the help of Grandpa who read a passage from the Bible. I'm sure there was a law against such a marriage, but effective law enforcement was a long way from Oklahoma Territory. As far as Kate and I were concerned, the outside world had no reason to meddle in our business, and we felt our marriage was as legitimate and sacred as if it had taken place in a cathedral.

Momma arranged for a Cherokee midwife to help Kate when her time came. The depth of the emotions I experienced was something I was not prepared for. Bad Wing Crow, the tough, fearless gunman melted away when the baby arrived.

The first thing I did, when I held little James, was to pick up his perfect little left hand. Tears filled my eyes as I counted and gently held each tiny finger, and I thought about the long and tortuous path we'd all taken to get to that moment.

This was an improbable family we'd put together, and Oklahoma Territory was a unique and improbable place. A place where skin color made no difference. For the sake of Kate and little James, I hoped it would stay that way for a long time to come.

There was also a sense of security in this loosely organized settlement of nearly three hundred Cherokee farmers. Nearly all of the men were like Joe and Johnny Black Fox. They were hard working and peaceful, but strong and virtually fearless at the same time. After the brutality and betrayal of the Trail of Tears experience, their tolerance for being pushed around was all used up. I could see no reason why any outsider would want to interfere with our lives here, but I pitied the man who tried.

I hung my revolvers on a hook soon after I arrived in the Territory and haven't taken them down since. Nonetheless, the stories of Bad Wing Crow lived on, and his legend grew bigger with each telling. I found it amusing. When somebody brings it up, I just say; " Bad Wing Crow? No, I'm asked that a lot because of my hand, and I've heard of the guy, but I'm Sam Tucker."

Jim Powell

Jim Powell

Author Jim Powell is a lifelong horseman and outdoors man who has lived his life in Minnesota and the Black Hills of South Dakota. "Bad Wing Crow" is one of two works of fiction he has written. He also produced a book of poetry called "The Phantom Poet of The Black Hills".

Having a degree in psychology from the University of Minnesota, Powell likes to get into his character's emotional and interpersonal struggles.

Bad Wing Crow

Historical reference: This book is not modeled after any one of the many African American cowboys of the 19th and 20th century west. However, there are some interesting parallels between the fictional story of Bad Wing Crow and the lives of two historical characters: Bass Reeves and Nat Love (pronounced Nate).

Bass Reeves (1838-1910) was born a slave in Arkansas. He escaped to Oklahoma Territory while serving with his master in the Confederate Army. He was the first African American Deputy U.S. Marshal and served in that capacity in Arkansas and Oklahoma Territory. He rode a big grey horse, had cross-draw holsters, and claimed to have captured 3,000 felons including three who sat horseback with their guns drawn. It is also said that he shot and killed 14 outlaws while never being wounded himself. Bass is reputed to be the inspiration for the creation of the Lone Ranger.

Nat Love (1854-1921), also born a slave, left Tennessee at age 15 and went west. He became an excellent horse trainer, a cowboy, and an expert marksman. After winning a shooting contest in Deadwood, SD, he became known as Deadwood Dick. As a cowboy and a trail boss, Nat fought many battles with outlaws and Indians. While in Arizona, he was wounded in a battle with a war party from Yellow Dog's tribe. He was taken captive, but spared because of the bravery he had shown in the fight. In Yellow Dog's band there were a number of individuals with African ancestry, and that may have helped Nat as well. When he recovered from his wounds, he escaped on a stolen horse. Nat spent his later years working as a Pullman porter for the Denver and Rio Grande Railway.

CPSIA information can be obtained
at www.ICGtesting.com
Printed in the USA
FFHW02n2231100918
48253117-52024FF